The bestselling authors of *Cherished Moments*:

ANITA MILLS, a former teacher of history and English, has turned her lifelong passion for both into a writing career. Karen Robards, author of the *New York Times* bestseller *Maggy's Child*, says, "Anita Mills is going to be a romance superstar!" Anita Mills is the best-selling author of *Secret Nights* and lives in Plattsburg, Missouri.

ROSANNE BITTNER, bestselling author of *Song of the Wolf*, makes her home in Coloma, Michigan, and is the author of more than 30 books with five million copies in print. *Romantic Times* says, "Readers of Rosanne Bittner can expect high-quality, well-researched love stories. For those who have not read her, you're in for a treat!"

ARNETTE LAMB, a *New York Times* bestselling author, "ignites readers with her unforgettable love stories and has a tremendous gift for writing genuine, warm, humorous, sensual love stories" (*Romantic Times*). She lives in Houston, Texas, and is the bestselling author of *Chieftain* and *Maiden of Inverness*.

CHERISHED MOMENTS

Anita Mills
Arnette Lamb
Rosanne Bittner

ST. MARTIN'S PAPERBACKS

Published by arrangement with Longmeadow Press

CHERISHED MOMENTS

Library of Congress Catalog Card Number: 93-47563

ISBN: 0-312-95473-5

Printed in the United States of America

St. Martin's Paperbacks are published by St. Martin's Press, 175 Fifth Avenue, New York, NY 10010.

Longmeadow hardcover edition published 1994
St. Martin's Paperbacks edition/May 1995

10 9 8 7 6 5 4 3 2 1

Contents

CHERISHED MOMENTS

Memories

by Anita Mills

✻ ✻ ✻

Near Whitby, Yorkshire: November 11, 1815

*I*t was violent, even for a North Sea storm, and the sound of relentless waves pounding upon the rocky seashore seemed far too close. Above the water's roar, the bitter seawind howled, blowing and sucking at the cottage's windowpanes. Bolts of lightning lit the small room, sending a cat behind the woodbox, where he crouched, his green eyes round with fear.

"Merowww," the animal cried pitifully. "Merowww-wwww."

Charlotte Winslow reluctantly put her brush into the

❀ ჳ ❀

water jar and stood back to survey the poster. No, she decided, Madame Rondelli appeared utterly insipid, when by all accounts the Italian diva was a striking beauty. It had to be the pomona green gown Mr. Burleigh had suggested. It simply was not rich enough to stand out.

But before she changed it, she would have to wait until morning, when the light was truer. Just now, her eyes were smarting from the smoking whale-oil lamps. Leaning over, she blew them out, darkening the room eerily, leaving only the red-orange glow of the hearth's fire.

"Meowwwww," Rex howled insistently. *"Meowwwww-wwwwww."*

"I shall be done in a trice," Charlotte promised him as she deftly cleaned her brushes.

A flash of lightning lit the room, then vanished as thunder rolled loudly through the small cottage. The cat cringed. "What a coward you are," Charlotte murmured, bending to pick up the animal. "You are a disgrace to your name, Rex, for there is naught kingly about you at all." Taking it to the chair nearest to the fire, she crooned soothingly, "It's all right, you poor big pussy cat. Poor kitty, poor big kitty," she whispered against the soft, orange fur.

Her hand stroked the cat's back, calming it. The big tomcat settled against her chest and purred loudly. Across the narrow room, her mother's old clock valiantly counted out the hour. Eight o'clock, she realized wearily. She'd been so absorbed in trying to finish the theater poster that she'd not stopped to eat her supper.

But she'd hoped to be finished with the playbill ere

now, for she had to begin Madame Cecile's fashion plates before she lost the money she'd been advanced. Briefly, she allowed herself to think of the modiste's utterly exquisite, shamefully expensive designs. The gowns of a young female's grandest dreams, she reflected, sighing. She could still remember those dreams—dreams fifteen years had made but a distant, treasured memory. Once there had been a time when she'd had fancy gowns, when she herself had had an abreviated season filled with parties, routs, and grand balls.

She caught herself before she dwelt on what might have been. No matter how eccentric her life must seem before the world, it was still infinitely better than that of being a governess to grubby little boys or a companion to a crotchety old woman, which was the usual fate of females too highborn to be parlor maids and too poor for anything else. No, she reminded herself resolutely, she had no wish to be like her younger sisters, whose every letter betrayed their unhappiness.

But to Sarah and Kate, it still seemed impossible that Charlotte could wish to live alone without so much as a maid or elderly female relation for propriety. Or that she would wish to live in a simple cottage perched between the moors of Yorkshire and the cliffs above the North Sea. A godforsaken place, Sarah had called it. Utterly improper for a female of good but impecunious breeding, Kate had declared. In truth, Charlotte lived near the village of Whitby for two very compelling reasons—her cottage was cheaply had, and its remoteness from London allowed for a necessary deception.

She sighed again and looked down at Rex. "I suppose after I have made my tea, you will expect to share a bit of mutton stew with me, won't you?"

As if it understood, the cat snuggled closer and kneaded its paws against her muslin skirt.

"If I were a Buddhist, I daresay I should think you were a notorious rake in your last life," she decided. "You have a definite propensity for working the wheedle, you know."

"Merowww."

"But at least you try to talk to me, don't you? I vow I should not know what to do without you for company. Sometimes, I find myself going into the village on the smallest excuse, when if the truth be known, my purpose is but to hear another human voice."

Easing the animal off her lap, she stood and took her ancient teapot from its niche inside the hearth, murmuring, "Quite enough water for one, and as Mr. Burleigh has paid me for last month's work, I think I shall use fresh tea leaves tonight. And once I have had my tea, I shall warm our stew."

"Merowww. Merowwwr."

"I suspect you are ever so much more comfortable a companion than a man, for most of them are utterly selfish and neglectful," she observed. "Only yesterday, I overheard poor Mrs. Bottoms complaining to Mrs. Wilson that Mr. Bottoms meant to be off to sea again, that he'd only been home long enough to put another loaf in her oven, as she said it. That will make eight, if you can but imagine coping with such a number. And she has the cheek to pity me. Fancy that, will you? I may have no husband about, but then the only mouths I have to feed are yours and mine. And I think I do rather well at that, if I may say so myself." Glancing down at the huge marmalade tabby, she smiled. "At least you do not look deprived in the least."

While she spoke, she made her tea and set it aside to steep while she fetched the cream pot. Just as she was about to strain the leaves out of the steaming brew, she paused, thinking she'd heard someone shouting outside. No, it had to be her fancy. It must surely be nothing more than sound of the howling wind.

But there was no mistaking the pounding on her door, nor the jiggling latch. Startled, she hesitated for a moment, then called out cautiously, "Who goes there?"

The answer was lost as rain peppered the windows like shot. Rex's hair stood on end as he backed behind her.

She tried again. Moving closer, she shouted through the door, "Who are you?"

"William Beggs!" he yelled back. "Coach went over the side—took th' horses with it! Gor blimey, but we was nearly killed! And th' earl's 'urt real bad! We got to 'ave help, missus! Mebbe yer mister—?"

Hearing the panic in the man's voice, she threw the latch, and he hurried inside. Water from his cap ran down his face, and his cloak dripped a puddle on her floor.

"'Pon my word!" she gasped. "Whatever—?"

"Horses bolted. We was—" He stopped to gulp air, then spilled his words, running them together. "I was drivin'—we was bound fer Durham when th' team shied. Wheel hit a rock and over she went quicker 'n Jack! God aid me, missus, but 'twasn't me fault, I swear it!" He caught his breath again, then rushed on, choking out, "Lord Rexford's hurt bad—'e jumped, but th' door caught 'is leg—took 'is boot plumb off, it did and 'e hit 'is head when 'e fell. 'E's out, 'e is, missus. I came down the road and saw yer light, I did."

For a moment, her world stood still, and she could only stare at the shaking man before her. He'd said Rexford, she was sure of that. But while her heart paused and her stomach knotted, she echoed hollowly, "Lord Rexford— did you say 'tis Rexford who is hurt?"

"Aye, missus. 'E's got ter 'ave 'elp, or 'e ain't survivin'. If yer 'usband . . ."

It was as though the years had faded away, and she could see the earl's handsome face, the shine of his black, waving hair, the reflection of Lady Conniston's chandeliers in his brilliant blue eyes, the warm smile that lit his face. What grand hopes she'd had of him in what now seemed another lifetime ago.

But by some stroke of ill fortune, the earl lay injured nearby, and she was going to see him again. Collecting herself, she moved to take her cloak down from the peg. "Where did you wreck?" she asked purposefully.

"Just beyond the bend in th' road, missus," William Beggs said, pointing with his hand. "If ye got a man as could—"

"There is none at home just now, I'm afraid."

"But 'is lights is out—'e don't know nuthin', and that's without saying 'is leg's broke by the look o' it, and 'is head's cut real bad. Ain't no sight fer a female, missus," he protested.

"I am accounted to have a strong stomach," she declared flatly. Turning quickly, she went to a drawer and retrieved a stoppered bottle. "I think there is plenty of laudanum," she decided.

"We was going ter Durham," he mumbled. "Be in a real takin', 'is mum will, when 'e ain't there. And God aid the man as tells 'er, for the old harridan's got a temper worse'n 'is, she 'as."

Charlotte disappeared briefly into her small bedchamber, then came back with a rolled blanket. "It'll be soaked in a minute, but at least it will provide some cover against the wind." She hesitated, then crossed the narrow room to the tea she'd prepared. On a night like this, Rexford was going to need something warm. "Do you have a flask?" she asked.

"Aye, but—"

"But you left it in the coach," she finished for him.

"Nay, but . . ." Reluctantly, he reached beneath his soggy coat and pulled out a flat bottle. "Got a bit o' rum in it," he admitted, handing it to her.

"That won't hurt—at least I don't think it will." She held it up to the firelight. "There's not much, anyway." Taking off the lid, she poured some of the hot tea into it, then added a little of the opiate. "Perhaps this will ease him."

"But yer a mort—a female," he muttered disgustedly, following her out the door. "And ye ain't even big enough ter 'elp lift 'im, I'll be bound."

"There's no time to waste!" she shouted as she threw

open the door. Without waiting for him, she pulled her cloak closer and forced her way through the driving rain, stumbling almost blindly up the narrow, muddy road.

Her face stung, and her cloak provided no warmth against the biting wind. She turned around, trying to back into it, but the steep drop between road and sea made that dangerous. The sound of the roiling sea hitting the rocks below was too near for a misstep. The coach driver caught up to her, catching her arm, and pulled her to the inside of the road.

"O'er there!" he yelled. "'E's over there!"

Struggling under the weight of her soaked cloak, she sloshed to where Rexford lay upon the ground. As lightning flashed, she could see he did not move. Another bolt showed one leg turned at an unnatural angle to his body. She pulled the rolled blanket out and dropped to her knees to place it over him.

"Damme, Thomas! 'E still ain't come to 'is senses?" Beggs asked.

"Naw," was the grim reply. "He ain't doin' nuthin'." The fellow looked at Charlotte. "Devil a bit! Billy, ye was s'posed ter fetch help, and ye brung a female!" he howled indignantly. "'Is lor'ship's in need o' more'n 'er, I can tell ye."

"Damme if there was another body ter be found—and 'tis *Mister* Beggs ter ye, Tom Tittle!"

Forgetting maidenly modesty, Charlotte slid her hand beneath the unconscious man's shirt to feel of his skin. His flesh was chill and damp. "He's losing his body heat!" she shouted over the wind at them.

"E's breathing, ain't he?" Beggs yelled back.

She moved her hand over the earl's rib cage. "Yes, but 'tis labored!" Reaching to touch the injured man's head, she felt through his wet hair with nearly numb fingertips until she found the lump at the back. It was sticky with blood.

"His scalp is torn, but I don't believe his head is fractured," she murmured to herself. As she spoke, she moved her hands down over the blanket to his lower leg. She did not have to uncover him to feel where the bone came through the skin. She looked up at the hovering driver and coachman. "You were quite right, Mr. Beggs, it is broken!"

Rexford lay there, vaguely hearing them, his whole being paralyzed by the hot, searing pain in his leg. He'd taken a ball, maybe worse, and without help he was going to die in this godforsaken place—he was going to die in the mud in Spain. He had to stay awake if he were to live—he had to let them know he was still alive. Otherwise, he'd be stacked with the corpses.

"Unnnhhhhh—unnnhuhhhhh."

"Why, e's comin' ter 'is senses! Lawks a mercy, if 'e ain't! Look at 'im, Mr. Beggs!"

"Leftenant . . ." he whispered hoarsely as she leaned close to hear. "Leftenant Howe—is he—?"

"Eh?" Behind her, Tittle was momentarily taken aback.

"Promised him . . ." He struggled, but could not sit up. "Got to tell him . . ."

"You are all right, my lord!" Charlotte shouted above the wind. "There has been an accident, but you have survived!"

"Don't let them cut—don't let them cut it off," he gasped.

"Gor blimey, but 'e's out of 'is 'ead, ain't 'e?" Beggs cried. "'E thinks as 'e's still in the bloody war! Hit ain't th' peninsula, milord!" he yelled into his master's face. "Ye done came back from there, ye know, and Boney's been beat, 'e 'as! Aye, and ye done as much as any ter see it!"

With an effort, the earl managed to open his eyes. Blinking blankly, he tried to think. "Sorry about the boy . . . sorry . . . but I—"

"You aren't in the war, my lord. You are in Yorkshire, just outside Whitby," Charlotte told him loudly. "There has been a carriage wreck."

"My leg. I cannot move it. I . . ."

"'Tis broken." She leaned closer and cupped her mouth so that he could hear. "We shall have to send for the doctor. In the meantime, we shall give you a bit of laudanum to ease you."

"No," he croaked. "Don't . . . want anything. Got to keep my leg. . . ."

It was obvious that he was too confused to understand, probably because of the force with which his head had hit the rocky road. In any event, it would do him no good to lie in the cold mud. Wiping wet hands on her wet cloak, she looked up. "Can you carry him as far as my cottage, do you think? I know we ought not to move him, but he cannot remain here."

"Aye." William Beggs looked to his coachman. "Well, Thomas, are ye game fer it?"

"'E's a 'eavy bloke, but, aye," Thomas Tittle responded.

Despite the earl's refusal, she gestured to the driver for the flask. Taking it, she opened the bottle and held it to the injured man's lips. "You are going to need this, I assure you."

Still dazed, he pushed it away. "No . . . got to . . . get up," he gasped.

"Mr. Beggs, you'll have to hold him, else he will strangle," she ordered.

"'E's got the devil's own temper," the driver warned her. "If 'e says 'e don't——"

She reached to touch the injured leg, and she felt the earl's whole body go rigid. Again, she put her mouth close to his ear, telling him, "You shall wish for more than laudanum ere you are inside." She waited until Beggs braced his shoulders before holding it to his lips again. "Try to take as much as you can," she said as she tipped it.

He pushed it away. "No . . . don't want . . ."

"Nonsense." Looking up, she appealed for help. "Mr. . . . er . . . Tittle, is it? Can you straighten his leg ere he is lifted?"

"Aye, missus!"

Excruciating pain shot from his shin to his hip, and nausea washed over Rexford, nearly overwhelming him. This time, when she put the flask to his mouth, he took great gulps of the mixture. As his driver eased him down, he closed his eyes briefly. "Damn," he muttered through clenched teeth.

She started to explain that they were going to take him

to her cottage, but her throat was raw from shouting. And whether he understood at this point did not truly matter. She stood, then waited as the two servants thrust sturdy shoulders beneath the earl's arms and crossed arms behind his soaked back, lifting him from the muddy road. A flash of lightning lit his face, betraying eyes closed against nearly unbearable pain.

"Hit ain't far, milord," one of the men assured him.

Despite the storm that tore at them and the slippery mud beneath their feet, they managed to carry him the short distance to her cottage. Soaked to the skin and cold beyond bearing, she trudged ahead of them to open her door.

"You can put him in the chair by the hearth," she said, removing her dripping cloak. Leaning over, she wrung out her hair, then pushed it back, where it clung to her face and neck. "You'd best get him out of his wet coat while I prepare the bed."

"Aye."

Picking up her two cruzie lamps, she carried them to the fire, where she handed one to Beggs. "There's enough wick left, I think, but there's not much oil. I hope it will last until we are done." Lighting the other one herself, she took it with her into the small bedchamber. "I shall be out in a trice," she promised as she closed the door.

She undressed quickly and found dry clothes. Her teeth chattering, her body shivering from nerves as well as cold, she managed to pull them over her head. As she dragged a comb through her dripping hair, her stomach growled, reminding her that she'd still not eaten. But there was no help for that, at least not until Lord Rexford was gotten to bed and Dr. Alstead summoned. As the last button was fastened, she turned her attention to the room.

He was going to bleed onto the bed, she knew, and yet there was nowhere else to put him. Pulling off the coverlet, she removed her sheets and replaced them with old, worn blankets.

The room was too cold. He would have to have a brick heated for his feet, else he'd never get warm. How humble everything was, she thought as she surveyed the plain bedstead, the small table, the cabinet that served for her wardrobe, and the flat wooden box where she stored everything else. Definitely not fit for a man of Rexford's means. Picking up the lamp, she went back to the main room.

The earl was leaning back, his eyes closed, his teeth clenched, his face ashen beneath his wet, wavy hair. She moved closer, drawn as much by curiosity as by memory. And as the lamplight caught the glint of silver amongst the black at his temples, the faint lines at the corners of his eyes and mouth, she realized with a start that he was no longer the grand buck of her youth, but rather a man close to forty. It just didn't seem possible, for she'd always remembered him as being boyishly handsome. She'd always remembered him as he'd been that night at Lady Conniston's ball.

Beggs looked at him and shook his head. "Gor, but he's a bloody mess, ain't he?" he murmured, breaking into her thoughts.

"What? Oh . . . yes . . . yes, he is," she managed.

The earl's eyes opened, and as he stared upward she

was struck by the same brilliant blue. In that at least her memory had not failed. Looking into those eyes, she felt anew the pang beneath her breastbone. Would he even remember her at all, she dared to wonder.

"How bad is it?" he croaked.

She fought the urge to lie to him. "Well," she answered cautiously, "I daresay it must be better than it looks just now. I expect we shall know a great deal more when you are cleaned up, and when Dr. Alstead sees your leg, of course."

"The ball . . ."

"Ball's out, milord," Beggs reminded him. "Ye ain't in Spain no more."

"Hurts like the devil." As he spoke, he clenched his jaw, biting down hard against the pain. "Don't want to lose the limb."

"Hit's just broke," Tittle reassured him.

But Charlotte was by no means certain that the leg could be saved after being snapped like a stick. Exhaling, she forced herself to take charge again. "As it is some distance to Dr. Alstead's, if we do not clean your wounds ere he gets here, they will fester," she stated matter-of-factly. "And my father used to say there was nothing worse than a bone infection."

He'd closed his eyes again. "Was he a doctor?"

"No. But we raised sheep and horses at Buckley, and he was forever treating them for nearly everything. I think Papa once wished to be a surgeon, but his father felt it quite beneath a Winslow." She looked down, hoping for a glimmer of recognition, but there was none. Hiding her disappointment, she asked, "Do you wish for more laudanum? If you take it now, it ought to work before the doctor gets here." As she spoke, she lifted the wet blanket up to examine the leg.

"No." As he felt her fingers touch him, he forced himself to look first at her, then down to where the sharp edge of his displaced bone broke through his muddy, blood-soaked breeches. He didn't have to be told now, he'd seen enough on the battlefield to know he'd be damned fortunate to keep anything beneath the knee. "All right," he decided.

She took the laudanum bottle and poured the rest into a cup. As she went to dip from the water bucket to dilute the opiate, Beggs spoke up. "'Is lordship was dec'rated by the Regent, ye know."

"Oh?" she murmured politely.

"Aye. 'E fought th' Frogs, 'e did, until 'e was wounded at Salamanca," the man declared proudly.

"Most noblemen of my limited acquaintance stayed home, I'm afraid."

"Guess ye know the neighborin' Quality, eh?"

She started to retort that she'd had her moment amongst the ton, then bit the words back. It didn't matter anymore, anyway. It didn't even matter if Rexford didn't remember her. Indeed, it would be less humiliating if he did not, she told herself resolutely, for the last thing she would want of him would be his pity.

Bringing the cup back, she held it for the earl. "Go on, drink," she urged him. "None of this is going to be pleasant, I'm afraid."

He opened those blue eyes again, nearly unnerving her. "I know." He swallowed half of it, then pushed it away, grimacing. "Enough. 'Tis enough."

She put the empty vessel on the table, then reached beneath the battered cupboard to retrieve the dishpan, a cake of strong lye soap, a clean cloth, and her sharpest knife. The cat rubbed against her leg and looked up at her reproachfully, making it plain that he resented company. She stopped to pour a saucer of milk and set it on the floor before she carried her supplies to the water bucket. Ladling another dipper of cool water into the washpan, she told herself that no matter how inclined she might be to retch, she must not give over to the weakness.

Taking care not to spill it, she brought the pan back to the fire, where she added steaming water from her teapot. She swished it around, then tested the temperature.

"Lean him forward, and hold him lest he faints," she ordered Beggs. "The laudanum has not taken full effect yet, so he is going to feel this."

"'E ain't no man-milliner, I'll be bound 'e ain't. Tough as the Iron Duke 'imself, 'e is."

But contrary to Beggs's belief in him, Rexford felt utterly sick. The last laudanum had hit the pit of his stomach, and on top of the mixture he'd had before, he was having to swallow to keep it down. He was dizzy, far too dizzy, and everything in the room was moving while he struggled to keep what little dignity he had left. He bent his shoulders and held his head with both hands, trying to fight each new wave of nausea.

Charlotte wrung out the cloth and began washing the matted, sticky hair above his nape, revealing the nasty gash she'd suspected. His wet, muddy shoulders shuddered as she touched the raw scalp.

"I'm sorry," she said. "If you feel the need, go ahead and curse, or whatever you wish. I assure you I am not missish in the least."

"If I wished to curse, I would," he gritted out.

She tried to be matter-of-fact, but for all her appearance of assurance, she'd never been closer than a country dance to him or any other man before she'd brazenly felt of his body in the road. She rinsed out the bloody cloth. "This ought to be stitched," she murmured, "but having no experience beyond watching Papa sew up a lamb torn by the miller's dog, I shall not attempt it. Besides, the leg is in greater need of attention."

Working intently now, she poured out the contents of the pan, then refilled it. Picking up the knife, she sought the seam of the expensively tailored, close-fitting breeches. "At least there is no boot to remove, which is a blessing, for your leg is already quite swollen." Taking care not to cut him, she used the tip of the blade to rip the seam open, exposing his shin.

"Gor blimey!" Beggs gasped, turning away. "Tom, ye got ter 'old 'im, fer I ain't up ter it."

Charlotte's stomach knotted as she looked upon the jagged bone that punctured the skin. Where the bone had snapped, thick, congealing blood seeped from the marrow. Afraid to actually touch it, she hesitated.

"Go on." As he spoke, the earl closed his eyes yet again to stop the spinning room. "Do what you have to, and get it over and done."

"I'm . . . I'm going to pour water over it, then leave it to Dr. Alstead," she answered. "After that, we'll get you out of your wet clothes and into bed."

Whether from the opiate or from the combination of it and the rum, he felt almost detached despite the intense, hot ache of his broken bone. Until she poured the soapy water over it. Every nerve between his hip and his foot was on fire. He jerked in reflex, then everything went black.

"Damme if he ain't swooned!" Tom Tittle exclaimed.

"If he has, it is a blessing," Charlotte murmured.

As cold as she still was, she could feel the perspiration on her forehead. She wiped her face with the back of her hand, then went back to work, flushing the wound until she was satisfied that it was as clean as she could make it. When she was done, she rose, shaking, and went again into the area that served as her kitchen to find a cloth. Tearing it into strips, she came back and wrapped it lightly over the break. Standing again, she exhaled her relief. She looked into the admiring gaze of the nearest coachman.

"Ye got the 'ealing gift, missus," Beggs declared.

"You'll have to get his wet clothes off and put him to bed," she said wearily. Handing over the knife, she added, "Use this to cut what does not come off easily, and when you are done, see that he is between the blankets. In the meantime, I shall warm a brick for his feet and write a note to the doctor."

She waited until they had taken him into her bedchamber, then she found her writing supplies, carried them to her eating table, and sharpened a pen. Dipping it into her ink, she composed a plea to Alstead, telling of the accident, adding, "As I doubt he can be moved, his lordship will be needing whatsoever nightshirts and other clothing you may spare," before signing it, "Your obedient, etc., Charlotte Winslow."

While the hastily fetched physician examined the earl in the other room, Charlotte sat staring absently over her scarce-touched stew, while the marmalade cat curled contentedly at her feet. No, it did not seem possible that she was seeing Rexford again, that he was actually in her cottage. Not after the passage of fifteen years. If she couldn't see the remainder of blood spots on her floor, she'd be inclined to believe she was merely dreaming.

Not that she hadn't tried to follow what little gossip and news there'd been of him. She'd known when he'd wed. Indeed, she could still feel the pain that had cut through her breastbone like a knife when she'd read the announcement in the *Gazette*. As she recalled them, the words seemed to echo in her ears. "Henry, Duke of Fairfax, announces the betrothal of his daughter, Lady Helena Heversham, to Richard, Earl of Rexford. A spring wedding at Heversham Park is intended."

And she'd known that after Lady Helena died in childbed, Rexford had demonstrated his grief by going off to war, where he'd distinguished himself in the peninsular campaigns. The gossips had speculated that without his beautiful wife, he no longer wished to live, but that was a hoax if she'd ever heard one, for he'd fought against Boney nearly ten years before coming home.

Still, upon seeing him now, Charlotte was stunned by the changes aging had wrought. For a moment, she stared into the hearth, seeing him as she so often had, a young man famed nearly as much for his address as for his handsome face. Perhaps 'twas her memory that was faulty, she conceded.

On impulse, she rose to rummage in her sketch boxes, taking out a yellowed folder of pictures she'd drawn in what now seemed another age. Carrying it back to the table, she opened it gingerly. Shuffling through her drawings, she came to those of him, and for a long time she studied her favorite one as though she willed him to come to life again for her.

Closing her eyes, she allowed herself to think back, to see again the pretty young girl smiling at her from her mirror. And now it seemed as though Lady Conniston's ball had been but yesterday, as though she could still smell the clean scent of the Hungary water he'd worn that night. Just as he was in the picture she'd done of him, he'd been so very handsome, and his bright blue eyes had been so warm, so filled with admiration then.

Though he'd signed her dance card at other affairs, that night his manner had been different. He'd actually singled her out, dancing not once but twice with her, taking her into supper on his arm while the tabbies had watched and speculated between themselves as to the significance of every smile he gave her.

And from somewhere behind the potted ferns, she'd

heard Lady Leffingwell titter, "'Twould seem that Rexford means to fix his interest with the country chit. How vexing for all those who have cast such lures at him." "Why, she is but a nobody," someone had replied. To which Lady Lavinia had countered, "Pish and nonsense. There is good breeding on her mother's side, and Rexford certainly does not have to catch himself an heiress. Why"—Lavinia Leffingwell's voice had lowered, and Charlotte had strained shamelessly to hear the rest of it—"why, Arthur tells me all the Lindens cut up warm, and Richard's father was no different from the rest of them—left more than seventy-five thousand pounds to his only heir, not to mention all those houses. Though why he has let Beatrice remain at Durham, I am sure I don't know, for dowagers always amuse themselves by meddling. I ought to know, for I am one myself," she added definitely.

How heady it had been just to hear her name linked with Rexford's. Her fanciful mind had taken to the notion, going so far as to consider how Charlotte Caroline Maria Winslow Linden, Countess of Rexford, might sound. It had seemed impossible even then. .

And once again she felt that ache, the yearning that came with memories of what might have been. Usually, she forced her thoughts away, telling herself she had much for which to be grateful. But just now she had not the will.

She'd had every green girl's dreams then, daring to believe that a man of wealth and title could throw his hat over the windmill for her. As much as she'd wanted to hope Lady Leffingwell had been right, in the end she'd had to concede what she'd mistaken for interest had merely been kindness. She'd been so easily swept off her feet because she'd encountered far too few kind gentlemen amongst the ton. Most were too concerned with the cut of their coats, too filled with their own conceit to care for anything beyond themselves.

Anyway, none of it mattered anymore, for the green girl was long gone, her dreams dead, dashed upon the shoals of a grim reality. Instead of presiding over Rexford's table, she lived scandalously alone, far removed from the gilded, glittering ballrooms of his world. And by passing herself off as Charles Winslow to her clients, she earned everything from the roof over her head to the food on her table, something no respectable female would dare to admit.

But for one enchanted evening at Lady Conniston's ball, the most sought-after buck in all of London had singled her out for two dances. And beyond that, he'd asked her mother's permission to "take Miss Charlotte for a turn about Hyde Park tomorrow at five o'clock." How everyone had envied her that night. She swallowed, remembering her mama's excited chatter on the way home.

"Oh, I vow I am in alt, dearest! I must tell William that the economies we have practiced to bring you out have paid off most handsomely! Now I should have been content with a plain mister of substance, of course, but 'tis Rexford! Who could have thought it—Rexford! Mark my words, Charlotte, he means to make you his countess!"

How very wide of the mark her mama had been, she recalled regretfully. That night had proven to be the most fateful of her life, but for a very different reason. And if she lived to be one hundred, she'd never forget the subdued manners of the servants or the stricken look on her mother's face when Dr. Crowe had said her papa was dead of heart failure at forty-seven.

And so had ended her only London Season. They'd withdrawn to Buckley Hall to bury her father, then remained there to mourn him for the requisite year. But within a week the awful truth had come out in a visit from her father's solicitor.

"Mr. Winslow has made some rather unfortunate investments, I'm afraid," he'd explained apologetically. "He gamed excessively, you mean," had been her mother's acerbic retort. But it was worse than Mama or Charlotte or the younger girls could ever have imagined—Buckley Hall itself had needed to be sold, and the extent of debts to be satisfied had been utterly overwhelming, ending any thought of their ever returning to London.

She'd written Rexford, of course, apologizing for missing the turn about the park, explaining her abrupt departure. But she'd not been quite able to tell him all of it, for she'd not wanted his pity. And it was just as well, she supposed. After all, for all her hopes of him, he'd never so much as bothered to answer. To add to the pain, it had taken him but a year and a half to wed another. Miss March, who'd actually seen his countess, confided to Charlotte's sister Sarah that Lady Helena had been that year's reigning beauty. And so she'd had to put away her dreams of him and go on.

Once the proceeds of Buckley Hall had partially

settled William Winslow's staggering debts, his destitute family had gone to live with one of his wife's brothers, who had seemed to begrudge them every pea they ate. Finally, in the end, Mama's spirit had failed, and she died the year Charlotte turned twenty-one. Uncle Henry, under the guise of being helpful, had secured Charlotte a position as companion to a spiteful, ill-tempered elderly female. It had lasted a week.

"Ahem."

Startled, she looked up to catch Dr. Alstead's frown. "I'm sorry," she responded apologetically. "I'm afraid I was woolgathering."

"I said I shall require some assistance. While his lordship's coachmen hold him down, I would have you hand my instruments to me. He has refused any more laudanum, despite the fact I have told him 'twill be excruciatingly painful," he explained irritably.

"You . . . you aren't going to amputate the leg, are you?" she managed to ask. "I mean——"

"I'm going to have a go at saving it first, Miss Winslow," he snapped. "However, I might point out that the longer the delay, the greater likelihood of infection where the bone is exposed. And gangrene, if it sets in, will take the choice from me, I'm afraid."

"Yes, of course," she agreed. Quickly shoving her pictures back into the folder, she rose. "I did try to clean him up a bit for you," she added.

"So I was told. They said 'twas you as cut his breeches off," he said stiffly. "But then I suppose I ought not to be surprised, Miss Winslow, for to my notion you are a very singular sort of female."

As he spoke, he emphasized the word *singular* rather dampeningly, as though she'd committed some sin, when in fact all she'd done was live alone. She bit back a retort. It didn't make any difference what he thought of her, she told herself as she followed him back into her bedchamber.

Rexford's face was ashen, his jaw clenched tightly against the pain. Beggs looked up, then shook his head. "'E ain't having no more o' the medicine, missus. I told 'im—"

"Nonsense," she cut in shortly. Reaching for the bottle that the doctor had set out on the table, she unstoppered it and started to measure some into an empty cup.

"No," the earl gritted out.

"Don't be foolish," she chided him. "You will need it."

"Don't be wifely," he shot back. Even as he said it, he winced visibly. "I don't want anything."

"'E's a stubborn man, 'e is," Tittle maintained stoutly.

"We have already been through this more times than I care to count," Alstead muttered. "Man's an obstreperous fool, if you'd have my opinion of him."

"But *why?*" she persisted, her eyes on Rexford. "Without it, you will be in agony, sir."

For a moment, he squeezed his eyes shut, then reopened them as though his will could somehow master pain. "Because," he rasped out, "I have seen too many dosed into oblivion who have wakened with one less limb."

"You'll be damned sorry, but who am I to tell a nob like yourself how you ought to go on." Taking out a knife, the doctor shrugged, then nodded to the coachmen. "Hold him down like I told you, boys. If he screams, don't let him go, particularly not if you are the one as is holding his leg."

"I got 'im," Beggs promised. "'E ain't movin' none."

"See as he stays that way." Alstead handed Charlotte his surgeon's bag. "Keep it near and open, 'tis all I ask. Can you do that?"

"Yes."

He lifted the sheet off Rexford's broken leg, studied it appraisingly for a moment, then exhaled heavily. After casting one last warning look at Beggs, he went to work, slitting the flesh next to the exposed bone. The earl gasped audibly, stiffened reflexively, and bit his lip, drawing blood. At first, Charlotte thought he'd fainted, but the determined clench of his jaw told her he hadn't.

"Snapped like a stick," Alstead muttered. "Bring the lamp closer, will you?"

"Aye, guv'nor," Tittle responded promptly.

Charlotte kept her eyes on the break, watching as the elderly physician matched the sharp edges, joined them together, dug beneath to wrap some sort of cord around them, then finished by dusting the whole with basilicum powder. With each move he made, the muscles of Rexford's calf jerked, but Alstead did not seem bothered by it. Finally, he turned around and ordered curtly, "The threaded needle."

"Where?"

"In the pouch."

She found it and gave it to him. Despite unsteady

hands, he managed to take neat stitches, pulling the torn flesh together, closing the wound over his handiwork. It wasn't until he straightened up that she breathed her relief.

"Gor blimey!" Billy said. "Where'd ye learn ter do that?"

"In the colonies."

"Eh?"

Alstead looked across at him. "I served as surgeon under Gentleman Johnny Burgoyne ere you were breeched, boy."

"You was in the army?" Thomas asked, awed.

"Aye. Counter to recent opinion, Napoleon did not invent war nor the means to man's destruction," the old man reminded him dryly. "In my time, it was the damned rebels in America."

"What did you use to hold the bone, sir?" Charlotte wanted to know.

"Gut—boiled gut." Wiping his hands on his surgeon's apron, he returned his attention to Rexford. "Now let us look at that head. A few stitches there, and I am on my way." He nodded significantly, prompting the two coachmen to ease the earl onto the unaffected side. His tension gone, he began to whistle "God Save the King" rather tunelessly as he sewed. "There," he declared finally. "Gently put him down, boys."

The earl's eyes remained closed, his forehead wet with perspiration. "If the leg don't fester, you'll keep it. As for the head, the wound's in the hair, so you'll remain a handsome enough devil," Alstead told him. "Miss Winslow ought to be able to tend the dressing. If naught's amiss and I'm not called back ere then, I'll come day after next to look at my work. I've told this fellow"—he pointed to Billy—"how to make a crutch. Ever use one before?"

"Yes." Rexford's voice was scarce above a whisper. "When I was wounded before."

"Aye, I saw where the ball took part of the muscle. Guess bullets don't know the difference between a nob and anybody else, eh?" When the earl didn't answer, Alstead went on explaining, "If the leg is hot or if you are fevered, Miss Winslow is to send for me immediately." He leaned over Rexford's face. "No hill too high for a man as was shot at Salamanca, eh?"

"No."

"Demned fortunate you didn't bleed to death in Spain, you know. That ball couldn't have missed the artery by more'n an inch." Turning to take his bag, he added, "You'd best pay Miss Winslow to keep you, for it'll be weeks ere you ought to travel. And I daresay the foolish creature hasn't a feather to fly with, as the saying goes. Can't be much to be made in drawing pictures, after all."

She felt the heat rise to her face. "Oh, but I assure you—"

"Pride don't fill stomachs, missy," Alstead snapped. "And from all I've heard, he's got gold to spare. Yes, well, that's all I can think of just now."

Rexford took a deep breath, then exhaled. "My thanks," he managed tiredly.

The doctor looked to Charlotte. "He'll take the

laudanum I'm leaving for him now, no doubt about it. Eight drops in half a glass of water whenever he asks for it until tomorrow. Then no more than six and be sparing with it—four times to the day at most."

"And the dressing? You mentioned I would be tending the dressing," she reminded him.

"Oh, aye. Change it daily, and wrap clean linen loosely around it. Don't cut off any circulation. Tie it so as two fingers can be got between the string and the dressing. When you take one off, wash the wound with good soap, and be sure to keep it dry with basilicum. All there is to it." He glanced down at the earl again. "Keep him quiet—gruel today, food tomorrow. If you are wishful of it, I can send Mrs. Adams from the village for propriety."

"I scarce think him in any condition to compromise anyone," she responded dryly. "And I am not at all sure she would wish to come here."

"Humph! For a look at an earl, she might." Turning away, he rearranged the contents of his bag, then snapped it shut. "I am leaving another nightshirt on the chair. 'Tis too wide and too short, but it'll do for now. Well, you got these boys as can help you with him, I suppose, though where you are to put them, I don't know."

"There is a feather mattress on the truckle, or I might sleep in the other room on a chair."

He started to leave. "Give you one thing, Miss Winslow," he shot over his shoulder, "you never flinched so much as an inch."

"I shall choose to take that as a compliment."

"Meant it so." Alstead hesitated. "You know, with the least encouragement, you could bring Raggett up to scratch . . . fellow's not put off by your pictures."

"Oh?"

"Told Mrs. Adams you are still a fine-looking female, Miss Winslow. Though what he's to think of having Rexford here——"

"Mr. Raggett and I should not suit," she interrupted him hastily. "Indeed, but we have scarce spoken."

In the other room, she retrieved Alstead's spattered greatcoat for him, then saw him to the door. As he was about to open it, Rexford's coachmen emerged from the sickroom.

"'E says as we are ter see ye 'ome," Beggs told the doctor. "'E don't want ye fallin' over the cliff yerself."

"Young man——"

"If ye was ter let me 'ave the 'orn lantern so's we can get back, I'd bring it ter ye tomorrow," Thomas added.

"Tomorrow's today," the old man muttered, then he relented. "But as the night's half gone already, you'd might as well finish it at the Red Bull. If you haven't the blunt, I'll have the bill put down to Rexford."

"But 'is lor'ship——"

"After eight more drops of laudanum, he'll be beyond knowing, I expect." The doctor jammed his hat over his unfashionably long white locks, then bowed slightly. "Goodnight, Miss Winslow."

"Wait. I don't suppose you could see that Mr. Beggs is able to engage a horse, could you?" As Alstead seemed taken aback, she explained, "Lord Rexford's mother awaits him at

Durham, and I'd have her know what has befallen him. Well, she must be worried, I should think."

"Me?" Billy Beggs eyed her askance. "Ye don't know 'er, do ye? Nay, but it ought ter be Mr. Tittle as goes," he protested.

"And I thought ye was me friend," Thomas said mournfully. "I ain't going alone ter beard th' dowager, I tell ye."

"Well, someone ought to tell her he's going to be all right," she said, exasperated.

"I'll see they get word to Lady Rexford," the doctor assured her. "Goodnight again, Miss Winslow."

She waited until the doctor's tilbury was safely on the road, then she closed and latched the door. Alone now, she rubbed her arms against the chill air before moving to lay another log upon the fire. Poking it until it settled, she stood there, her hands outstretched, drawing warmth from the popping coals.

She supposed she ought to have welcomed another woman's assistance, but there simply wasn't any place to put Mrs. Adams. Indeed, if Rexford's coachmen hadn't gone with the doctor, she'd have had to put them on the floor.

She was tired, nearly too tired to sleep, and her mother's clock chimed once. One o'clock, and she still had to give the earl his pain-killing medicine. And in a morning certain to come too soon, she had to finish Mr. Burleigh's poster. Squaring her own aching shoulders, she walked into the bedchamber for one last look at Rexford.

He appeared to be asleep. In the faint light from the

smoking cruzie, he seemed younger, more vulnerable than before. The shadows played tricks before her, obscuring the silver sprinkled in his dark hair, the lines at the corners of his lips and eyes. Unable to resist the temptation, she reached to brush at the unruly hair with her fingertips. His eyes opened, startling her. Embarrassed, she stepped back.

"I . . . uh, that is, I was wishful of seeing if you slept . . . or if you had decided to take the laudanum now."

He stared up at her, his eyes betraying how much the leg throbbed. "No to both," he muttered.

"You are fortunate to still have your leg, you know."

"I'll be thankful tomorrow."

"Yes, well, if you are quite determined, I shall take my blanket and withdraw to the fire, my lord. Tomorrow, no doubt, either Mr. Beggs or Mr. Tittle will apprise your mother of the accident."

"I don't want to see her."

There was such bitterness in his voice that she was momentarily taken aback. "But you were going to see her, weren't you? I thought Mr. Beggs said—"

He passed a hand over his face, then shook his head tiredly. "I want her out of my house and my life. And I want her to take Sedgely and his simpering daughter with him."

"Oh."

Again he sucked in his breath and held it until he could speak over the pain. "My mother has misled them into thinking I wish to step into the damned parson's mousetrap again," he said finally. "Once burned, twice warned, isn't it?"

"Never having been burned at all, I cannot say." Feeling very awkward, she retreated. "If you do not mind it, I shall collect what I need and bid you good night, my lord."

"Wait—"

"Yes?"

"I'd take water . . . without the laudanum."

"Yes, of course." Turning back, she quickly dipped water from a pitcher into a cup. Leaning over to lift his head with one hand, she gave him his drink with the other.

He swallowed, then lay back. "My thanks."

She longed to ask him of his wife—if Lady Helena had been the beauty Miss March had reported. Instead, she reached for the blanket.

"God," he muttered, "what a sinner I must've been to deserve this."

"At least the Almighty saw fit to spare you the fate of your horses."

"Are you always so cheerful?" he gibed.

"No. Sometimes I am positively blue-deviled. Sometimes I wish for things I cannot have. And sometimes I worry that Mr. Burleigh or Madame Cecile will not like what I have done for them. But in the end, the Almighty always provides."

"Does He?"

"Perhaps not precisely in the manner I have wished," she admitted, "but I have never gone hungry, nor have I had to endure the importunities foisted upon females in service."

Bustling about the small room setting things right, she opened her cabinet and found her heavy woolen nightgown.

Moving to her storage chest, she took out her last blanket. When she finally turned her attention back to him, it appeared as though he had dozed off.

"Good night, my lord," she said softly.

He didn't respond until she reached the door. "Wait," he said again.

She stopped. "Did you need something else?"

"I don't know what I need."

"Oh." Then the obvious dawned on her. "Would you like for me to leave the chamberpot on the table so you can reach it?" Even as she asked, she could feel her face redden. Before he could say anything, she drew the folded blanket and nightgown to her chest like a shield. "I assure you I shall try not to be missish in such matters." Not daring to look at him, she reached beneath a corner of her bed and drew out the pot. Setting it beside him, she turned to leave again.

"You appear to be one of the few sensible females," he murmured, smiling faintly.

"Well, as there is no chambermaid—nor any other servant, for that matter—I expect I haven't much choice."

"Alstead called you Miss Winslow."

She had her hand on the doorknob. "Yes."

"And you mentioned Buckley Hall."

She felt her breath catch painfully. "It was my home—a long time ago, I lived there. My father was William Winslow." When he said nothing, she blurted out, "I am sure you will not remember me, Lord Rexford, but we were briefly acquainted. I was—that is, I am Miss Winslow—Miss Charlotte Winslow, to be precise."

Had he not been in such agony, he would have pursued the matter. He would have asked how she came to be alone in such a godforsaken, isolated place, but he didn't. "I see."

"You can be forgiven for not remembering, for I have not been to London since—well, I have not been there in the past fifteen years. And the acquaintance was the merest one, I am sure. But you were quite kind, I recall." She was rattling on, making a fool of herself, no doubt. "Yes, well, if I am to finish Mr. Burleigh's poster, I really must get to bed. I shall leave the door open lest you need to call for me. Good night, sir."

He stared after her, thinking he would ask more on the morrow. "Good night, Miss Winslow," he murmured.

But long after she left, long after he no longer heard her moving about in the other room, he lay awake, fighting the throbbing in his leg. A clock struck three, and he began to wish he'd not refused the drug. But he wouldn't give in and wake her. He closed his eyes and tried to think of anything, everything but the pain.

Fixing his thoughts on Charlotte Winslow, he considered where he'd last seen her. It could have been at one of Sally Jersey's parties. No, it wasn't. With an effort, he tried to remember how she looked then. As her image came to mind, he recalled his disappointment when she'd suddenly gone into mourning. He'd written his condolences to her, but there'd been no reply, indicating he'd been mistaken in her.

Fifteen years, she said. Then it dawned on him. He'd

last seen her when Meg Conniston had come out in one of the grandest balls of that season.

Unable to stand the pulsing ache in his leg any longer, he turned his head and saw the laudanum bottle. And as much as he hated giving over to the nightmares that were certain to come with it, he reached for it. There was still a little water in his cup. He unstoppered the bottle and poured liberally from it. Putting it back, he swirled the dose, mixing it, then he gulped every last bit down.

The raging storm had abated, replaced by a cold, steady rain. She shifted uncomfortably in her chair and pulled the worn blanket closer. It was without doubt one of the longest nights of her life. She slept fitfully, dreaming wild, fanciful dreams where she was young and Rexford was still coming to drive her about the park. And her mother was vowing to buy her all manner of dresses, even a ballgown from Madame Cecile's, saying it was no extravagance at all. Sarah and Kate were still at home, waiting eagerly to follow in her footsteps. And Papa was proud of her, so very proud of her.

But something was wrong. It was winter; she could feel the cold in her bones and smell the smoke from a winter's fire. Rousing, she stared about her, seeing the heavy shadows, the faint, familiar outlines of the furniture in her cottage. The wind must have shifted, for despite the glowing coals in the hearth, the room was chilly, the blanket inadequate.

Rising, she wrapped the blanket about her and hobbled on nearly numb legs to poke at the fire. What she needed was to lie down, to curl up in a bed for warmth. There had to be some other wrap, something else she could use.

Tiptoeing to her open bedchamber door, she listened for a moment, hearing only silence. Alarmed, she crept into the room and walked closer to her bed. The wick in the cruzie lamp was drowning, a small, valiant flame flickering its last in the sea of oil.

"My lord," she whispered, "are you quite all right?"

He didn't answer.

Her hand touched the blanket where it lay over Dr. Alstead's nightshirt. "You were quite the best of the lot, the grandest buck of your day, you know. We all thought so. There wasn't a female amongst the ton who did not cast out lures to you," she recalled softly. "But I expect war changes a man, doesn't it? The old things no longer seem so very important, I suppose."

Reluctantly, she drew her hand away to rub warmth into her arm. Moving stealthily to the other side of the bed, she reached down to pull out the truckle, hoping to find another blanket. Her cold, stiff fingers felt the feather mattress, but it was too heavy to pull out without waking him.

He'd never know she'd slept in there, she reasoned. Or if he did waken, she could say he'd called out, that she'd been afraid she might not hear him the next time. Parting with the small warmth of her worn blanket, she added it to the one on the truckle, then slipped under both of them.

Slowly, even so slowly, the cradling featherbed

warmed, giving back the heat to her body. The sound of rain beating steadily upon the roof combined with that of Rexford's rhythmic breathing to lull her. And this time when she slept, there were no dreams to plague her.

Moaning in his sleep, he tried to turn over. But his wound pained him. Cradling his head on his hard saddle, he listened to the sounds.

Somewhere in the distance, the church bells still tolled for the dead. As he lay there in the darkness, he could hear the screams, and he could smell the awful stench of burning flesh and of blood. It was hot, close, stifling within the confines of the tent. His leg burned as though someone had thrust a hot poker into the hole in his thigh. Gentler hands pushed his away from the bandage, while a soft voice told him he was going to live. But he knew she lied. He could hear the screams everywhere. Everywhere. He could smell the blood. He heard her summon the surgeon, he heard her say he was far too hot.

The light. The light was too bright, the tunnel leading to it oddly dark. He was being sucked into it, but he would not go, not yet. Bracing his legs against the pull, he struggled to stay. He could hear his own voice shouting hoarsely that he wasn't ready to die.

She heard him scream, and she came awake with a start, rolling her tired body from the truckle. The wick in the cruzie had gone out, leaving the room in darkness, forcing her to grope for the edge of his bed. She found one of his clenched hands.

"Too much blood . . . lost too much blood," he gasped, his fingers closing painfully over hers. "Hot . . . too hot . . ."

In truth, his hand was ice cold, and he was shivering

uncontrollably. She leaned over him. "You are all right," she said soothingly. "You are all right."

"Benson . . . Benson took a ball . . . saw him . . . took his head . . ."

"Shhhhh. You have a broken leg, 'tis all, my lord. It will mend, it will mend," she repeated over and over.

"Got to . . . stop the blood," he mumbled. "Losing too much blood."

"No, the wound has been closed." With her free hand, she brushed his hair back from his temples as one would for a fretting child. "You are all right, my lord," she whispered yet again.

"Thirsty . . . so thirsty . . ."

She glanced at the laudanum bottle and saw that it was nearly empty, indicating that he'd taken too much. Disengaging her hand from his, she tucked the blanket closer about his shaking shoulders, promising, "I shall get you a drink of water in a trice."

"Don't go—don't leave me to die—don't . . ." He fought the blanket, tearing it away, grasping for her arm.

"You are not going to die, my lord, you have a broken leg," she said more loudly. "You are not in the peninsula, you are near Whitby in Yorkshire."

"The Frogs . . ."

"We beat them."

"Cotton—did Cotton . . . ?"

"It is over. We won at Salamanca, sir. We pushed them back all the way to France. We have beaten the French, and it is over. Boney's gone into exile, and the czar has been here to celebrate our victory."

"The rain . . . I still hear the rain," he mumbled. "Worms everywhere—in the tents—everywhere."

"The rain you hear is on my roof," she answered patiently.

Clearly he was as much out of his head as he'd been when he lay in the road, and it was no use to try making him understand anything just now. She tucked the blanket about him again and rose to get him his drink of water. There were still enough live coals in the fire to give the main room an orange glow and outline the doorway. Shivering herself, she crossed her arms over her old nightgown, holding in what little warmth she could.

She put another log onto the waning fire, then felt along the mantel for her box of wicks. Finding it, she drew out one and took it to the lamp. With her fingertip, she fished out the black speck of the last one before inserting the new one. The oil was low, but it ought to burn a little while. Carrying the lamp back to the fire, she lit a piece of tinder, then the floating wick.

When she returned with lamp and cup, he'd tossed the covers from his shoulders again. Sitting down on the edge of the bed, she tried to rouse him.

"I have brought you some water, my lord. You need to drink, for you have taken too much of the opium."

"Give it to Thompson . . . or one of the others," he rasped out. It was as though she were in a room of ghosts.

"They have already had their share," she said firmly, putting her arm beneath his shoulders, lifting him. "It is your turn to drink."

The flickering flame from the lamp reflected eerily in his glazed eyes, frightening her. "You've got to drink," she said again, holding the cup to his lips. "You must drink as much as you can."

He swallowed obediently, then pushed the rest away.

"No, take some more."

"The others . . ."

"They are being tended also," she murmured soothingly. "Come on, just a bit more."

He took another drink, satisfying her for the moment. Sinking back against the pillows, he closed his eyes. "Hell—I have seen hell," he whispered hoarsely. " 'Tis war. War is hell."

"You are dreaming merely," she said, persisting. "And you are freezing cold. In truth, so am I."

He nodded as though perhaps he understood her. She sat there until she could stand the cold no longer. Rising, she reached into the truckle bed and struggled to pull off the feather mattress. Straightening, she peered intently into his closed face.

Still fearing the overdose of laudanum, she spread the mattress over the bed, then she crept between it and the blanket that covered him. Turning against him, she reached out to pull the featherbed over both of them.

Someone was pounding loudly at the cottage door. She stretched reluctantly beneath the weight of the feather mattress, until she felt the body next to hers. It all came back to her then. Embarrassed, she gingerly eased away from him and sat up.

Light already came through the small window. She looked back at Rexford, but he was breathing evenly. Grateful for that at least, she rose and dressed quickly behind the cabinet door. Taking the blanket above the mattress, she hurried into the outer room, where she dropped it into the chair, then went to answer the door.

It was Dr. Alstead with two crude crutches and what appeared to be short slats. She pushed back her tangled hair and stood aside. "'Tis rather early, indeed, but I wasn't expecting you," she murmured. "I'd thought Mr. Beggs or Mr. Tittle—"

"'Tis nigh to eleven o'clock. And both of them have already left for Durham. Neither wished to face Lady Rexford alone," he recalled dryly. "I collect she is a Tartar of the first order." His gaze went past her to the dead fire. "Quite an unpleasant night, eh?"

"Yes. I think he overdosed himself, for he believed he was at Salamanca, and I could not convince him otherwise."

He nodded. "Best not to try. Fever's not up, is it?"

"No. Quite otherwise, sir."

"He was chilling?" he asked, frowning.

"I think it was that the hearth does not heat the bedchamber. I finally put the mattress from the truckle over him."

He glanced to the blanket that had slid from the chair. "You must have frozen yourself."

"I had the fire," she lied.

"Is he better this morning?"

"I don't think he is awake yet."

He set aside the crutches. "I forget sometimes that the nobs are slugabeds. Don't encounter too many of 'em myself." He measured the narrow pieces of wood appraisingly, then apparently satisfied, he murmured, "About the right size, I'd say." Carrying them with him, he sought his patient.

"Feeling more the thing, eh?" she heard the old man ask.

To her surprise, the earl had pulled himself up in the bed. For a moment, he regarded Alstead balefully.

"Which complaint would you hear first?" he countered sourly.

"Miss Winslow said you had a bad night. Leg pains you, I suppose."

"Yes."

"And the head?"

"Like the very devil."

"How long since your last dose of laudanum?"

"I don't know," Rexford muttered. "God, but it feels like an army marched through my head. And my mouth tastes as though I have drunk all the rotten rum in London."

"A little vinegar in water will take care of that. Any problem with nature?"

Rexford looked up at Charlotte's red face before he answered. "No. Where's Beggs?"

Ignoring the question, the physician laid the slats on the bed.

"You are going to splint the leg," Charlotte decided.

"Aye." Alstead addressed Rexford. "Going to hurt, no two ways about it, but you'll feel better when 'tis done." He lifted the feather mattress and blanket off, then removed the makeshift dressing. "Hmmmmm. Well, it looks better than I had expected. A little warm to the touch, but that is the body's way of healing a wound."

Charlotte peered curiously over his shoulder. Where the jagged bone had protruded from the skin, there was an irregular row of stitches and a large bruise.

"Got to keep it dry." As he spoke, the doctor opened his bag and took out the can of basilicum. "Infection breeds in moisture," he murmured, dusting his handiwork. "No baths until 'tis healed. Oh, no harm to a wet cloth now and then, but always dry the area after," he went on conversationally. "Can't keep a wound too dry." He took out a rolled bandage and began wrapping it around Rexford's lower leg. "Don't make a mess of it. Got to overlap it just so. There. Ought to keep the splint from rubbing."

Picking up the slats, he lined them up on both sides of Rexford's calf. "Thought I had measured about right," he observed with satisfaction. "Miss Winslow, as you have assured me you aren't missish, would you please hold them in place?"

"Yes, of course."

"Just get on with it," the earl gritted out.

"Even with these, I don't want any weight on the leg," Alstead said. "Nothing short of a miracle you are alive," he murmured as he worked. "Way I see it the Almighty must've knocked you the other way for a purpose. Divine intervention, I'd say. Ever think of that, my lord? Ever consider there might be a purpose?"

"No."

"Always wondered why a nob like you wanted to risk getting your head blown off in the war," the physician went on. "Ponsonby went, but then that was expected. Long military tradition in the family. I suppose the same could be said for Lord Longford," Alstead admitted judiciously. "Mad Jack's son, after all. I guess some of you fellows go for the excitement, eh?"

"I don't know," Rexford gasped.

Feeling that the physician had overstepped his manners, Charlotte spoke up. "Perhaps his lordship chose to serve his country against Bonaparte."

His face white, the earl managed to measure out his words. "No wars are just, and only fools fight them."

Alstead straightened up. "Well, it's not precisely pretty, but it'll serve to get you to the privy and back, I think. Seeing as Miss Winslow is an unmarried female, she won't have to worry over the pot, eh?"

"Alstead," Rexford growled, "you are over the line."

The doctor shrugged. "A pot's a pot, and without a maid to do it for her, I expect she's not entirely ignorant of my meaning." He turned his attention to her. "He will need help to stand, for he cannot bear weight on that side."

The earl shook his head. "I'm too heavy for her. 'Twill have to be Tittle."

"Yes, of course, when he gets back, my lord. But for now——"

"Beggs, then."

"Both gone to Durham."

"No, by God, they have not!" The earl looked toward Charlotte. "Is this your doing?" he demanded furiously. "I told you I had no wish to see her!"

"I sent them," Alstead answered for her.

But Rexford wasn't listening. "I gave you no leave to meddle in my affairs, Miss Winslow!"

The vehemence in his words stunned her. "Whether I sent them to tell her or not, she is your mother. She has a right to know you have nearly been killed, doesn't she?"

"No!"

"Here now, sirrah!" the doctor snapped. "I had it of your coachmen that you were on your way to Durham to see the countess."

"To send her packing to her own property!"

"Of all the ungrateful——Lord Rexford, Dr. Alstead may have saved your leg for you!" Charlotte reminded him angrily. "We both thought you meant to visit her!"

"Visit her! My mother, Miss Winslow, is the last creature on earth I should ever wish to see," he declared, biting off each word and spitting it at her. "And do you know what you have done? She'll be here fawning over me in a trice!"

"She's your mother!" Collecting herself, she tried to speak more rationally. "If I had a son, I should wish to know if he were hurt."

"Very affecting, but you don't have a son, do you?" Rexford reminded her sarcastically.

"No, of course not."

"See here, sirrah!" Alstead snapped. "'Tis enough, I say! I am sure Miss Winslow has done nothing more than is proper. If Lady Rexford comes, no doubt she will give the appearance of propriety."

The earl's jaw worked visibly before he spoke. "Whether she comes or not, let me make one thing plain to the both of you. No matter what is said, hell will freeze before I succumb to matrimony. I will not be trapped by some ridiculous notion of honor again. Not ever."

"And I have not the least notion of trapping anyone," Charlotte replied stiffly. "Now, if both of you will pardon me, I have quite a lot to do. I do work for my living."

As she walked out, Alstead continued to look at Rexford. "That was quite uncalled for, my lord."

"I don't want my mother here," the earl muttered, looking away. "I cannot abide her or the silly creatures she is forever trying to foist on me. One wigeon for a wife was quite enough, thank you."

"I fail to see where that touches Miss Winslow. You are, after all, dependent just now on her charity." The elderly physician snapped his bag shut and turned to leave. "If nature should call, I expect you will have to fend for yourself, though how you will manage emptying that chamberpot while on crutches, I am sure I do not know. But then, that is your dilemma, isn't it?" he said more mildly. "Good day, my lord."

"Wait!"

"I am sure I am not the one in need of an apology, sir."

"'Tis not that." When the old man hesitated, Rexford took a breath, then asked, "What do you know of Miss Winslow?"

"Very little. If you would pry, I suggest you inquire of her."

"I'm asking you."

"For all that she lives alone, a situation I cannot approve for a female, I know of no scandal," Alstead admitted grudgingly. "She came here without so much as a maid or female relation, possibly eleven or twelve years ago, causing a great deal of comment at the time. Somehow she managed to persuade Mr. Jenkins, then owner of this land, to lease this cottage to her—it was empty then. I believe Mrs. Bottoms said she pays twelve pounds per year. Not a princely sum, but no doubt 'tis all she can afford."

Despite his earlier anger, Rexford was appalled. "I see."

"Anything else I could say would be purely speculation, my lord, so I shall choose to leave it at that. Good day, sir."

After the doctor left, Rexford lay back on the pillows and stared at the ceiling. In the outer room, he could hear her moving about, maintaining a steady conversation. He had to listen for several minutes before he realized she was talking to an animal.

Miss Charlotte Winslow had come to a sad pass, he reflected soberly. The pretty, smiling girl who'd once spoken of books and roses was not only on the shelf but also she was eking out a living on the wild Yorkshire coast, reduced to living in a twelve-pound-per-year cottage. As much as he tried not to think of her, his thoughts turned to his dead wife.

Helena. He'd never forgive his mother for that. How he could ever have let his mother and Fairfax push him into offering for the creature was beyond belief. They'd all cheated him; aside from the girl's beauty, there'd been nothing. Absolutely nothing. And when he'd found her boring beyond bearing, she'd committed the greatest perfidy of all, saddling him with another man's brat before she died.

That was another score he wanted to settle with his mother. She had no right to blame him for Helena's indiscretion. He'd never failed to pay the simpleton's bills, nor had he denied her anything beyond himself.

He smelled food, and the growl in his stomach reminded him he was hungry. Even as he thought it, Charlotte rapped lightly on his door, then stepped inside, carrying a steaming bowl with a towel. As she crossed the room, he tried to guess her age. She was perhaps thirty-three or thirty-four, but her figure had remained trim, her dark eyes bright within an oval face, her step purposeful. And while she was far beyond that first bloom of youth, she was possessed of a dignity that Helena had never had, making him ashamed of his earlier outburst of temper.

"Your breakfast, my lord," she said stiffly.

He caught the bedstead and pulled himself up. "What is it?"

"As it is rather hot, I shall set the towel beneath it," she said matter-of-factly. After lowering both to rest on his lap, she started back toward the door. "Call me when you are done."

"Wait." He looked down and saw what appeared to be exceedingly thin oatmeal. "What is it?" he asked again.

"Dr. Alstead said you were to have gruel today, food tomorrow."

He dipped the spoon, then let the stuff spill back into the bowl. "Look, I did not mean to rip up at you. My anger is with her, not you."

She favored him with a disbelieving look. "Lord Rexford, I can recognize a wheedle when I hear it. Whether you are sorry or not, 'tis still gruel. For your own good, of course," she added sweetly.

"Heartless jade," he muttered.

"If you don't eat it now, I will save it for supper."

"You could at least stay."

"As I am not a wealthy nobleman, I'm afraid I have not the time."

With that, she was gone, leaving him to wonder. Sighing, he dipped the spoon again and carried it to his lips for a taste. He'd been right—it was thin oatmeal mixed with something else.

"What the devil is this?" he called out.

She came back to the door. "I told you, 'tis gruel."

"I would not feed this to a dog. You cannot have tasted it."

"Well, as I am never ill, I've not actually made any before," she admitted, suppressing a smile. "But it ought to be sustaining. 'Tis barley water, oatmeal, and pork jelly. Perhaps I forgot to add the salt. If so——"

"It needs considerably more than salt," he muttered. "And what, pray, did you eat?"

"I had a coddled egg and toast."

"Then I shall have the same."

"Perhaps tomorrow."

"Tomorrow?" he howled incredulously. "No, by God, *today!*"

"Are you always so obstreperous, my lord?" she inquired mildly.

"Come take this pigwash before I toss it!"

She shook her head. "I suspect if I got close enough, you might box my ears," she answered.

"No, my dear," he said tightly, "I should be more like to strangle you."

"Yes, well, I do not mean to put it to the touch. I believe I shall wait until you have eaten."

"I need coffee. I cannot eat until I have had my coffee."

"I should like to oblige, but I have none." Seeing that his face had darkened ominously, she offered, "But there is tea, should your lordship wish it."

"No chocolate?" he gibed sarcastically. "I thought all females doted on the stuff."

"Alas, no, it is rather dear." Stooping down, she picked up a huge orange cat. "Come on, Rex, I daresay he does not like animals today either."

He'd tried to apologize, he decided resentfully. But as he looked down on the gruel she'd made him, he felt distinctly out of sorts with the world. Of all the things he would be disinclined to taste, pork jelly must surely rank first. Nonetheless, to appease her, he had to attempt eating it.

In the outer room, she unfurled her poster and fastened it deftly to her easel. Stepping back, she viewed it critically, deciding she'd been right last night—the green definitely needed to be brighter. As for Rexford, she was severely disappointed. For whatever reason, the dashing gentleman of her youth no longer existed. This earl was far too bitter.

"Come take it!" he shouted. "I'm done!"

She went back to the bedchamber door. "You ate all of it? Or did you pour it into the chamberpot?"

"If you must know, I held my nose and drank it."

She collected the empty bowl and spoon, then put the towel over her arm. As she started to the door again, she could feel his eyes on her. "Is something else the matter?" she asked over her shoulder.

"Were you always like this? I seem to recall you had a better temper when you were younger."

She eyed him oddly for a moment, her expression fixed, then she recovered. "Well, perhaps memories play tricks on the both of us, for I seem to remember you were quite gallant."

"*Touché.* How old are you now, anyway?"

"How old are you?" she countered.

"Nine and thirty. And you?"

"You don't have a very precise memory, do you?" Relenting, she admitted, "I don't suppose it matters anymore, but I am three and thirty—four and thirty in June."

His gaze rested momentarily on her worn smock and the mobcap on her head. He supposed she wore the latter for dignity, but he didn't like it.

"You ought to get rid of that, you know."

"Of what?"

"That ridiculous thing on your head."

She reached up to touch it, then smiled. "Oh, but I shall not, for it signifies that I have reached an age where I need not be governed by silly proprieties. Think on it. If I were to dress like a simpering miss, there is no telling what sort of gossip might go around, is there?"

"It marks you for a spinster."

"I cannot think what else I could be considered. And with you here, there might be some to call me fast."

"Put it on when company comes," he suggested.

"And what if I should forget it?"

"Baggage."

She lifted an eyebrow at that. "I think I prefer heartless jade, my lord." She reached for the door. "You may have to call rather loudly, for when I work, I tend to become rather absorbed."

"You aren't going to stay and visit?"

"No. Alas, but Mr. Burleigh awaits."

"Is that what you call that poor cat?"

"The cat is Rex."

"At least spare me five minutes."

"As long as I don't mention your mother?"

"As long as you don't mention her."

"All right." She hesitated. "I suppose I ought to offer

my condolences for the loss of your wife. I read of it in the papers, you know. I understand you have a daughter." It was as though his face closed for a moment. "Forgive me, it was impertinent of me to pry. I should not have asked about your private life."

It was a question he had to steel himself to answer. "There is a girl," he said finally.

To her, it was an odd way to put it. "How old is she? Your daughter, I mean."

Again there was that rebellion within his breast. "Sophia is nine, I think—yes, nine," he said more definitely.

The moment was awkward, for clearly he had little wish to speak of the child. "I really must get busy, my lord," she said quickly.

"And you—how is it that you never wed?" he asked her, trying to keep her there a bit longer.

"I had no dowry," she said simply.

"And you never had a *tendre* for anyone, I suppose?"

Her chin camp up. "Yes, there was someone," she admitted, "but he never came up to scratch, I'm afraid."

"You ought to have gotten yourself a husband and children."

"Really? How very odd of you to say it, particularly when you seem to have so little regard for the notion yourself."

"Deceit makes for a damnable husband, Miss Winslow. A woman cannot trap a man into marriage and expect him to love her for it."

"If I were younger, I should try to remember that, but

as a confirmed spinster, I am resigned to leading apes in hell with the rest of my unmarried sisters."

He watched her leave, thinking she moved with a great deal of grace. Thirty-three. It didn't seem possible. He closed his eyes and remembered how close he'd come to pursuing her. She'd been pretty then, but it was more than that. She'd had a good mind and such an engaging smile that he'd begun to enjoy her company, to look forward to seeing her at all those interminable routs and balls a fashionable fellow had to endure. It was all coming back to him. He could even remember the gown she'd worn to the Conniston ball. It was white, with a rose satin sash, and as she'd danced with him, the scent of roses had wafted from her hair.

His leg throbbed, bringing him back to the present, but he was determined to take no more laudanum, not after the night he'd had. And now he had to get up either to use the damned chamberpot or to hobble to the privy. He swung his leg over the side of the bed, catching the splints on the bedcovers. For a moment, he thought he would faint, but the intense pain finally subsided. Somehow he managed to stand on his good leg, steadying himself as the room spun around him. Holding on to the bed, he reached for the crutches, retrieving one, knocking the other to the floor.

She came running at the thudding sound and saw him standing there. "What do you think you are doing?" she demanded.

He hated being an invalid. To cover his embarrassment, he snapped back, "It ought to be obvious, Miss Winslow."

She stared at him, thinking he looked rather ridiculous in Dr. Alstead's voluminous nightshirt, his bare legs showing beneath it. To relieve her own tension, she giggled.

"What, pray tell, is so damned amusing?"

"Nothing," she managed, sobering. Keeping her eyes averted, she walked to the table and picked up the chamber-pot. "Here."

"You were right—you aren't the least bit missish," he gritted out.

She felt the heat rise in her cheeks. "Actually, I suppose I am in some things, but I shall no doubt overcome it. Uh . . . if you will but call, I'll come back."

"You ought to smile more often, you know. I seem to remember it became you."

"Another wheedle, my lord?"

"No." He waited until she had her hand on the doorknob. "Your nose is green, Miss Winslow."

"Is it?" She rubbed at it with a finger. "Yes, I daresay it is," she admitted. "Now, if you will pardon me, my lord, I should like to finish my project."

It had taken her half a day before she was satisfied with her work. She made the last few strokes quickly, enriching Rondelli's gown, then stood back to admire it. After putting her brush in the water and wiping her hands on her smock, she took out her writing supplies and smoothed a piece of paper. Should she perhaps reduce her bill because the picture had been finished late? Casting a look across the room to it, she decided against that. Very carefully, she made her distinctive letterhead, then wrote out her invoice beneath it.

"Lud," she heard him groan.

Startled, she looked up, nearly oversetting the inkpot. Rexford was bracing his body between a crutch and the door facing, leaning his head against the jamb, grimacing from obvious pain. Afraid he was going to lose his balance, she hastened to help him.

"What on earth are you trying to do *now?*" she demanded, exasperated.

"Too damned weak," he muttered.

"Of course you are. Of all the idiotish—"

"Got to sit. Sorry for the nightshirt, but—"

"Lie down, you mean," she said. Thrusting her shoulder beneath his arm, she tried to steady him. He weaved slightly as she slipped her arm about his waist. "Come on, you are going back to bed."

"I'm not an infant, Miss Winslow," he managed through clenched teeth. "I want to sit up, by the fire."

It was cold in the bedchamber. It always was when the wind blew, she had to admit that. "I don't know if I could get you up from the chair," she ventured slowly. "All right," she decided.

She walked him slowly, steadying him as he struggled between her and the crutch. By the time he sank to the chair, beads of perspiration shone on his forehead.

"I thought I could do without it, but . . ."

Knowing that he meant the laudanum, she hurried to

get it. When she returned he had his head turned toward Mr. Burleigh's poster.

"You did this?" he asked, surprised.

"Yes. I hope it looks like Madame Rondelli," she murmured, measuring the opiate into a cup.

"My compliments. It's a very good likeness."

"You've seen her?"

"Yes." He took a deep breath and held it for a moment, trying to soften the throbbing in his shin. "So you are an artist."

"Actually, it is *Mister* Winslow who draws." Walking away from him, she explained, "Charles Winslow had to paint it. Otherwise, Mr. Burleigh should never have engaged me, and I should have starved." She dipped water into the cup as she talked. "Charles is rather prolific actually, for he not only does the pictures for playbills but he also draws fashion plates and illustrates an occasional book."

"But there isn't a Charles Winslow."

"I am sure there must be one somewhere, but I'm afraid I don't know him," she admitted. "When I first conceived the notion of doing this, I sent my drawings around to publishers, theaters, and opera houses. And of course they were scarce opened ere they were discarded. So after I came here, the deception was born, and Charles manages to keep the roof over my head." She smiled rather impishly, adding, "And given my distance from London, none is any the wiser. I merely ask to be paid in tender rather than by draft, which they quite count as my artistic eccentricity."

"My compliments."

She'd half expected him to disapprove, but he was looking at the poster again, nodding. "I know it must seem rather odd to you, but——"

He shook his head. "Actually, I was thinking you have more talent than half those who——" He stopped, his eyes fixed on the window. "Damn," he said under his breath. "Double damn and wish for hell."

"What?"

"My mother," he said tersely.

"Lud."

"Precisely." He tried to rise without putting weight on his splinted leg and couldn't. "Sorry," he muttered.

Already someone was knocking. She quickly stirred the mixture with her finger, then handed it to him. Smoothing her smock over her faded dress, she considered snatching off the mobcap, then decided against it.

"Yes?" she said, opening the door.

Beggs stood there, his hand raised to knock again, and behind him, Tittle was securing the reins. Charlotte tried to smile at the woman before her.

"You must be Lady Rexford," she murmured politely.

The dowager surveyed the room with marked disdain before turning her attention to Charlotte. "I am, and I am come to take my son home," she announced coldly.

"But he cannot be moved," Charlotte protested. "Indeed but he cannot walk unaided, and Dr. Alstead says——"

The countess's lips thinned, her disapproval obvious. "We shall see about that, shan't we? I should never trust a country bonesetter."

"Dr. Alstead was once an army surgeon," Charlotte managed stiffly.

The older woman fixed her with sharp blue eyes. "Yes, and I am sure we know what they are—Mrs. Winston, is it?" she asked, her brow lifting. Her gaze dropped to the spattered smock and the worn gown beneath. "Dear me."

"No, I'm afraid I *don't* know what they are," Charlotte responded evenly. "And it is *Miss* Winslow, my lady."

"They are drunks and sots, the lot of them. Ask Rexford, for they very nearly let him bleed to death in Spain. Though why he went there in the first place, I am sure I don't know." Swishing past Charlotte, she spied him. "Well, Richard," she declared acidly, "'tis a fine pond where you have brought your ducks to swim this time."

"Mother," he acknowledged grimly.

"The Sedgelys were most distraught, Richard, particularly dearest Meg. She's such a lovely girl, truly she is. But I assured her I should have you safely home ere the morrow."

"Did you now?" he murmured wryly. "How unfortunate I am unable to travel."

"Well, you certainly cannot stay here. The place is drafty as a stable," she sniffed.

"I have no complaints."

"Indeed? And who, pray tell, will play propriety?" Lady Rexford snapped. "But of course I am sure Miss Winston must count your accident a gift of divine Providence," she added knowingly.

Charlotte bristled. "The name is Miss Winslow, Lady Rexford, and I assure you—"

"No, Miss Winslow, 'tis *I* who will assure you," the dowager retorted. "For all that he is possessed of wealth and title, Rexford is far too cognizant of what he owes his name to be embroiled in a *mésalliance* or a scandal."

"Cut line, Mother! You've said more than enough!"

"Nonsense, Richard. I want her to know that I shall not stand idly by and watch her ingratiate herself above her station. And we quite understood, Miss Winslow?"

Two red spots rose in Charlotte's cheeks. "Really, madam, there is no need for this," she managed evenly.

"You will apologize on the instant!" Rexford shouted at the dowager. "Miss Winslow has saved my leg!"

"Of course you may expect reasonable compensation," Lady Rexford continued smoothly. "Shall we agree upon twenty pounds? Obviously that is quite a sum to you."

Furious, the earl lunged to his feet. As searing pain shot up his splinted leg, he staggered, catching at the chair for balance. Charlotte reached out to him, but she was too late. The chair toppled over, and he crashed to the floor, sending the startled cat scrambling for cover.

Heedless of the other woman's presence, Charlotte dropped to the floor beside him. "Of all the cork-brained things to do . . . well, this is outside of enough, my lord," she muttered, examining the splint. "Did you think I cannot defend myself?" Before he could answer, she asked almost angrily, "Did you hurt anything else?"

"Miss Winslow, have you no sense of decency?" the dowager demanded. "He is scarce covered!"

"A pox of propriety," Charlotte snapped, sitting back

on her knees. "Do you want him to lose the leg or worse?" She looked up. "Most physicians would not have tried to set it, you know, for the bone did not break evenly. As it is, there could still be an infection."

He lay there, scarce able to move for the agony. "Don't touch it again, I pray you," he whispered.

"We've got to get you up," she told him. "You only had four drops. Would you have more?"

He shook his head. "Rum."

"Rum is scarce fit for a gentleman, Richard."

"See if Mr. Beggs or Mr. Tittle has any," Charlotte ordered brusquely.

"I beg your pardon?"

"Please. Rum is sometimes used for surgery, I am told. Can you not see how badly he has been injured?"

"Well, I am sure——" Lady Rexford stopped. "Yes, of course."

"And ask them to help get him to bed also."

"Sorry," Rexford murmured. "Useless."

"Just for now," Charlotte reassured him. "In a fortnight, you'll feel much better, and within a month or so, you'll be all but well."

"I'll send her packing," he mumbled. "Won't have this."

The laudanum was beginning to take effect, she could see that, and yet she wondered if it would be enough. She reached to take his hand, squeezing it. "You survived one of Boney's bullets, my lord. You can survive this also."

He didn't answer.

Lady Rexford returned to stand over her. "I had this of Beggs." Looking down, she asked, "Is he any better?"

"Until we move him."

"Do you need a glass for the rum?"

"No." Charlotte took the coachman's flask and opened it. Leaning over the earl, she said distinctly, "One swallow, my lord."

As she held it to his mouth, he drank.

"'E don't look good," Beggs observed from behind the dowager.

"Right peaked," Tittle agreed.

"We are going to move you, my lord. Don't try to do anything yourself," Charlotte told Rexford. "Just keep the leg straight."

He nodded.

At least it was easier than it had been when they'd carried him in the rain. This time the splint helped, and between them, they got him back to bed. Charlotte lingered to cover him with the blanket and the featherbed off the truckle.

When she came out, Lady Rexford had discarded her traveling cloak and was standing before the hearth. Turning around, she asked, "He is all right, isn't he?"

"No." Charlotte took a deep breath, then let it out. "Unless he was sitting too close to the fire, he has a fever."

"But he cannot!"

"I think so."

Both women waited in the outer room, one pacing nervously, the other sitting. By tacit agreement, neither spoke. Finally, Dr. Alstead emerged from the bedchamber.

It was Charlotte who spoke up. "How is he, sir?"

"Well, the leg does not appear infected, which I count a blessing. Oh, there is some swelling, of course, but the wound itself is not hot to the touch."

"Then whatever—?"

He turned to Charlotte. "Perhaps the ague, perhaps the onset of a lung infection."

"A lung infection!" the dowager gasped. "But he cannot!"

The doctor regarded her for a long moment. "Madam," he declared, "if he has lungs, they can become infected. And if he doesn't have them, he is dead."

"If it is the ague?" Charlotte asked.

"It'll run its course. Be damned sick for a few days, but then 'tis over."

"But he has not been coughing," Charlotte said, encouraging herself.

"I got that out of him. Been too sore, he says. Daresay he may have cracked a rib or two with the rest of it."

"Perhaps if I took him home—"

Alstead looked at the countess as though she'd lost her mind. "It will be weeks before he can be transported anywhere in any comfort. Just now it is more important to keep him quiet and as comfortable as may be. We will treat the symptoms, of course."

"He despises gruel," Charlotte said.

"So he told me. Pork jelly, eh?"

"A *restorative* pork jelly, I believe the label boasted. It was a gift for a sketch."

"Might as well give him what he wants. Make up honey and vinegar if he coughs, onion poultice for congestion, and give laudanum for pain."

"And for the fever?"

"Willow bark tea. Not too strong, mind you."

Charlotte sighed. "Perhaps I'd best write down the recipe for the poultice."

"Common enough one."

"Yes, but I am never ill, and I cannot say I have ever mixed one."

"Lard and onions, that's all. Cook 'em until the onions are shiny but not soft. Put it on while 'tis still warm. Every four hours for half an hour. If that doesn't work, thump him."

"Thump him?" Lady Rexford said faintly.

"Pound his chest to loosen the phlegm. Beyond that, if he gets markedly worse, send for me, and I'll blister him. At this stage, I don't favor a purge or a blood-letting."

After he left, Charlotte broached the problem of sleeping to Rexford's mother. "There are only two beds—the one he is in and the truckle. I have exactly three usable blankets to my name, and one featherbed that can be used for a cover when the weather is too cold. I am afraid I simply do not have any place for you or Mr. Beggs and Mr. Tittle to sleep, nor do I have any shelter for your horses. There, I have said it."

"And just where do you intend to sleep, Miss Winslow?" the dowager asked archly.

"I had thought to ask the men to move the truckle out

here. If I give Lord Rexford the blankets, I shall need the fire."

"I see."

"There are lodgings to be had in Whitby, my lady."

For a long time, Lady Rexford stared into the fire. "No," she said finally, "he may not wish it, but I intend to stay here. He is, after all, my son." Raising her eyes to Charlotte's, she decided, "I shall take the truckle, and you may take the chair."

"Lady Rexford, this is my house."

The dowager looked daggers at her. "At twenty pounds, I should think you handsomely paid for it. Thirty pounds, young woman, is as high as I mean to go."

"I don't want your money . . . or his," Charlotte answered evenly. "I want him to live."

At that, Lady Rexford looked away. "He wishes me at Jericho, I am sure, but I will not leave him like this."

"No, of course not." As much as she disliked the older woman already, Charlotte could almost feel sorry for her. "As you say, he is your son."

"It was not always like this, Miss Winslow. He once was a kind, generous boy."

"And now he is a man of thirty-nine," Charlotte observed dryly. "Sit down, and I shall brew some tea."

"You do think he will be all right, don't you?"

"I hope so, but he may limp."

"He has limped since he came home from the war, Miss Winslow."

"Yes, of course. He took a ball, didn't he?"

"And it was such folly. He did not have to go. But after Helena . . . well, it does not signify now."

Charlotte measured tea leaves into the teapot, then got out cups and saucers. "I shall have to fetch the cream," she murmured, excusing herself.

When she returned from the cold cellar, Charlotte saw that Lady Rexford stood before the opera house poster. The woman turned around. "You live with an artist, Miss Winslow?"

"I drew that."

"Really? How very odd, to be sure."

"Actually, I much prefer painting to rearing other people's children."

"It looks very much like the creature," the dowager conceded.

"So Lord Rexford said."

The older woman's lips thinned in disapproval. "Well, I daresay he ought to know. But I shall say no more on that head, save that she is a grasping harpy. I have no use for opera singers, I'm afraid."

"Nor artists, apparently," Charlotte muttered.

"A mother wants more for her son, Miss Winslow. Above all else I would have him happy. There can be no happiness in a succession of lightskirts." She looked up. "You sell these pictures for a living?"

"I am afraid I must. It puts food on my table, you see."

"Yes, that is a consideration, I suppose. Unless of course you get your clutches into my son," the woman added slyly. "You would not be the first female I have bought off, you know."

"Lady Rexford——"

"But as we are thrown together for the moment, I shall say nothing more on that head."

"No wonder he does not come home often."

The woman blenched, then recovered. "That, Miss Winslow, is none of your affair," she snapped.

"No, it isn't. Well, in any event, if you should suffer a surfeit of boredom while here, you may look at my sketchbooks for amusement. I keep them in that box by the larger chair."

Rexford's mother looked again at the watercolor of Madame Rondelli. "You are rather talented," she decided.

"Actually, I had a rather good instructor at Miss Finch's Select Academy for Females at Chester. He told me I should not waste my time drawing poor flowers if I could master people." Charlotte moved away to strain the strong tea through a cloth. "I still dislike doing the flowers, for I can never quite do justice to them. To me, only God can make a credible rose."

"You went to Miss Finch's?"

"Yes."

Sitting down, Lady Rexford appeared to study a worn rug for a moment. "Surely you can afford a maid."

"I have been here so long I should not know what to do with one."

"But the cooking, the keeping of the house——"

"There is but Rex and me." Seeing that the dowager's

eyebrow lifted anew, she explained. "Rex is my cat—for Reginald," she lied, handing a cup of tea to the woman. "I do not particularly care for chopping wood, but then I daresay a maid might cavil at that task, anyway," she added, taking the other chair.

"But if you went to Miss Finch's, you must have been properly presented," Lady Rexford murmured.

"So long ago I can scarce remember it. It was fifteen years ago. After my father died, I couldn't afford to return to London."

"Yes, gaming is the bane of gentlemen, isn't it?" The other woman stared pensively into the fire, and the conversation ended. For a time there was no sound beyond the clinking of cup against saucer and the logs popping in the grate. "My husband died young, leaving me but Richard, you know," she said ever so softly.

Finally, Charlotte could stand it no longer. "I quite understand what you fear, Lady Rexford, but I am not so green as to think he would care for me. At thirty-three, I am quite on the shelf."

"Yes, of course you are," the woman murmured, her voice nearly too low to hear. Setting her cup aside, she rose. "I should like to sit with Richard, I think."

"As Mr. Beggs and Mr. Tittle must surely be freezing, they will wish to put up in Whitby, I should think. Would you mind terribly if I were to ride in with them?"

"But how will you get back?"

"I am used to walking, and I do not truly mind the cold." Rising also, Charlotte carried the cups to her sink, then moved to roll Mr. Burleigh's poster. "This must go out to London today."

"Oh. Well, I am sure we shall not need you at all." The dowager went to the small, distorted window and stared out absently. Then she turned and walked to the bedchamber to watch over her son. "But you'd best get coffee, for Richard does not like tea in the morning," she said over her shoulder.

Between the laudanum and the rum, he slept too soundly to disturb. She sat there, looking into his face, remembering him as a grubby little boy, and she felt an intense loss. There had been a time when he'd run laughing across the terrace, when he'd come in from a romp with his dogs and put muddy handprints on her wide, full skirts. And she could remember how his boyish grin had lasted far past his school years. Until Helena.

She heard the cottage door open, then close. And she could not help thinking how very different Miss Winslow was from Helena. Very gently, she leaned to touch her son's brow, feeling the heat beneath her fingertips.

"She still isn't for you, my son," she whispered. "An earl needs a wife of breeding, a girl like Miss Sedgely."

There was no change in the rhythm of his breathing, no sign that he heard. Sighing, she stood and walked slowly back into the other room.

She surveyed the place Charlotte Winslow called home, thinking the girl must never know how close she had come to snaring Rexford. No, it was better to let that lie, to pretend it had never happened. After all, she could not have known just how foolish Helena would prove.

She walked to the box beside the larger chair and lifted the lid. There were several sketchbooks inside, and a folder beneath. Curious, she set the books aside and carefully took out the folder. She opened it, and her breath caught. For a long time, she stared at his handsome face, committing it to memory, until she could no longer see through her tears.

Charlotte's face was ruddy from the cold when she stepped inside and threw the latch. Seeing that Lady Rexford sat before the fire, the sketchbooks on her lap, she moved closer.

"How is he?"

"He hasn't stirred since you left."

"And his fever?"

"It remains the same."

"At least that is something," Charlotte said, taking off her cloak. Walking to hang it on a peg, she added, "I brought more willow bark."

"I cannot think it his lungs, for there is no rattle."

"'Tis more like the ague. Mrs. Bottoms says it is going 'round just now."

"I think so." Seeing that the younger woman carried a bowl, Lady Rexford asked, "What is that?"

"Word travels fast here, 'twould seem, for Mrs. Bottoms, who can scarce abide me, sent up cabbage soup 'for his lordship the earl.' So now we have a choice at least— cabbage soup or boiled mutton and potatoes."

"I have a French cook at home." The dowager caught herself. "Yes, well, I daresay you will make what you like."

"The soup, then. Rexford ought to be able to eat it."

"He cannot abide soups. But," the older woman sighed, "It is probably a great deal better than the dreadful things he ate during the war."

Charlotte transferred the soup to the hanging kettle, then suspended it over the fire. "Odd he should have chosen to go," she said casually.

"So I said, but Helena had just died."

"I understand there is a daughter," Charlotte added, holding her hands out to warm them at the hearth.

There was a brief pause, and when she spoke again the dowager's voice was strained. "Sophie is nearly ten now. She's quite lovely, really."

"And he left her for the war? That is, it seems rather unnatural to me, but then Papa and I were always close."

"She isn't Richard's, for all that she bears the Linden name. He was furious when Fairfax refused to rear her."

"And you have her now?"

"Yes, she lives with me, Miss Winslow. I would not let him repudiate her."

"The poor child."

"She was the daughter I never had, you see," the dowager answered slowly. "I'd had hopes of Helena, of course, but that was a mistake. So now I have reared Sophie."

"He must have loved Lady Helena enough to wed her. I cannot think how she could have wanted to play him false, but then—"

"A man's sense of duty and honor can be manipulated, Miss Winslow." As Charlotte looked down at her, she nodded. "Once. She was my goddaughter. A duke's daughter, and she was so very pretty. He ought to have worshipped her."

"And he did not."

"No. And when he would not live in her pocket, she quickly assembled a court of her own. In turn, he amused himself elsewhere. Now I can quite see they never suited. She needed constant admiration more than affection. In the end, it was a tragedy, Miss Winslow. When Helena died, I had to name the babe myself. Sophia Eugenia Linden."

"And Miss Sedgely?"

"I thought to rectify my mistake. Meg is a dear, sweet, obedient creature, not nearly so empty in the cockloft as Helena, I assure you. She is the sort of female who could settle him down, I think. And the blood is good enough to pass to my grandson."

"Don't you think Rexford ought to decide that?"

The dowager's face clouded, then she sighed. "Well, I am sure if I were to recommend the greatest paragon alive, he would dislike her."

"Lady Rexford, why are you telling me this?" Charlotte asked suspiciously. "I cannot think you can possibly wish to wash your linen before a stranger."

"It doesn't matter. If it were left up to him, I daresay he would not wed again."

"Which seems a pity. I knew him once, when I was presented. He was young and handsome then, and every girl I knew had a *tendre* for him. And of course he played the gallant for all of us."

"He would."

Charlotte sighed. "I was such a green girl then. I was like all the rest. I even wrote him when Papa died." Then, afraid she'd said too much, she hastened to add, "But of course I can quite see everything different now. You must not think I expect anything from him, for I am older and no longer given to foolish notions."

"I should hope not, in any event."

"Knowing that marriage has passed me by, I have become content enough to paint here."

For a moment, the dowager stared at the licking flames as though she could read them. "Yes," she said finally, "I expect it has."

It was in the ensuing silence that they heard him cough. "If you will watch the soup, I will give him the honeyed vinegar," Charlotte offered.

"I expect he would spit it in my face if he could."

"No."

"He's a bitter man, Miss Winslow."

"Yes, I can see that."

"He was coming to Durham to send me packing, wasn't he? I sensed it, you know. I was so frightened I summoned Meg and her family to support me, thinking he would not do it before them. It was foolish of me, for he would no doubt have cleared the house of all of us. I thought if he could see her with Sophie, he might be brought to relent."

"You are telling the wrong person, my lady. You ought to speak to him."

"But you can remember how he was."

"He is not the same man now." Charlotte stirred the mixture with her finger, then tasted it. She shuddered visibly. "He may very well spit it back at *me*," she decided.

When she got into the bedchamber, he'd pulled himself up into a seated position, and yet he was still coughing. "Is she still here?" he asked between paroxysms.

"Yes. She's worried about you."

"No." He coughed again. "She merely wishes to manage my dying also."

"You are not dying." Heedless of propriety, she sat down on the edge of the bed and poured a large spoonful of the cough mixture. "Here."

"What is it?"

"I don't know," she lied. "It is for your lungs."

"Naught's wrong with my lungs," he gasped.

"Would you rather that I made the onion poultice?" she asked patiently.

"No."

"Then you'd best take this. Here." As she spoke, she carried the spoon to his mouth. "Open up."

"I am not a child—*arrrgh!* What the devil is it?" He choked, then nearly collapsed from more coughing.

"One more," she coaxed hopefully.

"When pigs fly," he answered balefully.

She reached to touch his head. "Are you too hot?"

"I'm freezing," he croaked.

"I'll bring you a hot brick and some tea."

"Rum."

"Tea. Actually it is made with willow bark for your

fever." She slid off the bed and started to leave. Stopping at the door, she turned back for a moment. "She loves you, you know."

He favored her with a withering look. "She's bamboozled you."

"She told me about Sophia."

"She had no right."

"Children are innocent. Besides, this one bears your name."

"Miss Winslow—"

"All right. It isn't my business, is it?"

"No. And I despise meddlers."

As she came out, Lady Rexford waited. "Is he any better?"

"No. I'm going to make the poultice and the willow bark water. But," she added, "I don't think he is any worse."

He lay there, reflecting that for all her tart words, Charlotte Winslow was possessed of a soft heart and a kind nature. And she deserved so much more than what she had been given in life. She was the sort of female a man ought to wish for, a woman who could keep a man's interest, who wouldn't suck the lifeblood out of a husband with incessant, petty demands. He almost wished he could go back and live that summer over.

But he'd written her that once, and she'd never answered.

Within the week, it became obvious that the earl merely suffered from a bad cold. And while the dowager did not go home, she took lodgings in Whitby, coming to sit with him while Charlotte worked. The result was an uneasy truce between mother and son.

It was not until Charlotte went into the village again that Lady Rexford was entirely alone with him. He sat bundled before the hearth, reluctantly holding a very determined, purring cat.

"At the risk of turning you against her," the dowager ventured finally, "after watching her these days past, I must admit I was mistaken in Charlotte. She has a great deal of kindness, doesn't she?"

He eyed her warily. "Yes."

"And common sense. She is so very calming, don't you think? Was she always like that, or don't you remember?"

"I remember nearly everything about her," he admitted.

Encouraged, Lady Rexford pushed a trifle harder. "As I recall it, you nearly fixed your interest with her."

"I cannot think how you would know. You were much too busy foisting Helena on me."

"Yes, and it was a tragic mistake, Richard. I know that now."

"I don't want to speak of Helena."

"But there is Sophia to consider."

"Mother—"

"Richard, the child is here! As much as you may wish she had never been born, she is here! Look how many children Oxford has had to accept, and scarce a one as looks like him! Indeed, it is speculated that perhaps Ponsonby even——"

"Can you and Charlotte not leave well enough alone?" he demanded angrily. "Now she even asks of her."

"Richard, there is no help for it, the child bears your name. And she deserves a mother. If you cannot love her, at least give her a mother who will!"

"I should strangle Miss Sedgely within a fortnight!"

She retreated abruptly. "I wasn't speaking of Miss Sedgely precisely."

He regarded her narrowly. "What new face is this, Mother?"

"It is not a face at all, I assure you. But I am old and tired, and I no longer wish to brangle with you. Indeed, but I have been thinking of retiring to the house your father provided for me."

"Is this some new scheme?" he demanded suspiciously.

"I am prepared to concede Meg is no match for you."

"And I am sure that within the twelvemonth you will be advancing another candidate," he gibed. "It is not in your nature to leave me alone."

"But I shall try, Richard. I shall try."

"There is a new wheedle——out with it."

"There is none. In fact, I should not like to discuss this further."

"Thank you," he muttered dryly.

"Miss Winslow is a remarkable artist, don't you think?"

"Yes."

"One must admire her for daring to follow her heart's work," Lady Rexford murmured. "There are those who think her exceedingly odd."

"And you were one of them," he reminded her.

"But that was before I actually looked at her drawings. And I am not speaking of posters or fashion plates, Richard." Reaching down, she opened the box by her seat. "Has she ever shown you any of these?"

"No."

"You ought to look at them."

"Mother—"

"No, there are people you will recognize on the instant," she assured him. "It is most enlightening. Go on," she urged.

He regarded her quizzically, then opened the first book. As he turned the pages, he realized Charlotte Winslow had recorded her one short Season in sketches. There was Maria Sefton, her head bent, listening to gossip from Sally Jersey. And the Regent, not in caricature as he was so often depicted anymore. But by the shape of his body, one could tell he wore a corset.

"I had no idea she could do this," he admitted. "She couldn't even publish them under her own name."

"Yes, well, most men think us poor, weak creatures incapable of anything beyond the vapors. Though Miss Austen has done well, I must say."

He was still looking through the sketchbooks. She waited until he had finished, then she held out the folder.

"But these are the best, Richard. I believe she has poured her heart into them."

Curious, he opened the folder carefully and was utterly stunned. It was as though he stared into a mirror that had not changed with time. Although it had been done in pen and watercolor, there was a glint of humor in his eyes, a sensual, almost Byronic softness in the mouth. And the tousled hair that fell forward in a reluctant Brutus had no gray. He gazed at it, wondering how she'd done it, how eyes made of ink could pull him into them.

"There are more, Richard. She did them all from memory. She has held you in her heart all these years."

"My God. I had no idea . . . no idea at all."

"She wrote to tell you that her father had died, that there was no money for another Season."

"Did she tell you that? Did she tell you I wrote her also?"

"No. She never knew it. I don't even think she knows I have seen these." She raised her eyes to his. "But I know, Richard, because I burned both letters. I wanted better for you."

It was some time before he could bring himself to speak. "I see," he said heavily. "Why do you tell me now?"

"I wanted you to see yourself through her eyes. You are yet young enough to correct my terrible mistake." Holding back tears, she leaned across to take his face in her hands. "I hope I have made my last match for you." Releasing him, she stood up. "Now, if you do not mind it, I shall walk back to the village. I need air, I think."

He sat stone-still until she opened the door. Then he let out his breath. "Thank you, Mother."

Charlotte came in smiling. "Well, I shall eat for a year at least," she announced happily. "Mr. Burleigh has not only sent his schedule, but he has also commissioned a twelve-month of work. And so I told your mother when I met her." Aware he sat in shadows, she stopped. "Why didn't you light the cruzies?"

"The smoke makes me cough," he said. "But I did manage to drag a log onto the fire. It wasn't an easy task, Charlotte."

Her breath caught with the realization he'd used her Christian name. When she looked at him, the warmth in his eyes nearly unnerved her.

Her hands shook as she turned away to take off her cloak. "Well, I must say you do not look any worse for it."

"Do you remember the Connistons' ball?" he asked softly.

She was glad he couldn't see her face. "Why do you ask that?"

"I think I fell in love with you that night."

Her throat constricted, and her heart thudded painfully beneath her breastbone. "I remember it like yesterday," she whispered. "I have never forgotten it. I can still smell the Hungary water you wore."

"I can't dance anymore, Charlotte. I may not even walk properly, you know." He stood awkwardly on his crutches.

Tears scalded her eyes as she turned around. He was

smiling crookedly, almost boyishly at her. "Miss Winslow," he asked softly, balancing himself with one arm, "will you do me the honor of becoming my wife?"

Without hesitation, she went to him. As the other arm closed around her, she clung to him, burying her head against his shoulder. "Yes. Oh, yes," she managed, choking back the tears. "I have loved you such a long time, Richard."

His arm held her tightly. "God, but I wish I'd done this fifteen years ago," he whispered against her soft, rose-scented hair.

She could hear his heartbeat beneath his shirt, and she could feel the solid warmth of his chest. Charlotte Winslow Linden, countess of Rexford. Her heart almost sang at the very sound of it.

Flowers
from
the Sea

by Arnette Lamb

❀ ❀ ❀

Acknowledgment

My deepest appreciation to
Alice Shields and Joyce Bell
for their creative expertise.

And to Pat Stech, the eagle eye.

Dedication
For Louththia Garrison Dinn
of Columbus, Indiana

Thanks, Tish, for being a mom to me.

May 1680. Scottish Isle of Arran

*T*oday she would learn the secret of the grave.

Her heart pounding, Lily Hamilton crouched behind an abandoned fisherman's shed on the beach at Brodick Bay. As a child she'd played here, always searching for Spanish coins, usually settling for bits of colored glass.

Behind her, the towering, snow-capped peak of Goat's Fell loomed in the darkness. Soon the yellow glow of dawn would turn the mountain to gold and flood the cove with light. The bay was empty and quiet now, save the gentle lapping of the surf. The fishing boats had already sailed on the tide. The merchant ships were away, plying the Irish trade. Near the shipwright's cottage, her uncle's barkentine rested on wooden runners at the dry dock, the hull scraped clean of barnacles and a new rudder jutting from the stern.

The village families had yet to stir. Fearing discovery from a more dangerous source, Lily stole a glance over her shoulder at her home, Hamilton Castle. The massive stone structure lay hulking in the gloom. No one could see her. Not yet.

Although spring had come to the island, the wind blew chilly, whipping off the swells of the Firth of Clyde and biting to the bone. Shivering with both cold and anticipation, Lily huddled deeper into her tartan-lined cape and clutched her sack of keepsakes.

Today the man would come.

The eastern sky grew luminous. Perched on the battery of cannons nearby, gulls heralded the coming of the dawn. Lily scanned the bay. To her great disappointment, no three-masted ship rode the waves. Not yet.

She did not doubt his arrival; he'd been tardy before. Once each year for over a decade she had watched his ship cruise into the bay. She pictured every detail of his past visits. At first light he would stand at the prow and stare in the direction of Goat's Fell. After a long moment of what she suspected was prayer, he flung a bouquet of roses into the bay.

Today she would find out why.

Why did he toss a bundle of the very same primroses that grew in only one place on Arran? Who was buried in that lonely grave beneath the dying bush? Upon discovering the grave twelve years ago, Lily had asked her kinsmen about it. They called her fanciful and ordered her to stay away from the high glen. But she knew that the remote burial plot, marked by a cairn of smooth stones and an alien rosebush, was linked to the stranger who made a yearly pilgrimage to Arran. The roses were the key.

Driven by wistful desperation, she willed the ship to appear. When a sliver of the sun appeared on the horizon, she reverted to a childhood method. Squeezing her eyes closed, she repeated what had become a constant prayer: "He must come. He must come."

She opened her eyes. Joy soared through her, for there, at the mouth of the bay, sailed the ship. Lily knew about ships. On her eighth birthday, her grandfather had given her a finely rigged pinasse and declared it her dowry. The demise, only two years later, of that precious vessel and the painful repercussions from its loss had changed her life.

Today her life would change again.

Wanting to run to the water's edge, yet knowing from past experience that the stranger would abort his mission if he saw movement on the beach, she watched his ship round the point. Only when he had sailed fully into the bay, would she make her move.

The ship rode high in the water, a sign the hold was empty. An old canvas, weighted with sandbags, draped the prow and covered the name of the vessel. The practice of concealment was common, but only when sailing into un-friendly waters. She would also ask him why he cloaked his ship. Surely he had no quarrel with her people. The Hamiltons of Arran had only one enemy: Clan MacDonnel of Ardrossan.

Over twenty years ago, upon the death of Oliver Cromwell, the MacDonnels had celebrated the Lord Protector's passing by creeping into this bay, burning the fishing boats, and razing the village. The MacDonnels' bid to control the lucrative commerce of the islands failed when the Hamiltons retaliated. A clan war was waged, and the enmity continued today. Like a hungry beast with an insatiable appetite, the feud had eaten away at the prosperity of both clans.

Lily's mother, still nursing her only child, had been an early casualty. As the years passed, uncles, cousins, and friends followed. Even Lily's dowry ship had fallen prey to the MacDonnels. For her marriage portion, she now possessed the dubious gift of a lifetime's witness to the oldest and most destructive clan war in Scottish history. No decent family would offer for her; the other clans had long since turned their backs on the Hamiltons and the MacDonnels. Even the command of King Charles II had failed to stop the feud.

Lily's hopes for a peaceful life with a kind husband and children of her own had long since crumbled. She despised her kinsmen, for they were prideful men who thirsted for power and thrived on revenge. Longing to escape Arran, she had studied hard in hopes of gaining a position as governess for a family in Glasgow or Edinburgh. But without her father's reference and her uncle's blessing, she was doomed to an empty life.

Tears blurred her eyes, but Lily willed them away. Today was a day for ceremony and discovery.

Today was her birthday.

Focusing again on the ship, she saw activity near the bow. The anchor splashed into the bay. The ritual would soon begin. Squinting she searched the deck. Crewmen scurried in the rigging. The helmsman manned his post. The stranger had yet to appear.

As she waited, she recalled her past birthdays. Over the years she had stood on this very spot and pictured the stranger in many fanciful roles: Landless adventurer paying tribute to the sea, devoted admirer paying homage to a lost love. From the age of eleven, Lily had measured her own growth against the changes in the dark stranger. The year her menses had begun, he had sported a manly beard. The spring the parson's son had given her her first kiss, the stranger had worn a baldric housing a shiny new sword. On her nineteenth birthday, when her father had forbidden her to again broach the topic of leaving Arran, the stranger had come barbered in the Dutch fashion still favored by the flamboyant Stewart king. Sometimes she thought of the stranger as royalty. She always thought of him as her special birthday guest.

Then she saw him, and her breath caught. For the eleventh time in as many years, he rose from the companionway and spoke briefly to the helmsman.

As always, he wore black. Garbed in a cockaded hat

and a caped greatcoat, he looked like a courtier answering a royal summons rather than a man performing a sentimental ritual. Against his dark clothing, a splash of pink identified the familiar roses.

This year he would not throw them into the bay. Lily would not scoop them from the water and trek up the hill to place them on the lonely grave. Today she would tell him that the rosebush on the grave was dying.

Today she would find out who was buried there.

The moment he began the walk to the bow of the ship, Lily stepped from the shelter of the fishing shed. Waving her arms, she yelled, "Stop!"

Like a hawk sighting prey, he turned, the flowers still clutched in his hand. He produced a spyglass and raised it to his eye. Even from one hundred yards away, she felt the intensity of his gaze.

She'd spent a sleepless night contemplating this moment. To fill the hours, she'd washed her hair and chosen, then discarded, a dozen different gowns. For convenience and warmth, she had decided on a serviceable and moderately flattering dress of dark blue wool. Her cloak was new, a birthday gift from her uncle, the duke of Hamilton. She wore no jewelry; her mother had left her none.

Flustered by his lengthy scrutiny, Lily strove for composure. She tried to smile. Her cheeks trembled with the effort. He probably thought her a waif. Or worse, lacking in the head. Then he lowered the spyglass and stared into the rigging as if contemplating what to do. Silently, she beseeched him to understand. Again he peered at her through the glass.

She pushed back the hood of her cloak. The wind whistled, chilling her bare neck and ears. Sending him an honest appeal, she mouthed the words, "Please, I must speak with you."

He barked an order. Half a dozen men raced to lower a wherry over the side. Two burly sailors clamored into the small boat and rowed straight toward her.

She had hoped the stranger would come ashore. For over a decade, she had longed to meet him. She wanted to tell him about the day she had discovered the grave and the then-thriving rosebush. She wanted to commiserate with him on her yearly journey up the mountain to place his tribute of roses on the grave. He *must* know that a summer drought followed by a harsh winter spelled doom for the alien plant.

Disappointment choked her, for she must relay her message through a third party. There would be no meeting, no reminiscing. She wouldn't be able to tell him how cleverly she defied her family and absented herself from Hamilton Castle on her birthday every year, just so she could put the roses where they belonged. There would be no opportunity to become friends.

The ship's boat scraped land. A burly seaman stood up, a woolen cap pulled low over his brow, his face weathered by the wind and sea.

"Please tell the man in the cape that the rosebush on the grave is dying," Lily said.

"Climb aboard." The seaman extended his hand. "I'm to fetch you to him."

Surprise snatched her voice. Dare she risk her reputation for the chance to talk to him? "Who is he?"

"The captain."

Turning toward the sun, she studied the captain at length, looking for evidence of what she knew: He was a man of good character, a man true of heart.

With a wave of his arm, he beckoned her. Giddiness buoyed her senses. If she were discovered boarding or leaving his ship, she'd be condemned for a harlot. She almost laughed out loud at that. Being a dutiful daughter had gained her nothing, except unlimited access to her uncle's library, a new cloak every year, and the pitiful title of spinster.

Caution ignored, Lily picked up her sack of treasures, lifted her skirt above the sea foam, and stepped into the wherry. The small boat surged up and over the swells. Sea spray tickled her nose and coated her lashes. Scanning the shore, she saw smoke rising from the chimney of the baker's shop. The alehouse was quiet, same as the other buildings. Sunlight winked on the windows of Hamilton Castle and had indeed turned the peak of Goat's Fell to gold.

Hoping her other expectations proved as solid, she phrased a practiced speech in eloquent terms. But when she stepped on the deck, words failed her, for she found herself nose to chin with a man so startlingly handsome she couldn't help but stare. He possessed a bounty of manly attributes. High cheekbones, a strong jaw, and an elegantly sloping nose bespoke nobility, yet his shoulders were as broad as a stone mason's and his legs long and slender, like that of a horseman. A neckcloth of fine black silk complemented his sun-bronzed skin and contrasted sharply with eyes so deeply blue they rivaled the midnight sky.

"If you've come to flatter me, lass, you succeeded admirably."

He spoke in cultured tones flavored with only the slightest of Scottish burrs. Or was he Irish? No, he was too tall and familiar in what her grandfather termed, "the Scots way." Blushing, she said, "It's just that I pictured you differently."

He cocked his head. "Why would you picture me at all?"

Embarrassed to her soul, Lily blurted, "The rosebush is dying."

Dipping his head, he studied his gloved hands, now empty of his floral tribute. "Rose?"

Why was he pretending ignorance when petals littered the deck? She snatched up a handful. "This rose."

Rather than being interested or grateful for her participation in his yearly quest, he seemed troubled and uncomfortable, his gaze sliding away and his throat working nervously. "What know you of that rose?"

Murmurs spread among the crew. Lily grew uneasy, for the meeting wasn't going as she had expected. He was her special guest. They should rejoice in each other's company and celebrate their common bond. "'Tis exactly like the one that grows up there." She pointed toward Goat's Fell. "On the grave hidden in the high glen."

His jaw grew squarely taut. "I know nothing of a grave on Arran."

Knowing he lied and wondering why, she pulled an old scarf from her canvas sack. "Here. See the flowers." She laid the fresh petals on the cloth. "They are the same."

His large hand dwarfed the scarf, yet he held it with care. "'Tis the needlework of a child."

The crew occupied themselves with busywork—scraping brightwork and wielding holystones—but their interest strayed to her. Their surreptitious scrutiny did not trouble Lily, for she'd grown up around seafaring men. The captain, however, made her conscious of the fact that she was an unescorted female on a shipful of strangers.

Feeling as if she'd stepped onto a crumbling cliff, Lily struggled for solid ground. "Of course it is." She took back her keepsake. "I was a child when I stitched it."

"Who are you?" he asked.

"Lily."

"Lily . . . ?"

She hesitated, fearing that he, too, would scorn her for her family name. Her association with this man was pure, untainted by clan wars. She wanted to keep it so. She did not favor her relatives; her hair was red, and she stood as tall as most of her clansmen. "Just Lily."

A sly grin lifted one corner of his mouth. "I should have known."

"Known what?"

Ruefully he murmured, "You're not the sort of female that usually hails our ship. But the times are a-changing."

Mortified, she glared at him. "I'm no strumpet, and I expected better of you."

"You signaled. I responded." He tipped his hat and turned away.

"Wait! Don't you care about what I've done?" Years of questions tumbled in her mind. She chose one. "I don't even know your name."

He stopped, the wind ruffling the exotic plume in his hat, his shoulders blocking out the rising sun. His crew shared curious, expectant glances. Slowly, he turned and looked not at her but at the shoreline.

His was the searching, fearless expression of an adventurer. Hers was the wistful gaze of a hopeless romantic. Lily chastised herself for the fanciful observation. He was simply a man, albeit a dangerously attractive one. She was a woman with a mission. "Who are you, sir?"

Placing a hand on his chest, he said, "I am but a man of the sea who mourns the loss of a vessel. The last ship I captained wrecked upon those very rocks."

He was also an inventive liar. News of a shipwreck moved on the wind in Brodick Bay. No such tragedy had occurred since a Spanish galleon had run aground. She'd been nine years old at the time. "I don't believe you."

He looked insulted, his features smooth with disdain. "A pity then. Now, if you'll excuse me, I have a cargo to deliver." He signaled to the burly sailor who had fetched her. "Spanker, return her to shore."

Angered by his swift dismissal, she lifted her chin.

"Unless you traffic in goosedown, Captain, your hold is empty."

Regal indifference turned to interest. His keen gaze studied her from the coil of braids at the crown of her head to the sand that coated the toes of her walking boots. Indecision softened his noble features. "What know you of ships and cargo, Lily?"

Past injustices tormented her, but Lily shelved them; she had information to gather and a rose to save. "I had a ship of my own once, a French-made pinasse as fine as this vessel. But I did not come here to talk about my life. I came to ask—"

"You sailed often?"

If he could be evasive, so could she. "Much as I would enjoy nattering on with you, I must not. Tell me about the grave."

He raised one brow. "Tell me about your ship."

"The grave," she said through her teeth.

"The ship," he insisted.

She knew better than to engage in word games she couldn't win, but pride and fear drove her on. "Don't you see? I cannot linger with you."

He crossed his arms as if to say, I'm waiting.

Resigned to the queer turn of events, she answered honestly. "I sailed on my ship only once, but I was allowed to play on the deck when she was in port." Lily had carved her name on the bulkhead in the main cabin, but she didn't think he'd be interested in that any more than he cared to make friends with her.

"Play?" Again, his wary gaze strayed to the shore. "Did you also embroider ships on handkerchiefs?"

An unrealness gripped her. They should be discussing the ritual that bound them. "Mock me if you will, but rather you should thank me for tending that rosebush."

"Why do you care? I do not."

Could she tell him that her happiness and her future had somehow become entangled with the grave and the dying rose? No. He was too cold and forbidding. She couldn't hide her disappointment. "You, sir, are a liar."

Movement on the ship stopped. "You, madam, are dismissed."

His coldness wounded her deeply. All the better, then, that time was running out. She must glean the answers and quickly. "*I* want the roses there. *You* want them there. Why else would you come here every year?"

His eyes glittered with challenge. "You claim to have seen me here before?"

She hadn't expected defensiveness or denial. "Of course I have. For eleven years."

He laughed. "Hear you that, Forbes?" he said over his shoulder. "This lass claims to have charted my comings and goings for over a decade."

A portly, dignified man dressed in brown velvet knee breeches and a matching coat joined them. Doffing his beaver hat, he bowed from the waist. "I'm John Forbes, purser of the Go—"

"Thank you, Forbes." The captain cut him off before he could reveal the name of their vessel.

A horn blared from the shore, signaling the ship had been spotted. Lily's heart sank, but she pressed on. "Who is buried in the grave? Please, I must know."

"Perhaps you would care to share breakfast with me, Lily."

She fidgeted. The meeting was going all wrong. An uneasy suspicion niggled. What if he were a MacDonnel? Impossible, her better judgment said. A MacDonnel wouldn't brave enemy territory on a sentimental journey; they were bloodthirsty killers. Perhaps he was sorry for insulting her. "Thank you, but I must decline. I care more for answers than for food. Did you dig the grave and plant the rosebush?"

His gaze drilled her, and she felt rooted to the deck. "A woman who thirsts for knowledge. How novel."

Although wounded by his sarcasm, Lily hid her pain. "Insult me if you will, but——"

A cannon boomed. Gulls screamed. Whirling, Lily saw a solitary figure on the beach near the battery. He held a torch. He wore a Hamilton plaid. Drat!

Water splashed about thirty feet off the stern. The cannonball had gone wide and short.

"Anchors aweigh!" bellowed the captain as he whipped out the spyglass and scanned the shore. "Haul out the mains."

Crewmen shinnied up the masts. Like snakes slithering upward into the rigging, the halyards uncoiled. The windlass began to squeal. Over the din, the captain shouted orders to the mate.

To her dismay, Lily saw a stream of tartan-clad Hamiltons pouring onto the beach and running for the battery.

"Hard about, Master Bonaventure," said the captain. "Get us the hell out of here."

"Turning to, Captain," answered the helmsman.

Another cannon boomed.

Into the rigging, the captain yelled, "Pile on the muslin."

The sails fluttered, then began to sheet home, catching the stiff breeze. The ship listed into the turn, righted, then lunged toward the mouth of the bay.

The second cannon shot also fell short.

"Forbes," barked the captain. "As soon as we catch the currents, bring that woman below."

Lily's heart sank. "Nay. I must go back. I'll row myself ashore or swim." Even as she spoke, the wherry was hauled onto the deck. She raced for the rope ladder.

The captain caught her halfway there.

Near panic, she considered pleading, but discarded the weak option. Staring up into his eyes, she looked for a glimmer of honor. She saw intelligence and determination. "You cannot keep me. I'm sorry my family fired on your ship, and you don't have to tell me who is buried there. I swear to respect your silence."

"Your family?" Hatred hardened his mouth and his hands tightened on her arms. "You're a bloody Hamilton!"

She started. "Let me go. I do not share their quarrels."

"Quarrels?" Pushing her away as if she were a leper, he

turned on a heel and strolled toward the aft hatch, his cape billowing in the wind.

She went cold inside, and her skin turned to gooseflesh. Until the day they wrapped her in her father's tartan plaid and laid her to rest, she would remember the condemnation in the captain's eyes. Her gallant adventurer had become an ordinary man who hated her, not for herself but for the crimes of her kinsmen.

Forbes stood at her side. "Come with me."

Why had her kinsmen fired on the ship? Had the one clansman seen her in the wherry? Her mind a muddle of confusion and misery, Lily murmured, "Why is he keeping me? 'Tis cruel and unfair."

"On my grandmother's soul, I swear the captain is neither of those things."

His loyalty was understandable; no seaman worth his salt would gainsay his captain. But if her kinsmen knew she had boarded this pinasse, they would follow in hot pursuit. She glanced at the shore. Brightly garbed in the red, blue, and white Hamilton plaid, the clansmen scurried around her uncle's bark, preparing to launch the craft.

Her spirits plummeted. Without cargo, the Hamilton ship could overtake the pinasse if the men worked quickly enough. With her uncle away in Edinburgh her father would captain the family ship. Better this pinasse escaped capture, for the Hamiltons would offer no quarter. "Where do we sail, Mr. Forbes?"

He fumbled with his hat, and his gaze wouldn't meet hers. "I'm not at liberty to say."

Something was badly amiss. If it weren't so preposterous, she could think this ship a MacDonnel vessel and the captain her enemy. But that was absurd. They were merely afraid of the Hamiltons. Or were they? Secrets abounded here, and she intended to ferret out every one.

"I can find my own way, Mr. Forbes." So decided, she crossed the deck and entered the companionway. Carpet covered the steps and leaded glass lanterns lighted the way. Although like the *Valiant Lily* in design, this pinasse was luxuriously appointed. The musty, sweet smell of tobacco permeated the air. At the end of the hallway, the door to the master cabin stood open.

She paused on the threshold and saw the captain locking a wardrobe. He'd removed his cape. Over the full-sleeved silk shirt, he wore a quilted leather tunic, and his black velvet breeches were tucked into bucket-top boots. Now hatless, he had secured his overlong hair with a ribbon at his nape.

Spying her, he stood, slipped the key into his pocket, and motioned her into the room.

The cabin was richly furnished, the chairs cushioned with quilted damask, the table set with pewter and crystal, the brazier inlaid with silver. A massive desk was cluttered with map rolls, pencils, an astrolabe, and other tools of the seafarer's trade. Sunlight streamed through a bank of mullioned windows at the stern. Lily couldn't help thinking about her own ship and the hours she'd spent exploring every nook and cranny of the vessel. But that was another dream long dead.

Her gaze strayed to the corner and the huge bed draped in velvet and scattered with familiar pink primroses. Curiosity turned to trepidation. "You cannot keep me here."

He followed her line of vision, and a smile quirked his lips. "Your virtue is safe, Lily Hamilton, but I'll not take you back. Your kinsmen would have a thing or two to say to that."

They would, but only out of pride. "'Tis wise to fear the Hamiltons of Arran, for they carry their grudges to the grave—especially if one of their kinswomen is dishonored." Let him make of that threat what he would.

Glaring at her, he loosened his neckcloth and pitched it on the bed. "Harboring grudges is surely your clan's one *admirable* trait, then, for the Hamiltons are masters at kidnapping and butchery."

There it was, the condemnation that she had expected. Again she had fallen victim to the crimes of her clan. The unfairness rankled, for she had thought her dashing captain above prejudice. He had a face better suited to merry laughter than stern disapproval. But she wouldn't be fooled by a winsome smile. He had condemned her, not for herself, but for her family name.

"I do not share their beliefs or their disputes, and I must return."

"To what, then?"

To what indeed, she wondered, picturing her apartment, a small parlor and a smaller sleeping room on the upper floor. She thought of her family, the men turned bitter by war and hatred, their women tired and cowed, their children eager to walk the familiar path of destruction. She had dreamed of leaving Arran, but not with her kinsmen giving chase and dozens of lives in jeopardy.

"Do you return to a beau?" the captain asked.

She couldn't help but laugh. She had no dowry, and her father refused to take money from the war chest to provide her with a respectable marriage portion.

"Aha!" He snapped his fingers. "A husband awaits you."

His eager expression depressed her more, for he was probably hoping she'd married into Clan Hamilton, rather than share their blood. Would that it were true. "Nay. I am a maiden who wishes to return with her good reputation, which will be ruined do you keep me. Put me ashore at Lamlash or Blackwaterfoot. I'll find my way home."

"You're old not to be wed."

"You're young to be so jaded."

He looked impressed, his gaze sharp, his interest engaged. "My apologies. I meant to say that you are bonny enough for a prince."

At his weak flattery, her temper snapped. "Don't patronize me. I have not wed, for reasons of my own. Now, thanks to your villainy, a cabbage farmer wouldn't take me to wife."

"A Hamilton without a fortune to buy her a husband?" He leaned against the cabin's center beam. "Pardon me if I don't believe you. And 'twas you who wished to speak with me."

Past reason, beyond decorum, she moved close to him

and poked his shoulder with her index finger. "Listen to me, you heartless bully." He backed up. She came on. "I have tended that grave for over half of my life. I have crouched on that beach on my birthday for the past eleven years and watched you unveil your pride. You're a beast to belittle my feelings for the plight of that rose." She poked him again. "And you're an ungrateful wretch."

His hand curled over her fingers, flattening her palm against his chest and holding it there. "I'm no hero, Lily Hamilton. I will not risk the safety of my crew to save your honor or a dying shrub."

Bright girlish dreams faded, and she couldn't stop the tears. "I'm sorry I came to you."

Softly he said, "I cannot say the same."

Puzzled, she frowned. "Why not?"

He gave her a smile that would have melted a harridan's heart. With his thumb, he brushed away her tears. "Because you are surely the bonniest lass ever born on that island."

She hadn't expected more pretty words. Flustered, she batted at his hand. "Please take me to Lamlash." The port city was so close by, she could walk home.

"I regret that I cannot, Lily."

Defeat weighted her shoulders, but she could not blame him. To make port anywhere on Arran would imperil his crew. "You know my name. Tell me yours."

He walked to the table, pulled out a chair and, with a wave of his hand, invited her to sit. "I'm Hugh, and the earl of Blackburn."

He hadn't named his clan or mentioned an alliance with an influential family. She scanned the room for a heraldic symbol, a tartan plaid, or a clan badge. She found a few personal items: a cask of French wine; a pair of blown-glass vases from Venice; and a stack of books beneath the windowseat. "Blackburn? I don't know that title."

"'Tis recently bestowed. Do you harbor ill will to those new to the nobility?"

"Of course not, but you didn't answer my question. Rather, you asked me one." When he gave her the bland, handsome stare she expected, she said, "I have six uncles and enough male cousins to man this ship. I'm familiar with the tricks men play with words."

"You do not yield to their superior intellect."

She fought the urge to huff. "I do not play their games."

He propped his arms on the back of the chair and leaned forward. Lamplight fell on his hair, turning the black strands to midnight blue, the same as his eyes. "Because you lose at their games?" he said.

Heavens, he was insufferable and disarmingly handsome. "Because I prefer to watch porridge spoil."

He laughed, and his eyes crinkled at the corners. He even had a dimple. The rogue. "Me thinks 'tis because you've grown bored with besting those rascally Hamilton men."

It was Lily's turn to shrug. She had little in common with her kinsmen. They fought battles; she helped patched up their wounds. "To where do we sail, my lord?"

"Where would you like to sail?"

He had intentionally asked her a question. She gave him a pained look. "To paradise—eventually—on the wings of angels."

His expression softened, and he chuckled. "That can be arranged. Now, sit, eat, and we'll chase away that fear I see in your eyes." He rocked the chair.

The table bore an odd feast—a bowl of nuts, a grainy yellow cake, a large ham, and a jar of what looked like thick whiskey. Not even if the king's own chef had prepared the meal, would she eat before learning their destination. "To where are we sailing?"

"To the American Colonies—eventually."

Her senses reeled. "I cannot go there."

"Why not? Do you find the colonists too primitive?"

"You know very well I haven't been there."

"I know you not at all, Lily Hamilton. Sit, tell me about yourself."

When she did not move, he heaved a sigh and stared out the open windows. "Have you a weapon?"

"I do," she lied. "I've a dirk sharp enough to cut out your gizzard."

He continued to gaze at the sky. "Not my heart?"

"You haven't one."

Grinning, he turned slowly toward her. "Bloodthirsty women disturb me. I merely thought to offer you a blade for your peace of mind. You need not fear me."

"You'll pardon me if I question your sudden concern. It rings hollow."

"Like my chest?"

"How can you jest when my future stands in ruins? You should have let me go in the wherry."

"What future? You hate your kinsmen. I suspect you have no marriage prospects. Why not go adventuring with me?"

She sent him her most withering stare. "You have the reasoning power of an oyster."

"And you have the tongue of a viper." He put a hand near his cheek and flapped his fingers against his thumb. "With you nipping at me constantly, I'm not certain I'd survive a long voyage."

She couldn't help but smile. "Then tell me what I want to know. Who is buried in that grave?"

"Sit down."

"Not until you answer me."

"On my honor as a . . . man of the sea, I do not know. Now will you sit?"

He had not intended to swear on his occupation, of that Lily was certain. Why did he conceal his family identity? The more she looked at him, the more certain she became that he was not one of the dreaded MacDonnels. They were fair of face and hair, traits from their Viking ancestors. Given an hour alone in his cabin, she would find out his family name. Joining him at the table seemed a reasonable start.

When she sat down, he took the chair across from her. "These are corn cakes—from the colonies."

She tasted the crumbly cake and found that it had a rich, nutty flavor, stronger than wheat or oats.

He handed her a napkin. "Do you like it?"

"Yes, but I'm unfamiliar with the grain."

"The natives call it maize." As he spoke, he piled her plate with ham. "The kernels grow in a husk, six or seven to a plant. The colonists farm it, but the natives harvest it at random."

So fondly did he speak of the New World, Lily felt bound to say, "You sound as if you like the colonies."

"Aye." He pulled a stopper from the bottle of thick brown liquid and drizzled a puddle on her plate. "Try it."

She did and found it sweet. "Delicious. Are you a merchant ship?"

"Aye, 'tween the king's isles and Chesapeake Bay."

From the smell of the ship she knew he normally hauled tobacco, but was curious to know if he would tell the truth. "Your cargo?"

He hesitated, mischief glimmering in his eyes. "Goosedown."

Lily didn't know whether to laugh or groan. He shouldn't be so witty, so companionable. But he was.

"You have a bonny smile," he said.

"You have an empty hold."

He shook his head. "I think I pity your cousins and uncles."

"I'll tell them that when they board your ship."

Propping an elbow on the table, he rested his chin in his palm. "On second thought, 'tis likely I'll have to pay them to take you back."

With your life, if you do not let me go, she almost said.

But friendly banter offered a respite from the danger they faced. "Are you wealthy, then?"

"In spirit"—he declared, spearing a forkful of ham—"I am as rich as the king." He popped the meat into his mouth.

"Are you a Stewart? You have their look about you."

"Again, you flatter me, Lily. Master Bonaventure swears I favor the Brodies."

"Oh, nay. They come from Norse stock."

"You sound well traveled, Lily. Why not add the New World? 'Tis a bountiful land with a handsome native people. The soil is so rich, 'tis said the seed willingly flies into rows as straight as a new mainmast, and weeds keep to their own. For an entire season, the sun shines so brightly the men must shield their eyes and the ladies protect their delicate skin."

So much sun seemed impossible, especially to one from the cloud-misted isle of Arran. "I've heard the natives are savages."

He grew serious. "No more savage than the Hamiltons and the MacDonnels when they cross paths."

At least his condemnation was fairly divided. She could only hope to change his mind about one Hamilton. "You swear you take no side in the feud?"

He turned agreeable again. "I swear that I despise all quarrels, save those with greedy harbormasters and flame-haired vixens. . . ."

She grew shy, thinking how seldom anyone on Arran praised her hair or appreciated her outspoken nature. In more than appearance, she was different from her people.

"With eyes the rich shade of chestnuts. . . ."

A flush heated her skin. She searched for a quip but her mind was content to savor his compliments.

"And a taste for adventuring."

He had steered her off course. She couldn't go traipsing across the world with the earl of Blackburn. Blame for her predicament was hers, but she would not compound her mistake with more unseemly behavior. She had come seeking information. She would not be deterred. "Why do you cloak your ship?"

Hugh MacDonnel had no intention of telling the clever Hamilton lass. He couldn't believe his luck. Fate had dropped the sweetest plum on the Hamilton tree right in his lap. His father would empty his treasury to get his hands on her. The MacDonnels would dance in the street, did they possess this bonny prize.

Hugh didn't for a moment believe her long-suffering tale of waiting and watching on the beach. There was no grave and no rosebush; his sister would have told him so. The scarf was not proof. Lily could have patterned her poorly embroidered roses after the flowers he tossed into the bay. The Hamiltons were using her. Unfortunately, Hugh MacDonnel had taken the bait. How badly did they want her back?

The clansman in him stirred to life, and he felt a devilish need to seek carnal revenge. His father would praise him for slaking his lust between the thighs of a Hamilton wench.

Wench. The undeserved slander shocked Hugh, and he

quickly tamped back the demon inside. He'd long ago turned his back on the politics of his clan. He would not now become a supporter of their destructive ways, even for a tumble with a shapely virgin.

"Why do you bring the flowers?" she asked.

Not for a moment did he believe she would understand his devotion to an older sibling; she was a Hamilton, living amid discord. "'Tis a private concern."

"'Tis a sentimental quest," she corrected in that bold tone he was coming to expect and to favor.

"Attach no soft-hearted ideal to what I do in Brodick Bay. I come here for someone else."

Her saucy smile boded ill. "Coming here for someone else is sentimental in itself. Admit it, Captain, you're a gallant."

She had spun girlish dreams about his visits here. A lie would put an end to them. "Not if I'm paid to do what I do."

Disappointment glazed her eyes. Seeing vulnerability, Hugh pressed on. "That's what you thought, isn't it?" For effect, he laughed. "You'd have me coming to Arran for nostalgic reasons. Admirable, Lily, but short of the mark."

Bless her, she rallied, demanding, "Who pays you then?"

Since he'd acquired his first command, Hugh had distanced himself from the feud. His family had disdained his lack of interest. When that hadn't worked, they'd bought him a title to entice him back to Scotland. But Hugh Alexander MacDonnel had found his home an ocean away, among industrious people who cared more for harmony than tradition. Only for the love of his older sister did he navigate Brodick Bay every spring, a bundle of primroses in his hand.

"You *do* bear some concern for the grave. I see it in your eyes."

He'd have to hide his feelings better, for among her other qualities, Lily Hamilton could ferret out a soul better than a priest. But, by the saints, she was a pleasure to look upon, her eyes a soft warm brown and her hair the glorious shades of a harvest fire. He'd wager his tobacco plantation that as a child she'd had a spray of freckles across her nose. Now her complexion glowed like new ivory. His gaze kept straying to her mouth, the perfectly symmetrical bow of her upper lip, and the fuller one below. He could make a banquet of her mouth.

"Who is buried there? A sweetheart? When did you fall in love with her?"

A few moments ago, Hugh realized, for Lily Hamilton's romantic nature begged to be coddled and shared. And her body—only a cloistered monk could ignore her lush curves and lithe limbs. But she, of all women, was forbidden to Hugh MacDonnel, for he would take no spoils in a war that he despised.

Curse his soul, he wanted to believe her, to find a bright spot in the dark war between the Hamiltons and the Mac-Donnels.

"Please talk to me. I've watched and waited for so long."

Her earnest plea dashed his introspection and inspired

a challenge. "Over a decade you said. That would have made you six or seven at the start."

She had a lovely way about her, both retiring and exciting at once. "I was eleven"—she demurred—"when first I saw you."

He gave her a skeptical frown. She couldn't possibly know so much about his life. She couldn't be two and twenty either; she didn't look a season over ten and seven.

"You don't believe me. Very well, Captain Hugh. You wore no hat that first year or cloak. 'Twasn't dawn yet, and the bay was becalmed. You carried a torch, which you also dropped into the bay."

Hugh had been clumsy with cold that year. She must have shivered, too, if she'd been standing on the shore. Which he doubted. No child would venture out alone on such a mission. One of her kinsmen had seen Hugh and passed the story along. But that brought up another question. "Why did you not sound the alarm?"

"Because of the roses." Using the tines of the fork, she cut into the ham. "I'd just found the grave the year before."

His sister had not mentioned a grave. When asked the reason behind her request that Hugh deliver the roses, Fiona MacDonnel had said, "'Tis for an angel." An odd statement, for her knowledge of Arran and the Hamiltons stemmed from the most bitter episode in the clan war. Did Lily know what had happened to Fiona on that island so many years ago? No, she wouldn't have been born then, and the abduction and ransom of Fiona MacDonnel had been a closely guarded secret. "How did you locate this grave?"

She seemed to settle in, resting easy in the chair. Between bites, she studied the furnishings. When she tilted her head back, he couldn't help but stare at the graceful column of her neck. At length, she said, "I ran away from home."

"A lass of one and ten? Why?"

Her gaze level, she said, "An injustice done to me by my kinsmen."

No doubt she'd seen her share and more of the cruelty of which her clansmen were capable. The bitterness of Edward Hamilton, a high-ranking chieftain, knew no rival. Or did she, like her kinsmen, enjoy the strife? "What injustice?"

Her lips thinned, and she again studied the cabin. "They lost my dowry ship to the MacDonnels."

They might well get it back, too, if they had managed to launch that barkentine and catch a fair wind. Before remodeling, his *Golden Thistle* had born the name *Valiant Lily*. How fitting, he thought, watching her comport herself with dignity. A spoil of the clan war, this pinasse had been part of Hugh's majority. The ship had also been her dowry. "That is why you haven't wed?"

Pride shimmered around her. "Why I haven't wed is as you say, a private concern."

"A clever reply." One thing was certain. Hugh Mac-Donnel had no intention of alienating Lily Hamilton. He was content to simply admire her beauty. A Hamilton? The notion was laughable. When her clan bred true, they were rightly called pigeon-faced. He hadn't exaggerated when he said she was lovely enough to please a prince. Why, then, had her father not found her a husband? She needed no financial inducement to grace a man's table and share his bed. No doubt her father was holding out for the highest bidder. 'Twas common knowledge that the Hamiltons would turn a profit on the cairns of their ancestors. What price would they pay to save her virginity? Could Hugh take it? He didn't know.

"Who is buried in the grave?"

He could be relentless, too. "A duke's daughter has much to recommend her."

"The duke is my uncle." She gave him a piercing look. "Edward Hamilton is my father."

Hugh shivered inside at the name of the monster who had sired her. Edward the Angry, they called him. With a single-mindedness born of evil, he kept the feud alive. "What of your mother?"

Her hand stilled and she looked down. "Dead at the hands of the MacDonnels. I was but a babe."

So that had been the source of Edward's vengeance. Sympathy squeezed Hugh's chest, not for the butcher of Arran, but for his daughter. She'd been a motherless babe in that den of thieves. Yet how many MacDonnels had the Hamiltons orphaned? Enough. "I'm sorry, Lily."

With the ease of long practice, she composed herself. "I'll keep asking you about the grave."

"Then we shall often be at an impasse."

"How can you refuse me after all I've done? My kinsmen deny the grave exists."

"As do I."

"Then I'll take you to the glen. I'll show you the grave."

Hugh laughed, for he'd sooner swim the Atlantic than step foot on Arran. "Pardon me, but I must decline Hamilton hospitality."

"I pose no threat to you."

He almost choked. "No threat?"

"You're safe—once I explain to them. My kinsmen only bear a grudge against the MacDonnels."

On that statement of irony, Forbes appeared in the doorway, a cloth-covered basket in his hands. Hugh waved him inside. "What have you there, Forbes, treats from the purser's pantry?"

The always dignified Forbes lifted his chin. With his thumb and index finger, he whipped away the napkin. In perfectly clipped English, he said, "I thought my lady might enjoy a taste of something sweet." He came forward and held the fruit basket before her. "The figs are particularly fine."

She peered down, her excited gaze fastening on the contents. She chose only a fig. "Thank you, Mr. Forbes. I've always wanted to taste one."

Hugh watched her wrap her lips around the fruit in a manner so innocently provocative that he groaned inside. When she closed her eyes and hummed, savoring the taste, he felt his loins swell.

"Does my uncle's bark follow?"

The question dashed Hugh's ardor. She stared up at Forbes, who glanced at Hugh. He nodded.

Taking his cue, Forbes said, "Aye, my lady."

A worried frown scored her forehead. "They'll overtake us."

All things being equal, she would have been correct. But Hugh had done more to the *Valiant Lily* than change her name, add a few luxuries, and double her cannon. He'd square rigged her fore and main, leaving only the mizzen to lateen sails. No wonder Lily hadn't recognized her dowry ship.

The bark might get close, but the lumbering sea cow would not overtake the swift and near empty pinasse. "Who captains the Hamilton ship?"

"My father."

God's hooks! "Forbes," Hugh said as calmly as he could. "Inform Master Bonaventure that Edward Hamilton commands the bark."

The purser dropped the basket. "God be with us."

Her expression grew suspicious. "If you live in the colonies, how do you know my father?"

"His reputation is widespread," murmured a now sallow-faced Forbes, stooping to retrieve the spilled fruit.

"Don't fret, my friend," Hugh said. "Mistress Hamilton has assured us that her father butchers only MacDonnels." When Forbes glanced quickly from Lily back to Hugh, he added, "Have Bonaventure take evasive measures."

"What measures?" she demanded.

Feeling as if he were perched on a crossroads, Hugh

battled with his conscience. Arran was small, and according to his kinsmen, gossip traveled on the island air. He could put her ashore at Blackwaterfoot and be rid of her. He could also sail into a trap of her father's setting. Or he could keep her and outwit Edward the Angry. Or he could ponder the question a while longer. The latter held particular appeal to Hugh. "We sail to our summer moorings."

She rose. "Where is that?"

Hugh had no intention of telling her that, either. He had stowed his tartans, his log books, and his seal of office. Short of picking the lock, she wouldn't find a clue in this room to his identity. He'd tell her who he was, eventually. Why make her suffer needlessly? He couldn't return her, wouldn't return her. Her clansmen had seen him in the light of day and were now plowing the Firth of Clyde to catch up.

Since Hugh had yet to decide what to do with the extremely personable Lily Hamilton, getting away from her seemed the prudent choice.

He rose. "I'll speak to Bonaventure myself. Lily, you stay here."

To his surprise, she did not protest, but went back to the meal. Ah, well, she was a Hamilton, wasn't she, and schooled since birth in the art of intrigue. He would take defensive action. He'd begin by having the carpenter fashion a board bearing a new name for the ship. The *Golden Thistle* was about to take on another identity.

"Lily?"

At the sound of her name, Lily dragged herself from a

sound sleep. She'd been watching though the stern window and didn't remember closing her eyes.

Blinking, she looked up. The captain stood over her. In one hand he carried a string hammock, in the other two tankards of ale. His appreciative grin didn't bear contemplating.

She sat up and stretched the kinks from her back. Glancing out the window she realized the sun had set. She hadn't seen the captain since this morning. Several hours earlier Forbes had brought her a tray of cheese and bread, plus items for her personal comfort. At the behest of the captain, so Forbes had said.

"You slept well?"

Under the circumstances, his cordiality rankled. "You locked me in."

"Need I remind you that you are a beautiful woman on a ship with common seamen? This vessel has only one other private cabin. Bonaventure and Forbes share it."

He had a point. He also looked like a fox stalking a covey of quail. Who was he? From where did he hail? Her every attempt to spring the lock on his wardrobe had failed. His desk had yielded nothing in the way of identification. Her irritation grew. "How thoughtful of you."

"Sarcasm doesn't suit you, Lily." He raised the mugs. "Join me? 'Tis fresh from the purser's swipes."

Courage from a keg, her grandfather used to say. "You wouldn't be trying to get me tippered, would you?"

He tossed the hammock onto a chair. "You wound me,

Lily. You wanted to board this ship." Holding out one of the mugs, he said, "You've no cause to fear me."

In the course of a day, he'd changed from the forbidding stranger to the friendly host. With reservations, she took the offered tankard. "That wasn't my uncle's ship behind us this afternoon, was it?"

He clanked his mug against hers. "Many ships sailed in our wake today. Many more crossed our path. Any of them could pass along our direction."

She set down the ale. "Have you changed course?"

"Aye, and do not ask where, for 'tis better that you do not know."

The extent of the danger she was in made her wary. She wanted to run. To where? A shipful of unsuspecting ruffians who ran before her kinsmen's revenge? Back to a family who would shun her for a fallen woman? Better the devil she knew.

She sipped the ale and found it palatable, if weak. "Am I allowed on deck?"

"Are you offering to mend the jib?"

At his innocently worded question, laughter bubbled up inside her. Had she stumbled onto a renegade, a libertine captain? The possibility made her brave. "And if I am?"

Hitching his hip on the edge of the desk, he crossed his arms over his chest. "A noble sacrifice, but I could not allow a guest to labor so."

His shirt was open at the neck, and she found her gaze drawn to the mat of black hair that peeked provocatively from the garment. "You don't trust me."

As amiable as could be, he smiled. "Let us just say that I don't know you."

Her family name meant nothing to him save trouble. An earl surely had friends in high places. Perhaps he knew of a family in need of a governess. A family. Did he have a wife and children? "Are you married, my lord?"

"Are you making an offer for my hand?"

Caught off guard, she gave a huff of indignation. "Of course not. I was making conversation."

"Nay, I've not wed."

She shouldn't have been glad, but she was.

"And I seldom answer to 'my lord.' Captain will do."

"Tell me the name of your vessel, Captain."

His eyes shone with pleasure rather than pride. "She's the *Westward Angel*."

"Will we make port tonight?"

"Perhaps." He walked to the table and picked up the hairbrush the purser had brought her earlier. "Yours?"

"Forbes said you wanted me to have it."

"Ah, Forbes," he drawled. "Now there's your gallant."

"Ha! You are a gentleman, Captain Hugh."

As if to prove her wrong, he lifted his brows in invitation. "The bed is soft and made for two."

Mortification nibbled at her composure. "I'll take the hammock." Snatching it up, she moved away, but not half as quickly as she wanted to. She located the hooks overhead, but they were out of reach.

"Can I help?" He sounded much too agreeable.

"No. You've done quite enough for one day." She slid

a chair to the appropriate spot. Throwing the hammock over her shoulder, she lifted her skirt and stepped onto the chair.

The rope ends slipped easily onto the hooks. His hands moved effortlessly to her waist. "I wouldn't want you to fall."

His seductive tone made a pledge of his concern. Summoning bravado, she thought of a cheeky reply. "Not unless I landed in that bed with you."

As if she weighed no more than a pebble, he lowered her to the floor. He stood so close, she could see herself reflected in his blue eyes. Her adventurer. A man who, for one day each year, had brought purpose to her life. Another lonely soul paying tribute to a dying rosebush on an anonymous grave.

"Lord, Lily, you rob a man of his wits."

Then his lips touched hers, and his arms surrounded her, coddling her, drawing her into the shelter of his broad chest. A spicy sweetness flavored his mouth, reminding her of mulled wine sipped 'round the Hogmanay fire. Hogmanay, the day when a maiden's beau presented himself on her doorway and offered her food, drink, and the warmth of his fire. Year after year, she had watched and congratulated the other girls for their good fortune. No such suitor had come for Lily Hamilton . . . until now.

Like a raging thirst, a lifetime of loneliness demanded that Lily drink, and she did, savoring the wondrous new feeling of being cherished, valued, and wanted. But no sooner had one need been met, than other surfaced. Her head felt light and her breathing strained, as if she'd raced to the top of Goat's Fell and now teetered, ready to tumble off the peak. Seeking purchase, she clutched his waist to steady herself, and found warmth and a body taut with manly strength.

His tongue slid between her lips, and he murmured, "Open your mouth, Lily. Give me your sweetness."

At his provocative command, she snapped to her senses and jumped back, her hand drawn to her tingling lips. "Absolutely not."

His dreamy gaze slid from her mouth to her straining breasts, to her skirt, beneath which, her knees trembled. "You liked kissing me," he said, all powerful male.

The truth in his words only embarrassed her more. Maidenly protests rose in her mind, but she discarded them for the flimsy excuses they were. Never more than at this moment did she miss having a mother to confide in. Yet with stern conviction, Lily knew she would brave even her father's wrath for this man, this stranger's cause. "I would have us be friends, Captain."

A grin as big as Scotland spread across his handsome face. "Oh, aye, Lily Hamilton. I believe we will indeed be friends." He held out his hand.

Having no reply and less will to argue, she climbed into the hammock, although she knew sleep would be a long time coming. An odd silence pulsed between them, as if the air were charged with words unsaid and desires unfulfilled.

She sought a light topic. "If you'll tell me who pays you to throw those roses, I'll take the night watch at the wheel."

His chuckled sound devilishly male. "You'd run us aground in Ireland."

"Ah," she said, feeling smug, "so that's where we're going."

The bed linens rustled; he was settling in. "Pleased with yourself, are you?"

"Pleased?" She stared at the beamed ceiling and listened to the creaking of the ship and the flapping of the sails. "You say you want to be my friend, and yet I must trick you to gain the smallest bit of information. 'Tis poor ground on which to build a friendship."

"Ground littered with angry Hamiltons."

"I've told you before, I am not like my kinsmen. I would have your trust."

"The moment you boarded this ship you put a crew of innocent men in danger."

"Not apurpose. I came only because of the rose. Had you told me what I wanted to know, I would have returned home and . . ." She could not tell him of the lonely future that awaited her on Arran.

"And what?"

Her disappointments were her own, and until he confided in her, she would keep them to herself. Better she stay with the event that had brought them together. "I would have tried to save the rose, and I would have anticipated your next visit to Brodick Bay."

"Must you natter on about that piece of maidenly fiction?"

A quick glance at him confirmed her suspicions. "Why are you angry?"

He scowled. "Your husband will explain it."

Now she was completely confused. "You're just too prideful to admit your part in a romantic ritual."

At his huff of disbelief, she considered rolling out of the hammock and confronting him. Better yet, she would give him something to think about. "By the way, on my twelfth birthday, you sailed into Brodick Bay wearing a seaman's beard."

He fluffed his pillow. "Men often grow beards."

"You do not. Not in May."

Reaching to turn out the lamp, he gave her a sharp look.

It was a small victory for Lily, but progress all the same. She would hammer away at his resistance. She'd describe each of his visits to Arran. Eventually, he'd come to trust her.

"On the morn I turned three and ten, you wore a Dutchman's hat." She sat on a water barrel and busied herself mending the edge of a frayed sail.

The captain stood at the rail and surveyed the sea. "A Dutchman's cap?" he scoffed, not taking the spyglass from his eye.

The pinasse cut effortlessly through the swells and the wind felt like a gentle caress. Basking in the thrill of being at sea again, Lily grew brave. "You looked rather square-headed."

He sighed and slapped the glass against his thigh. "Best you get out of the sun, Lily, and not just to protect that pretty skin."

"Did you hear that, Master Bonaventure?" she said to the helmsman. "The captain believes me daft."

"This captain," Hugh said, before Bonaventure could reply, "thinks you are clever for a Hamilton. Too clever, perhaps, for the rustic pleasures of the May Fair."

That got her attention. "What May Fair?"

Giving her a sly smile, he motioned to the helmsman. "Master Bonaventure, enlighten our guest on the Irish custom of May Fair."

Ever willing to join in the conversation, the affable Bonaventure spoke in a booming voice flavored with the accent of his native France. "You, *la belle fleur*, shall witness the children of Erin at their playful and primitive best. A warning, though, eat not the food, for an Irishman has the palate of a swine."

The first mate, a Lowland Scot named Crossjack, jumped to his feet. "An' what would a Froggie be knowin' about food? They eat snails." He pretended to spit on the deck. "I ask you, what civilized man eats snails?"

Laughter drifted from the rigging and the bowsprit as the crew joined in. The nimble-footed Crossjack waved his stocking cap, extolling them to challenge the helmsman.

When her turn came, Lily said, "How ever do you chew the shells, Master Bonaventure?"

He rolled his eyes, but the battle of cultures had been

struck. A lengthy discussion followed on the eating practices of everyone from Turks to Quakers.

Lily only half listened, her attention straying often to the captain, who still scanned the sea. His stance was so familiar it filled her with a sense of destiny. She felt in the midst of a scene she had watched from afar. At twelve years old she'd prayed for God to change her into a bird so she could fly to his ship and share his ritual.

Was he thinking about her description of his visit to Arran eleven years ago? How would he counter her next testimonial?

"Ridiculous," was his reply. "I have never worn a lovelock."

Hoping to ease the imposing stiffness from his shoulders, she had recalled the occasion of her fourteenth birthday. Her ploy had backfired, for he stood straighter, his arms rigid as he took a turn at the helm later that afternoon.

Lily could not retreat. "Aye, your hair was almost as long as mine at the time, and ever so curly. You wore the lovelock draped over your shoulder, but the wind kept blowing it into your face."

"You are a spinner of tales, Lily Hamilton."

She sighed dramatically. "I imagine the look fell out of fashion, for the next year you wore your hair braided in a Frenchman's queue."

"There, you've tricked yourself up. I know not the first thing about plaiting hair." He jiggled his eyebrows. "I am, however, adept at *un*plaiting it. Shall I show you?"

He'd done the tricking and, as usual, Lily felt like the naive island girl she was. "You're a rogue."

"Thank you, but you needn't flatter me with words. Adoring glances will do."

Fuming, she said, "I'd rather . . ." No insult came to mind.

"Watch porridge spoil?"

He shouldn't have such a good memory, not when she had so little experience to draw on. Her mind shouldn't dwell on the kiss he'd given her, and her body shouldn't yearn for his touch.

"What's this," he drawled, "a Hamilton without a cutting sally?"

She had no clever reply, but thought of a way to take the wind from his sails. She began to whistle.

"Avast that noise!"

Ignoring him and the superstition she provoked, she strolled in a half circle behind him, warbling her best. She knew she was being rude, but couldn't help herself.

"I'm warning you, Lily. Cease this instant or you'll have a gale on us before sunset."

So, he *was* subject to sailors' tales. "Admit that you came to Arran wearing a lovelock."

He stared into the rigging, his neck muscles corded with tension, his too-long hair blowing in the breeze. She started whistling again.

"Crossjack will throw you overboard. The cook will refuse to light a fire. We will have to eat ship's biscuit and drink brine water for a week."

He looked so discomfited she knew she should retreat, and she would, but not just yet. "Who is buried in the grave?"

"I'm a sailor, not a seer. So leave off, Lily."

With a sinking dread she watched the first mate cut a length of rope. Working quickly, he tied what she knew was a square knot to ward off the gale winds her whistling might bring. As he looped the knotted rope onto a spoke of the helm, Lily ceased the torment. Crossjack didn't deserve ill treatment, only the captain did.

The next morning, Lily stood in the doorway of the master cabin. They had just docked in Wexford, Ireland, and Hugh, as she was beginning to think of the captain, had promised to take her ashore to the May Fair. Circumstances dictated that she refuse. Since he'd kissed her two nights before, Lily had tried to keep her distance. It wasn't that she feared his seduction. She was frightened by her own weakness. He had roused a need in her that neither time nor distance had filled.

Like a specter, the memory of the kiss stood between them. They conversed civilly, but Lily felt they were only marking time, and the uncertainty of what lay ahead for them troubled her.

He could rebuff her until the king scorned his many mistresses, but she would continue to describe his annual visits to Arran.

"You have a fanciful imagination, Lily," he had said earlier in the day.

Perhaps, but she also had irrefutable proof.

Now, shoring up her courage, she stepped into the cabin they shared. Her hammock still hung in place, a constant reminder that she must keep herself apart from him. He adjusted his cockaded hat, setting it at a jaunty angle. The cockscomb.

She cleared her throat. "The year I celebrated my sixteenth birthday, you came to Brodick Bay wearing a buff coat tied at the waist with a black sash."

As had become his habit in these circumstances, he sighed and gave her a courteous and infuriating smile. "You must have either the eyes of an eagle or you watched through a powerful spyglass to see so much detail as the sash 'round my waist."

She had expected his placating tone, and took no offense. Strolling across the room, she delved into her keepsakes. "Not necessarily. 'Twas windy that morn. Your sash caught on the thorns of the rose. When you could not untangle it, you tossed it into the bay with the flowers. I fished it out and laundered it. Here 'tis."

His facade of cordiality faded, and for the second time since boarding his ship, Lily sensed a chink in his armor of denial. He swallowed, and his steely gaze moved to the black silk. Then he took it from her.

"Tell me, Hugh. Who sends you to Arran? Who is buried in the grave?"

In reply, he gave her a lopsided grin and, holding an end of the sash in each hand, he flipped it over her head. With gentle pressure, he pulled her toward him. Like a child eager for the fair they were about to attend, she went willingly. His eyes burned with an intensity that warmed and chilled her at once. He must have sensed her hesitation, for he bestowed a brotherly kiss on her forehead. "An admirable try, Lily, but unconvincing. Half the gentlemen I know wear sashes like this."

Angry and unwilling to concede, she glared at him. "You're no gentleman."

His heated gaze roamed her face and settled on her mouth. "Much more of that, Lily, and I'll prove you right."

For all his nonchalance, he'd given her a warning. Ignore it, her woman's heart demanded. Step away from him, her dignity said. Obeying the latter, she yanked the scarf from his hands and returned it to her bag.

Under her breath, she murmured every curse she knew.

"Come," he said, as if the portentious exchange had not occurred. "Be of good cheer and I'll buy you a ribbon at the fair."

That did it. "You're placating me, and I like it not," she ground out.

"You're exciting me, and I like it well."

Her insides turned to porridge, and she vacillated between slapping his handsome face and rushing into his arms. Eleven years of waiting and wanting dragged at her scruples. She knew the reasons behind her weakness; she felt as if she'd known him all her life. He knew her not at all, and if she succumbed to his winning ways, she'd be no better than a woman of the streets.

Pride won out. Mustering good humor, she pulled on her gloves. "I'll try again, Captain."

He chuckled. "Then so will I."

If desire were a sound, it was his voice. Mortified at the thought, she stiffened her spine and preceded him off the ship.

Five minutes into the excursion, the starch went out of her, for the May Fair was all and more than Master Bonaventure had said it would be. Parti-colored stalls and booths marked with fluttering pennons lined the streets of Wexford. Merchants sold everything from Connemara marble to Brian Boru harps.

Hawkers enticed them to "dunk the duchess," a sport wherein a fashionably dressed woman sat on a plank suspended over a barrel of water. Spanker pitched a penny to the boothman, then pulled a handle, dropping the pretend duchess into the drink.

Laughing lads on stilts navigated the busy thoroughfares. Courting couples strolled hand in hand. At every turn she was reminded that spring was in the air.

On the edge of the fairgrounds, the fletcher harkened them to test their skill at archery. After considerable taunting from the crew, the captain paid tuppence and selected a bow. The target, a board fifty paces away, featured a likeness of the Lord Protector himself. Minutes later, Hugh shot four of five arrows between the eyes of Oliver Cromwell's image.

"Take your prize, my lord," said the fletcher, indicating a selection of scarves, ribbons, and garlands. "Pick a trinket for your lady fair."

With a hand on Lily's elbow, the captain held her there while he made a great show of indecision. From a batch of cloths, he pull out a black scarf and held it before her. "On second thought, not this one. The color is as common as a crow, and much too ordinary for you, Lily."

The implication was clear. He was belittling the evidence she'd shown him earlier in the day, because he had no intention of admitting the truth. She'd been a fool to cherish that scarf and attach romantic dreams to the wearer.

Sadness enveloped her. Feeling foolish, she turned away and moved into the throng of fair-goers.

Bonaventure appeared beside her. "You are troubled."

"He's a troll," she murmured, trying desperately not to cry.

"*Oui.* Perhaps he has good cause, no?"

Perhaps he did. In any event, she refused to let Hugh's stubbornness spoil her fun. Bother it. Bother him. She was in Ireland, a land she had never dreamed of seeing. Nothing would tarnish her day at the May Fair, and if she lived to be one hundred years old, she would never forget how much the captain and his crew had enriched her life.

Moments later the captain joined them, a garland of daisies in his hand, an apology in his eyes. "For you, my lady." He put the ring of flowers on her head.

Lily put dreary thoughts behind her and reveled in the day's pleasure. By the time they returned to the ship, exhausted and full to their gullets, she hadn't the will to challenge Hugh. Tomorrow would come soon enough.

Standing with her back to the prow, Lily watched Master Bonaventure tack his way north along the Irish coast. The ship's carpenter played a ballad on his new harp. The reclusive cook leaned against the bulwark and hacked off the tops of fresh carrots and leeks. The sharp smell of the vegetables blended with the salty air.

Barefoot and wearing canvas breeches, the captain walked the yards, inspecting the rigging.

Friendliness and compatibility were the order of the day. So happy was Lily, she wondered if she weren't back in her bed at Hamilton Castle, dreaming this voyage and imagining these people. Please, she prayed, don't let me awaken.

With a hand at her brow, she shaded the sun from her eyes and watched the captain descend the mainmast. Once on deck, he stopped near the cook and filched a carrot. Then he approached her, his strides long, his smile easy.

She felt as blessed as a newly christened babe. "To where do we sail?" she asked.

Mischief sparkled in his eyes. He crunched the carrot. "What's this? 'Tis almost noon and you've yet to bedevil me with one of your fables."

Being honest about his visits had yielded little success, so Lily spun a tale. "Very well. In the spring of seventy-five, you sported an elegant wig."

He waved the stub of the carrot for emphasis. "I do not wear wigs."

Undaunted, she flowered the tale. "'Twasn't just any wig, mind you, but a masterpiece of invention—curled at the sides and flowing down your back. Very stylish, Captain."

"I hate wigs!"

"Oh, but you flatter them so."

Cool anger smoothed out his features. "I tell you, Lily Hamilton, I'd sooner rake dung than wear a wig."

She batted her eyes. "You looked so fashionably handsome, I nearly swooned on the beach and ruined my heavy coat and gloves."

"Impossible. 'Twas unseasonably warm in seventy-five and I wore——" He stopped, realizing that she had baited him. Giving her an angry stare that promised retribution, he spat, "We sail to Bangor."

Inordinately pleased with herself, Lily clasped her hands. "Splendid. My uncle Seamus plies the Bangor port."

The music stopped. The captain towered over her. "Did I say Bangor? I meant Dublin of course." He glowered. "Why are you smiling?"

"Because my cousin Randolph will most likely be there."

Eyes narrowed, fists planted on his hips, he said, "Swear."

She summoned her sweetest tone. "On my honor as a . . . lover of dusted wigs and daisy garlands."

Frowning, he cast her a sideways glance. "Your cousin Randolph, you say?"

"Aye, a ham-fisted fellow with a surly crew. You'd not willingly tangle with that lot."

"Crossjack," Hugh yelled to the mate, who stood near the windlass. "Know you of a Hamilton sailor by the name of Randolph?"

The mate spat over the side in disgust. "Spawn o' Satan, so I've heard, Cap'n. They say he sleeps with a cat-o'-nines and flogs 'is crew fer pleasure."

"Then 'tis best we guard our backs well and conduct our business with haste."

They docked in Dublin just before sunset. More troubled than he was willing to let on, Hugh took Lily aside. "I haven't forgotten what you said about your cousin Randolph. You'll stay below while we are in port. We won't be long at our business."

Like a contented cat, she lounged on her favorite spot, the windowseat. "Of course."

But after the cargo of fine laces and bolts of linen cloth had been loaded, Hugh found his cabin empty and the window open. She'd escaped. Her bag of meager belongings was gone, as was the wilted garland he'd given her at the May Fair. She'd left him.

Spanker came rushing in. Huffing, he said, "I just come from the Harp 'n' Hound Tavern, Cap'n. Hamiltons are asking after the *Golden Thistle* and swearin' we kidnapped their kinswoman."

"Damn!" A passing vessel must have taken notice of them before the carpenter had altered the name of Hugh's ship.

"That ain't all. The best mate o' the *Sea Lion* said they'd got Mistress Hamilton back."

"What?" He should have been glad to see the last of her, rather than sad for his loss. She was trouble of the kind he'd forsaken Scotland to avoid. "Fare thee well to her," he grumbled.

"It ain't like that, sir." Now anxious, Spanker ducked beneath the doorway and stalked him. "I strolled past their ship an' I heard a woman screamin'. 'Twas awful, Cap'n. Sounded like they was fair killin' her."

Hugh's blood ran cold, then boiled. He'd scouted the *Sea Lion* earlier in the day and found Randolph Hamilton's crew sleeping on decks and his vessel in poor repair. The town's gossips disdained the slothful ship and dreaded her making port.

Screaming. Hugh ground his teeth.

"What'll you do?" Spanker asked.

"Wake the crew. Tell Master Bonaventure to ready the ship."

The big gunner started, banging his head on a ceiling beam. "Ain't you goin' after her?"

Ignoring him, Hugh unlocked his wardrobe and pulled out a black shirt and tunic and a razor-sharp dirk.

"You canna go alone, Cap'n."

"I will."

Spanker yanked off his cap and threw it on the floor. "Then you'll have to be givin' us all our pay tickets."

Hugh exchanged his dress clothing for the dark garments. "Pay tickets?" He laughed without humor and slipped the blade into the lining of his boot. "If I don't come back, Spanker, the damned bloody ship is yours."

"I'm going with you, and there it is."

Knowing the man wouldn't budge, Hugh rethought his plan. "All right. Load three wheel-locks and find Crossjack. I'll meet you on the gangplank."

"Aye, aye, sir. I've a bit o' conversin' to do with that scurvy Hamilton. A pistol whippin' should perk up his ears."

Ten minutes later they stood on the quay near the *Sea Lion*. A single lantern on the foredeck illuminated a group of crewmen who'd abandoned their posts to play at dice. The aft deck was empty, the hatch open. With Hugh in the lead, they crept across the darkened deck and tiptoed down the companionway.

An ominous silence pulsed in the close air. The foul odor of stale urine and sour sweat assaulted his nose. The urge to kill thrummed through him. Taking shallow breaths, he scanned the darkened companionway. Off the narrow hall were four louvered doors. The first two stood open, revealing the unkempt mess and the cluttered navigator's quarters. Both were empty of men, which Hugh expected, for according to Spanker most of the crew were downing pints at a dockside tavern.

Of the two remaining doors, the farthest would lead to

the captain's cabin. Bars of light seeped through the slats and onto the floor, which was littered with wilted daisy petals. The trail of flowers stopped before the closer door.

Hot anger pulsing through him, Hugh knotted his fists to keep from smashing down the door. Moving cautiously, he grasped the knob and was surprised to feel it turn in his damp palm. He eased it open. A smelly candle cast a faint yellow glow throughout the small chamber.

His heart stopped when he saw her. She lay on her side on the narrow bunk, her hair in tangled disarray. Her dress was torn at the shoulder, the exposed skin abraded.

Hugh rushed to the bunk and crouched beside her. "Lily?" he whispered.

She didn't, couldn't hear him.

He pushed her hair out of the way. A bruise the size of a man's knuckles darkened her jaw and cheek. Her bottom lip was split, and dried blood stained her chin.

Spanker came up behind him. "Blessed Jesus!" he hissed.

"Who's there?" shouted someone from the master cabin.

Crossjack peered over Hugh's shoulder. "Me an' Spanker'll pay your respects to her cousin," he said. "He won't be siring another Hamilton anytime soon."

"Or layin' a hand to a woman," Spanker put in. "Not when we're done with him."

The two men moved quietly from the room.

"Lily?" When she did not stir, Hugh touched her neck, but his hand was shaking so badly he couldn't find her pulse.

Over the fear ringing in his ears, he heard thuds and grunts from the captain's cabin. Desperate to get her to safety, he scooped her into his arms. Limp and light as goosedown, she made no sound. Hugh whispered a prayer for her safety and headed for the door.

Crossjack was waiting. "Poor lassie," he crooned, patting her head.

"You lead the way," Hugh told him. "Spanker, stay behind me. Let's away, lads."

"I hate men."

She could have cursed Hugh to hell in a haywagon and he wouldn't have cared. He still felt euphoric with relief. Somehow this lovely daughter of his enemy had worked her way into his heart. She was angry now, a very good sign.

"Even me?" he said.

"Oh, nay." Her brown eyes glowed with fondness. "How did you find me?"

Wanting to hold her and never let go, yet knowing it was wrong, he strove for lightness. "Well, lassie, 'twas a puzzle to be sure."

"But—" She smiled, then winced. "You're teasing me."

"Aye. How do you feel?"

Hesitantly she touched her cheek. "Awful. How do I look?"

Far too at home in my bed, he wanted to say. "Randolph paid a price. Spanker and Crossjack saw to that."

"When I first came aboard your ship, I thought them

ruffians. I was wrong, and I should have listened to you."
Her voice broke and tears pooled in her eyes. "I never
thought Randolph would hurt me. We played peevers and
tag as children. We learned to ride the same horse."

Hugh's heart went out to her. She had been sheltered
on that island, much the same as the women of Ardrossan
were shielded from the cruelty of their MacDonnel men.
Hugh was always surprised at the changes in his own father.
The chieftain of the MacDonnels could wage war for weeks,
spilling Hamilton blood and pirating their property, but
when he returned home he became the laughing, loving
husband and kindly sire.

"Randolph's a bully now, and suffering a thousand
times more than you," Hugh promised.

"Truly?"

"Sailor's honor."

"You avoided the question of how I look. Is it bad?"

His first impulse was to shrug, but from the moment
she stepped into his life, Lily Hamilton had shown a
strength of will that demanded honesty. In this matter he
could tell her the truth. "Your lovely cheek is bruised, and
your luscious bottom lip has a wee cut on it."

"You make it sound inconsequential."

Her bruises would heal but what of the injury to her
heart and her soul? What of her disillusionment? Protecting
her became vital to Hugh, as if his own life hung in the
balance. "You'll mend, Lily."

"What are you thinking?"

What could he say to her that would soothe and satisfy

at once? He couldn't blame her for running to her family; propriety dictated that she flee her abductor. A truth seemed his best choice. "I was thinking that you do not deserve such poor relations."

Her sadness seemed tinged with irony. "I think I know how the MacDonnels feel."

Guilt swamped Hugh, and his conscience urged him to bare his soul. Years of estrangement from the evil that gripped both his clan and hers stopped him. "You should have a loving family, Lily."

"Tell me about yours."

Her earnest plea went straight to his heart. Taking her hand, he threaded their fingers. Her knuckles were scratched, her once neatly pared nails ragged. Stifling a surge of renewed anger, he cleared his throat. "I have only a sister."

She looked not at him, but at their twined hands. "Were you friends as children?"

"Fiona is much older—ten years."

"Do you share the same mother?"

"The same father."

"What is she like, your Fiona?"

Fond memories warmed him, for Fiona had been the one calming force in his turbulent youth. Thoughts of her flourishing garden came to mind, but loyalty stopped Hugh from broaching the topic closest to his sister's heart. "She has hair like yours, except 'tis straight as a stick, so she says. From the time I could walk, I remember the teasing she suffered."

"Let me guess." With her free hand, Lily flipped a

strand of her glorious red hair. "The churchwomen gave her pieces of coal to keep the bad spirits away. The midwife sent her decoctions of lemon grass to fade the unlucky color."

Hugh had to laugh. "Aye. To this day she loathes the smell of lemons. As for the coal, she used to say she could warm the castle with the fuel of the superstitious."

"Where is the castle?"

It was natural that she should ask and prudent that he did not answer. "She doesn't live there. She lives in my mother's dower estate." He hesitated, then added, "'Tis in Wigtown in Dumfries."

Genuinely pleased, she squeezed his hand. "You're a Douglas, then?"

He couldn't lie, not tonight. "I'm a man who thinks you should rest."

Disappointment framed her features, and her eyes went out of focus. "Are we under sail?"

With the grace of a skilled diplomat, she had changed the subject. He should be grateful for the conversational reprieve. Instead, he felt an acute loss. "Full sail. We're Liverpool bound, to fill the hold with hats and stays and furbelows for the fashion-starved ladies in the Virginia Colony."

Looking up at him, she tried to smile. "Thank you for risking your life to save me."

A MacDonnel had saved a Hamilton. Only one person would believe the story. Fiona would also praise him for his gallantry. What his father would do didn't bear consideration. An understatement seemed appropriate. "'Twas nothing."

Modesty shined in her eyes. "'Twas gallantry at its best."

"Merely necessity. I've grown fond of your fables."

"Not as much as I anticipate your denials."

The friendly banter seemed natural to Hugh, and he wondered why other women did not cultivate the knack. Probably because the talent was natural with Lily. As was often the case, he didn't think of her as a Hamilton. Whether from his own estrangement from the feud or from her strength of character, he did not know. But he suspected the latter. She didn't deserve to pay a price for the sins of her clan.

"Hugh?"

He harkened back to the subject. "You feel grateful."

"If this is gratitude, then I'm a MacDonnel."

Would that you were, he lamented. Would that you were.

"What's wrong?" she asked. "You look sad. Or have I been too bold?"

Minute by minute he was falling more deeply in love with Lily Hamilton. The situation both troubled and thrilled him. "I just remembered something." He went to the desk and returned with a bag of coins. "Spanker took this money from your cousin."

Reasonably, she said, "I couldn't keep it. 'Twouldn't be right."

"A small price for your suffering, and sooner than not, dear Randolph would spend it on wine and women."

Her chin puckered with disgust. "He has a wife and two bairns to support."

"Then give the money to them." The words were out before Hugh could stop them.

"Are you taking me home?"

At the thought of letting her go, he rebelled. It took every ounce of strength to say, "If that is your wish."

She looked at him for so long he grew worried that she could see past his charade and into his MacDonnel soul. At length, she smiled a smile that eased his worried heart. "What I wish is to have three new gowns, a hat with fancy feathers, and a pair of slippers."

"Will tomorrow be soon enough?"

"Aye." Turning on her side, she drew his hand beneath her unmarred cheek and nestled into the pillow.

Hot desire, tempered by the need to comfort, spiraled through him. Observing the conflicting emotions made him chuckle. "You're wicked, Lily Hamilton. And a lot of trouble."

Her contented hum sounded more like a purr. "You're just miffed because you have to sleep in the hammock."

"Says who? You might need me in the night."

Shyly, she whispered, "I've never had a friend outside my clan, and I find that I am coming to need you."

"I should be crestfallen did you not. Oh, angel, you gave me a fright."

Lily decided he had a voice and a manner as smooth as

the molasses he favored. Gallant was too common a word to describe him. "And you've given me the time of my life."

"Rest now."

Rest? No. She couldn't help thinking of Randolph— his bitterness and disregard for her feelings. She had sought refuge with her kinsman. He'd called her a whore and accused her of taking a MacDonnel for a lover. Details of the evening rose like nightmares in her mind.

"You even sailed on their bloody ship," her cousin had said.

"Nay, Randolph. 'Twas the *Westward Angel*, a ship from the colonies."

He'd backhanded her then, knocking her to the deck. As she tried to flee, he caught her by the hair, dragged her below deck, and shoved her into a cabin. Between curses and accusations, he damned her for shaming him and all the Hamiltons. Sadly, she realized that he cared more for the family's reputation than for her feelings.

"You took a liking to that pretty pinasse, did you?" he said, his familiar face a mask of evil. "'Tis well you should, for it once belonged to you."

She had tried to reason with him, but blind rage had him in its grip. "How could you do this to us, lass? Have you no shame?"

"You're twisting the facts and making my misfortune your own."

In reply, he busted her lip and demanded to know the whereabouts of a MacDonnel ship named the *Golden Thistle*.

Baffled, Lily had said she did not know and reiterated that she had sailed on the *Westward Angel*.

"Liar!"

Her only prevarication had been the statement that her abductors sailed away after putting her ashore. Thank God they had not, for she shuddered to think of the further abuse she would have suffered at the hands of her kinsmen.

They had seen the last of Lily Hamilton. Even if she had to scrub floors to make her own way, she'd never return to Arran. Then she thought of the dying rosebush on the old grave. Forsaking her family would be easier than abandoning the lonely soul buried on her island home.

Through the haze of her dilemma she felt the captain pull his hand from hers. A moment later the cabin door opened and closed. Compounded by her unfulfilled promise, the loss of his comfort left her feeling acutely alone. She slipped into a troubled sleep.

In Liverpool, half the crew was granted shore leave. Upon their return four days later, the other men took an equal furlough. Crates and barrels of shoes and stays, books and china, had been secured below. The shallow-drafted pinasse rode low in the water. Enough room remained in the hold for a pair of hunters Hugh intended to purchase for his own stables.

By the seventh day in port, Lily's bruises had faded. The cook had prepared her favorite meals, and the crewmen went out of their way to cheer her. Between meetings with merchants and arguments with the harbormaster, the captain tended her wounds. Each time she asked him about the grave on Arran, he denied any knowledge of it. When she pleaded to know the name of the person who sent the roses, he stormed off, grumbling, "'Tis not my place to say."

Lily believed him.

On his arm, she visited the dressmaker and the cobbler.

They returned to find the watch relieved and ship manned by a sparse crew. The cook served the evening meal in the shadow of the mainmast. Afterward, Lily and the captain strolled the deck, taking in the sounds of Liverpool harbor and gazing at the full moon.

"Tell me about your title."

"'Tis an empty one, bestowed to keep me in Scotland."

"But you prefer the colonies."

"Aye."

"The women must be bonny there."

"Jealous?"

"Of their beauty? Nay. 'Tis their freedom I covet."

He wasn't surprised; she'd been a prisoner of Arran all her life.

"Tell me about the children in the Virginia Colony. Are the lads fostered?"

"Not usually. Most of the families are isolated by the size of their farms. Imagine if you can, a land so vast it has yet to be charted from shore to shore. A dozen Englands would fill the area we have explored."

"Surely the children are schooled in some fashion."

Her interest in the families didn't surprise him; as a

woman she would be concerned with hearth and home. "The wealthier families import English or Scottish tutors. The others use servants indentured for seven years."

"Seems a high price to pay for passage." It would be simpler for her to find employment here.

Hugh agreed that seven years was too long. Over the years, he'd seen hordes of eager faces pouring into the colonies. "'Tis the adventure they seek. Like you, they yearn for the freedom."

She nodded and turned her attention to the dock.

Hugh wanted to ask her again to come with him, but he couldn't, not until he told her the truth. If he bided his time and nurtured her love, perhaps she'd accept him for the man he was rather than the name he carried.

When he ordered the crew below, she asked. "Why did you do that?"

He guided her to the table but did not sit. "Since the cook put that trifle before us, I've had an unbearable urge to kiss you."

They hadn't touched the dessert. "Only since the trifle?"

"Step into my arms, minx. Your answer awaits."

Willingly she did, and as his hands caressed her shoulders and skimmed down her arms, she thought his embrace the sweetest dessert imaginable.

"Close your eyes, love."

Love. She liked the sound of that. Her eyes drifted shut.

"Open your mouth."

Thinking of the intimate kiss she'd once declined and regretted, Lily did as he asked.

A spoonful of the trifle touched her tongue. A smile of pure pleasure blossomed on her face. "Hum. I want more."

"Greedy baggage."

"More."

He stepped behind her and slipped his arms around her waist. Unable to resist, she leaned against him. When he nibbled her ear, her breath caught.

"Do you like that?" he breathed.

She shivered, but innocently said, "Like what? Are you doing something?"

He chuckled. "Turn around."

Lily couldn't say why she hesitated.

He put his cheek next to hers. Freshly shaven, his skin was smooth and warm, and she wondered if the rest of his body would feel the same.

"You're safe with me, Lily."

Considering the direction of her thoughts, it seemed logical to say, "Aye, as safe as a fat mouse in a den of hungry snakes."

His throaty laughter vibrated through her, and she turned in his arms, the velvet of her new dress rustling with the movement.

"Did I tell you that you look bonny tonight?"

"Yes. Before the beef and after the fish. Thank you again."

Smiling he touched the coil of braids at the crown of her head. "May I?"

Wary of seeming naive, she said, "I'll help."

"Absolutely not. I claim this pleasure."

Flattered to the tips of her new stockings, she watched him pull the pins from her hair. Silvery moonlight lined his elegant features, and she wondered for the hundredth time if he truly were a Douglas. His father must be powerful to buy him an earldom. But the ranking Douglas chieftain was only a viscount.

When Hugh buried his face in her hair, she forgot lineages and titles and gave herself up to his skilled seduction.

He groaned, then his mouth sought hers in a kiss unlike any he'd given her before. He coaxed her with tongue and lips, retreating now and then to let her take the lead. Her confidence grew and her own need soared until Lily couldn't hold back a moan of surrender.

"Are you sure, Lily?"

His gallantry was showing, and she loved him for it. "Aye," she whispered.

He swooped her into his arms and carried her below. Once in his cabin, he stood her by the bed. The moment her feet touched the floor, he laid into the kiss again. A whirlwind of pleasure churned inside her as his tongue thrust into her mouth, then withdrew. She gave chase, and he responded with a manly growl of satisfaction.

Warm, strong fingers traced the line of her shoulder and circled the column of her neck, then his lips followed the path. She felt his fingers work the laces on her dress, and she followed his example, but when her gown fell open and his hands touched her breasts, Lily went weak in the knees. She swayed into him, and he cupped her bottom, pulling her close, then shifting a little to let her feel how much he wanted her.

"Our bodies are very different," she confessed.

"Blessedly so." He continued to undulate against her.

She busied her own hands, mapping the muscles of his shoulders, arms, and chest. All adeptness, he loosened her petticoat and stays, then lifted her, leaving the garments to pool on the floor. Except for her stockings and garters, she stood naked before him, and the sight of her made him smile. "Sweetheart, you are bonny everywhere."

She flushed. "But you're still dressed."

"Not for much longer."

He ripped off his jacket and shirt, then yanked off his boots. His black velvet knee breeches hugged him like a second skin, and she couldn't help but stare at the bulge of his manhood.

Uncertainty made her suddenly shy. He must have sensed it, for, as he laid her on the bed, he looked deeply into her eyes. "Worry not, Lily. We were made to join."

From that moment on, she gave herself up to his loving, and when the sharp pain of his entry made her cry out, he paused, soothing and comforting with a gentle touch and whispers of encouragement. All patience, he rekindled her desire until she begged him to ease the beautiful torment. With one final thrust, he took her to a place of pleasure where she languished, feeling sated and thoroughly complete.

When their breathing slowed, he rolled to his side and pulled her against his chest. "How do you feel?"

Giddy to her soul, she laughed. "Like I kissed the pearly gates. And you?"

"Like I passed through them on the wings of angels." He hugged her. "You are wonderful, Lily."

The compliment warmed, yet she felt a chill of uncertainty. What would become of them now? Would he do the honorable thing and offer her his name? And what would that name be? She had an uneasy feeling that he lied, for not once had he mentioned the Douglas clan. She had asked the crew, but as she expected, they were loyal to their captain.

"What's wrong, love? You seem distant."

She hadn't the nerve to voice her doubts. In their short time together she had experienced more of life than she ever expected to see, and she couldn't bear for it to end.

Gathering courage, she looked up at him. "On the day we met, you asked me to go adventuring with you. Does the offer still stand?"

His eyes glowed with excitement. "You're sure?"

"I've never been more sure of anything, but you must make me a promise. When our voyage comes to an end, will you help me find a position as governess?"

Hugh felt as if he'd been gut-punched with a mainmast. He'd risked his life, and for what? For a woman who wanted only a dalliance with him and then a damned reference. Lord, he'd been wrong about Lily Hamilton. Earlier she'd asked him about how the children in the colonies were educated. Now he knew why.

He closed his eyes, willing sleep to take him and ease his bruised pride.

"Will you?"

"But of course."

Then she snuggled closer, running her fingers through the hair on his chest and sliding her leg over his. His body reacted with the zeal of a man too long at sea. Push her away, his pride said. Enjoy her while you can, his passion demanded.

Damning himself the weakest of all men, Hugh pulled her astride him and began suckling her breasts. When her glorious hair curtained around him, he was lost to all thoughts save those of her and the pleasure they shared.

He awakened hours later to find her sitting on his sea chest, her shoulders draped in a MacDonnel tartan.

"You despicable pirate."

Shaking off sleep, he searched for a reasonable reply. "Lily, I can explain."

"Explain what? How you tricked me into lov—" She gasped. "Into believing you."

The hurt in her eyes mirrored a soul of deep pain, and Hugh felt his insides twist with grief for her, for them both. "I'm sorry."

"You miserable snake."

She'd misunderstood his apology. "I meant that I'm—"

"A dung-eating MacDonnel."

That did it. "I see you couldn't wait to pick my pockets for the key to that wardrobe."

Her brown eyes turned dark with scorn, and her knuckles were white from clutching the tartan. "I grew cold because you took all of the blankets. I couldn't find my new sleeping gown, so I thought to borrow something of yours."

"An interesting selection, Lily. Admit that you were snooping in my belongings."

"Belongings! Don't you try to make the plaid of my enemy sound like an everyday cloak. A Douglas you said."

"You said it, not I."

"How could you deceive me so?"

"You wanted me, Lily."

Her throat worked and her eyes snapped fire. "You're a monster to bring that up."

"Bring what up? The fact that you love me?"

"Ha!" With her free hand, she swept her hair back and over her shoulders. " 'Twas lust and no more."

Ironically, he thought the colorful MacDonnel tartan a perfect foil for her country-fresh beauty. " 'Twas love, Lily."

"I'd sooner mate with a swineherd."

Quick as a cat, he grabbed her wrists and pinned her beneath him. "You *gifted* me with your innocence . . . after I gallantly gave you the opportunity to keep it. 'Are you sure?' I asked. 'Aye,' you purred."

She fought like a wildcat, but her strength was no match for his. Panting, she spat, " 'Twas *after* you kissed me senseless." Twisting and straining, she tried to free herself. "And you probably drugged my wine."

"You were as sober as a saint when you yielded your maidenhead."

"You took it."

"You enjoyed our loving."

"I loathed every moment of your pawing."

The jibe hit home, but he ignored his smarting pride. "Now you're sorry."

She quivered with rage. "You're a bloody MacDonnel."

"Not," he ground out, "a practicing one."

"Liar. You practiced your roguish ways on me, and fool that I am, I believed you sincere—gallant even." She laughed. "I hate you, Hugh MacDonnel."

"Nay, Lily, you don't. You're just angry because I didn't tell you."

Through her teeth, she hissed, "How astute of you. Get off me."

"Not yet."

Looking away, she closed her eyes. Hugh was desperate to make her see the truth and understand. "Did I ask you to board this ship?"

"I wanted to save the rose."

He pressed on. "Did I drag you to the May Fair in Wexford?"

"Nay."

"Did I turn a deaf ear when I heard that your cousin had beaten you?"

"Don't." Her voice was thick with misery, her eyes squeezed tight against the agony of betrayal.

Plagued by regrets, he searched for a way to get through to her. "Don't what, Lily? Don't fall prey to clan loyalties? Don't take joy in your company simply because my family and your family make war on each other? God, Lily, 'tis why I left Scotland." The admission drained him.

Her breathing slowed. "You don't know what the MacDonnels have done."

"Probably not, but remember what you said after Randolph abused you?"

He felt her relax, but only a little. "What?"

"You said you knew how the MacDonnels felt. We're people, too, Lily, and not all of us thrive on enmity." He thought of dear Fiona. "Some have suffered greatly at your father's hand."

She turned toward him, and his heart ached at the pain she could not disguise. "Is that why you seduced me—out of revenge?"

The accusation in her words kindled his ire anew. "You did a damn fine job of seduction yourself, Lily Hamilton."

"Don't you dare blame me for your rakish ways."

"Nay? Then let me refresh your memory. Before I made love to you the third time, you said your breasts ached for the touch of my tongue. You begged me to suckle you. You said your stomach floated like a cork every time I came into you. You said I made you feel like—"

"Enough!" She looked away. "I was besotted."

He saw the small love bruise he'd left on her neck. Nibbling her skin had been his first mistake. Pray God he'd made his last. Drawn again to her sweetness and eager to end the strain between them, he leaned close and touched his lips to the mark.

She bucked beneath him. "No."

Bracing himself above her, he looked into her eyes, then lower. Her nipples were stiff with desire, her skin flushed with wanting. Her teeth closed over the bottom lip and her nostrils flared.

"Don't you see what we're doing to each other, Lily? Forgive me for not telling you, but I swear in the beginning I did it to protect my crew. Later, I couldn't bear to lose you."

"Easy words to speak now."

She had a right to doubt him. He was bound to change her mind. "Look at me."

Slowly she turned toward him and the yearning he saw in her eyes rocketed to his loins. Only a MacDonnel tartan and Hamilton pride separated them. Desperate to possess her, he moved the cloth aside and settled between her legs.

"What are you—Oh!"

He found her moist and ready, and his head spun with desire.

"Our destiny is here, sweetheart. Since that morning eleven years ago when you saw me drop that torch into Brodick Bay."

She grew attentive. "You admit you came there every year?"

"Aye. Now admit you love me."

Minx that she was, she took her time. "I don't forgive you."

It was the best he would get from her now, but given time Hugh would hear her say the words. At the moment, though, his body craved a different commitment from her. "Open for me, Lily. I love you. 'Twas meant to be."

"What did you say?"

"I love you."

On a groan, she yielded, and he made them one.

"Sweet Saint Margaret," she whispered.

"Amen," he rasped.

When Hugh awakened, he was alone in bed. Fearing Lily had fled, he yanked off the covers and started to rise, but stopped, for he felt her presence and relaxed. Sitting on the windowseat, she wore a new gown of yellow linen. Her hair trailed over her shoulder and pooled in her lap. Had he selected a woman to grace his cabin and warm his life, he could not have chosen better than Lily Hamilton.

She looked up, and her winsome smile pleased him anew.

Oddly, he was reminded of his sister. "Good morning," he said.

As he expected, a maidenly blush colored her cheeks. "Good morning to you."

He patted the mattress. "Come. Sit with me."

Rising gracefully, she came to him with strength of purpose and excitement and, to his great relief, the promise of forgiveness. She sat beside him, and he pulled her into his arms. As his lips settled on her, it was as if he were seeing inside her. He instinctively knew that he'd only scratched the surface of her character. Next year, five years, ten, twenty years from now, she'd grow and polish and shine like a treasured keepsake.

When he drew back, she studied him.

He basked in her attention. "You've much to recommend you, Lily Hamilton."

Shyly, she said, "You know little about me."

"Precisely my point."

She opened her mouth, then closed it. After a moment's consideration, a smile blossomed on her face. "Thank you."

He thought his heart would burst with love. Before he could voice his feelings, she cleared her throat. "Now that . . . that we've . . . we've come to . . . to know each other better . . ."

"I love you. Will you marry me?"

She looked much too serious, her hands folded in her lap, her expression pensive. "Yes, if you will tell me two things."

A cold fist of dread knotted in his belly, for he knew what she would ask, and he hadn't the right to answer.

"Is this—was this ship once mine?"

It was the last thing he expected and the easiest to address. "Aye, 'twas the *Valiant Lily*." He couldn't help adding, "A fitting name. I'll have the carpenter change it back."

She pointed to the wardrobe. "I carved my initials there—in the bulkhead."

She'd imprinted herself on his soul, too, but he'd wait to tell her that. Anxious to see her handiwork, he pulled on his breeches and crossed the room. Putting his shoulder to the task, he swung the large piece of furniture away from the wall. There, in the bulkhead were the initials *LMH*.

He waved her over, and when she stood beside him, he draped an arm over her shoulder. "The 'M' is for . . . ?"

"Margaret, although I've never done it justice, particularly of late."

"You're too exciting for so common a name." Margaret was the patron saint of Scotland and often bestowed at christening. His sister Fiona and many of his cousins carried the name.

Lily knelt and touched the carving.

"How old were you?" he asked.

"Eight." Giving the symbol a final pat, she stood and faced him solemnly. "When I was ten years old, your family took this ship. The day I learned of it, I was so devastated, I ran away from home. That's when I found the grave." She placed her hands on his and, with her eyes, beseeched him to understand. "Who is buried there, and what is the significance of the rose?"

He pictured her young and heartbroken and bravely seeking solace. She'd found it in a grave he knew nothing about and a rosebush he knew very well. "On my soul, Lily, I do not know. I've never stepped foot on Arran. But I'll take you to the person who has."

She gave him a smile that filled him with love. "When?"

"As soon as I dress and speak with Bonaventure."

Moving around him, she opened the wardrobe. "Here." She handed him a shirt.

Laughing at her eagerness, he kissed her cheek, then dressed and went on deck.

Once the *Valiant Lily* was secured at Wigtown, in the Scottish Lowlands, Lily waited on the quay while Hugh hired a carriage. Excitement coursed through her. Soon her quest would come to an end. She would hear the name of the one who lay buried in the grave she had tended for so long. Then her future would begin. She would marry Hugh MacDonnel and travel to her new home in the Virginia Colony.

During the voyage from Liverpool, she had phrased a dozen letters to her father, telling him of her plans and describing the depths of her feelings both for Hugh Mac-Donnel and for her own clan. An apology for running away always crept into her thoughts, but Lily refused to ask forgiveness for following her heart. Her father would be angry, of that she was certain, for her cousin Randolph was surely home by now, spreading ghastly tales.

Bother them, and the devil take their anger. They probably wouldn't miss her anyway, so why write?

At the sound of approaching horses, she turned to see Hugh seated in an open carriage. Elegantly dressed in a blue velvet jacket and knee breeches, he handled the team with the same skill that he governed his crew. And her heart, she added, smiling at her own romantic musing.

Pulling back on the reins, he doffed his cockaded hat, then helped her up. She felt a burst of pride, for his towering height and dark good looks drew appreciative glances from the females they passed.

"If one more fellow tips his hat to you," Hugh grumbled. "I'll run him down."

Lily laughed. "Odd, for I was just thinking that the women cannot seem to stop batting their eyelashes at you and fiddling with their fans."

He leaned close. "Ah, 'tis well then."

They traveled through the busy town in companionable silence. When they had exited the city and turned west on the road that would lead to his property, Lily breathed in the fresh summer air.

"Happy?" he asked.

"Oh, yes. But why did you tell me you were a Douglas?"

"Because my mother was their kinswoman. 'Tis from her that I gained this estate." He pointed to a stand of birch. "See? There's Blackburn Keep, beyond the trees."

Peering through the forest, Lily spied a modest, vine-covered castle with only one tower and a large stable off to the right. The perfectly straight drive was lined with double rows of newly planted cedars. Their spicy scent blended with the rich aroma of heather and gorse. Butterflies and dandelion dust floated on the air. Spring lambs frolicked in a field, and a cow lowed in protest when the lambkins came too close.

"You cannot see the garden from here, but 'tis a glorious sight. Almost as lovely as you."

"You flatter me well, Hugh MacDonnel."

"I had an excellent tutor in"—he kissed her nose—"you."

Fighting back embarrassment, Lily again surveyed the beautiful landscape, lush with the promise of summer. "Stop that, Hugh. I have no intention of blushing like a maid when I meet Fiona." She still loved the sound of the name and anticipated meeting his sister.

"She'll love you as much as I do."

"But I'm a Hamilton."

At the entrance he slowed the team. "Fiona carries no grudges against the Hamiltons, even though she has more cause than most."

Lily grew nervous. "What do you mean?"

"Whoa." When the horses stopped, he secured the reins and stepped down. "Come, sweetheart." He extended a hand. "'Tis for Fiona to tell you."

A flustered housemaid let them in, fussing that his lordship should have sent word.

"Leave off, Polly," he chided the woman. "And tell me where I can find my sister."

"In the garden, my lord."

As Hugh led Lily through the castle, she was surprised to find no clan regalia or battle shields. Even the tapestries depicted peaceful scenes of animals in the forest and children at play. To her relief, she saw no captured unicorns or felled and bloodied boars. Even the portrait gallery was devoid of stern-faced MacDonnel chieftains. The prerequisite portrait of the king peeked from behind an overly prosperous potted plant. The family paintings were all of children. One in particular caught her eye, for the subjects seemed eerily familiar. A red-haired woman was seated on a bench in a garden of primroses, a strapping lad of about twelve sat at her feet.

"Wait," Lily said, wanting to get a better look. "That's you in this painting."

"And Fiona." He pulled her onward. "You should meet her in person first."

"I wanted to look at you."

He jiggled his brows. "You had quite a good look at all of me this morning."

"You were bathing."

"And you were helpful—deliciously so. 'Twas a thoroughly unforgettable experience."

"You're wicked."

"I'm besotted."

She was still laughing at his naughtiness when they stepped into the garden. Lily sucked in her breath, for the smell of roses was almost intoxicating. The ten-foot-high stone walls were blanketed in pink blossoms, as were the tunnel-like trellises that framed a sunny pond. Like the fountainhead of a trickling stream, this garden was the source of the sickly rose she'd tended for so many years.

"Fiona!" Hugh called out.

"Over here!" A gloved hand appeared above a half-trimmed boxwood hedge.

Heading for the shrub, Hugh lengthened his strides. Lily quickened her steps to keep up.

The woman wore a straw hat with a wide floppy brim that shielded her nose and eyes. Her mouth broadened into a smile and she rose, drawing off her gloves and fluffing out the skirt of her pale pink dress.

She looks at home, Lily thought, studying the woman who was slightly taller than herself. But why did she send roses to Arran?

Hugh's hand slipped from Lily's, and he scooped his sister into his arms and swung her around. Her pealing laughter sounded like that of a girl, not a woman who was ten years older than Hugh.

He whispered something to her. "Then put me down," she said. "So I can greet the lass."

He did as she asked, then took Lily's hand and pulled her forward. Her stomach tightened in anticipation, for although she did not know Fiona MacDonnel, she felt bound to her because of the grave and the roses.

Elbows in the air, head bowed, the overly slender Fiona MacDonnel worked at pulling the pins from her hat. "Had I known Hugh was bringing a special guest, I would have——" She stopped and stared at Lily.

Fiona's eyes were brown, and her nose quaintly turned up at the tip. Pretty did not suit her, for she possessed an uncommon elegance of form. Her upswept hair was straight and red, but shot through with strands of honey gold.

And the color was draining from her face.

"Who are you?" she asked in a fearful whisper.

Hugh moved immediately to her side. "What's wrong, Fiona? Are you ill? Have you labored out here all morning?"

She never took her eyes from Lily. With a wave of her hand, she said, "I'm fine, Hugh. Please, tell me your name."

Lily felt the old hurt rise. Hugh's sister wasn't as neutral in the feud as he thought, for she was obviously discomfited by Lily's presence. But wait, Lily didn't favor her clan. Hugh must have revealed her name during that whispered exchange.

Gathering her gumption, Lily curtsied. "I'm Lily Hamilton."

"Soon to be my wife," Hugh said.

Fiona seemed to shake off her confusion. "Forgive me, Lily. It's just that you remind me of someone. Who are your parents?"

Lily hesitated, fearful of the reaction. Put it behind you, her conscience said. Standing taller, she swallowed back her fears. "My father is Edward Hamilton, and my mother is dead. Her name was Margaret. She was a MacLean from the Isle of Mull."

Fiona's smile was bittersweet, and she nodded. "A MacLean, then. Welcome, Lily, to Blackburn Keep."

"Let's do sit." Hugh escorted them to a pair of benches near the fountain, the setting for the painting of Fiona and Hugh that Lily had seen inside. Their affection for each other was genuine, and familiar, as if they were old friends as well as siblings.

When they were seated, Hugh leaned forward, resting his arms on his knees, his hat in his hands. "Lily and I met because of the flowers. She swears there's a grave on Arran where someone planted one of your roses."

Hugh related the story of Lily's long mission to retrieve the roses and put them on the grave. Like a compass needle swaying north, Fiona's attention kept returning to Lily. When he'd finished, Fiona said, "How old are you, Lily?"

"Two and twenty."

Lightly, Hugh said, "'Tis a coincidence that I delivered your roses on her birthday all these years, is it not, Fiona? You've always been adamant about the day."

Fiona's mouth tightened and her eyes grew luminous with tears. Tiny lines framed her mouth, but she did not look her age, Lily thought. She looked heartsore and long suffering, as Grandpapa would have said.

Eager for an answer, Lily also leaned forward. "Who is buried in the grave?"

Covering her mouth with a graceful hand, Fiona shook her head. "I can—I cannot say just yet. Tell me, Lily, has your father wed since your mother's death?"

"Nay. He told me that he loved her well and would claim only her in heaven."

Fiona made a choking sound.

Hugh grew alarmed and knelt at his sister's feet. "Come, I'll take you inside. We can talk later."

"Nay." She pulled a handkerchief from the pocket of

her gardening apron and wiped her eyes. "The truth must out now."

Still, she watched Lily, who anticipated her long-awaited answer.

"When I was six and ten, the Hamiltons raided our Ardrossan home. I was taken hostage."

Lily's heart went out to her, for she suspected that the people of her clan had not treated this woman kindly. Yet Fiona did not seem especially sad, now that she'd begun to speak.

Sighing, Hugh's sister stared at the wall of roses. "I thought I would be ransomed right away, but I was not. Months passed, and rumors spread that the clans were yet again rallying behind our king, who was exiled at the time. Oliver Cromwell ruled our land. I thought the royalist cause was the reason my father had not bought my release.

"I came to know your father well." Again her tear-filled gaze strayed to Lily. "He was barely twenty at the time, and not at all pigeon-faced or angry, as they style him now."

Hugh stiffened. Lily's stomach grew queasy.

Her eyes closed, Fiona rubbed her temple. "As many other Scots, the Hamiltons were hiding a Catholic priest at the time." She looked up. "In November of fifty-seven, in a secret ceremony, I married your father, Lily. The next May I gave birth to you."

"Nay!" Hugh sprang from the bench and clutched his sister's shoulders. "Sweet God in heaven, nay. Say it isn't so, Fiona."

Her uncle. Lily's head spun. Hugh was her uncle. They

had committed the blackest of all sins: incest. She shivered with revulsion and hugged her stomach to keep from shaming herself.

Tears spilled down Fiona's cheeks. "There's more, Hugh."

"More?" His shock-filled expression must have mirrored Lily's own. Releasing his sister, he paced the pebbled path, never looking at Lily. Too ashamed, she knew.

"Please hear me out," said Fiona. "Lily was but three months old when my clan raided the Hamiltons. Your father and I thought that perhaps we could bring peace between our families. But when the MacDonnels stormed Hamilton Castle, your father bade me take you up to the mountain and hide in the woods. Unfortunately my father and his men saw me running away and gave chase.

"I made it as far as the high glen." Her voice dropped. "I had not fully recovered from the birth, and you were a healthy, fat babe. And the bonniest child in the world."

Her mother. Through a haze of guilt, Lily understood what else Fiona was saying. She was Lily's mother. "Why did you leave me there?" She couldn't say the word "mother."

Fiona's tears now streamed down her face. "I was weak from running. One of my uncles carried me, another carried you, but we were put upon by Hamiltons and separated. Later they told me there was an accident. They said you died there and swore they buried you in the high glen."

Lily felt hollow inside. In the same breath, she had gained a mother and lost the man she loved. Hugh still paced, his body rigid with anger and heaven knew what other torments.

"After I returned to Ardrossan," Fiona said, "I paid a man to go to Arran and find your grave. When he told me of the cairn there, exactly where my kinsmen swore they buried you, I sent him back with the roses." Fiona stood and held out her arms. "Oh, my darling Lily, you've been tending your own grave all these years."

Better she were in it, Lily thought morosely. Her only consolation stemmed from the knowledge that she would never have to visit the grave again or worry over the roses. She would never go to the Virginia Colony, either. She glanced at Hugh, and found him looking at her, his eyes filled with misery.

Sobs choked her. If she ever needed a mother, Lily decided, it was now. She rose, and on shaky legs, stepped into Fiona's embrace. Loving hands soothed her, rubbing her back, and a mother's voice whispered endearments Lily never thought to hear.

At the sound of retreating footsteps, Fiona held Lily tighter. "Don't go, Hugh," she called out. "There's no reason to walk away."

The garden was silent, save the chirping of birds and the bubbling of the fountain. Who would comfort Hugh?

"I've every reason to walk straight to hell, Fiona. I love Lily. I *have* loved her."

Against Lily's cheek, she felt Fiona smile. "Then look past that Stewart nose of yours and grasp the truth."

"You talk nonsense."

She gripped Lily's shoulders and held her at arm's length. "Fret not, my dear. All will be well."

Into the emptiness of Lily's soul poured a mother's love. Staring into Fiona's face, she understood why the painting had seemed so familiar, and she now knew why she did not favor her clan. But resemblances mattered not.

"Nothing can be well, for Hugh and I have—" Lily couldn't voice the horror of her sin.

Fiona lifted her brows in query. "You have anticipated your wedding vows?"

"God, Fiona," Hugh cursed. "Must you torment her so?"

Moving to Lily's side, Fiona held out her free hand to Hugh. "You are not my brother, and if you but think on it, you will see the truth."

He had crushed his hat, Lily noticed. The brim was curled and ragged from the force of his anger, and the exotic plume lay in shreds. Now, hope moved him toward them. "I will see what truth, Fiona? Do not cloak what you have to say. Tell it to me straight out."

"I did, Hugh. But you were not listening. Better I show you. Here, take Lily's hand. She needs your comfort, and I won't be long."

Her gaze still fixed on his hat, Lily watched him move close. Through a cloud of confusion, she saw her hand being placed in his. His skin was cold, as cold as her own.

Skirts flying, Fiona raced into the castle. The moment she disappeared through the door, Hugh dropped Lily's hand.

"She's your mother," he said without emotion. "I should have noticed. I think I did . . . see the resemblance . . . when I first met you. But nothing came of it, of course. I was consumed with—oh, God, Lily, I'm sorry."

She felt like a pillar of salt.

"Say something, Lily. Please. I'll go mad do you not."

Insecurity didn't suit Hugh MacDonnel. MacDonnel. The man she loved. "Fiona says you are not her brother."

"Pray God she speaks the truth."

Weakened, Lily leaned against him. He started, then wrapped an arm around her. She breathed in his clean, familiar scent, and wanted to embrace him but thought better of it. They would first hear what Fiona had to say.

When she returned, Fiona carried a large gilt frame, the subject of the work hidden. On the back of the painting, Lily saw spider webs and frayed edges of the canvas.

"Here." As excited as a girl, Fiona put the painting on one of the benches and turned it around.

It was a likeness of the king, Charles II. Captured in his voluminous Garter robes of royal blue velvet and white taffeta, the cross of St. George emblazoned at his left shoulder, the handsome Stewart monarch wore a mustache and a full wig of jet black curls.

"Well?" Fiona said.

The king's eyes and the slender, yet elegant nose caught Lily's attention. She looked at Hugh, who was frowning. On the king, that same look bespoke power and privilege.

"You do look like him, Hugh," she said.

"But not enough to declare him my father."

Most people would rejoice to claim such a relation. Only Hugh would think twice about affirming a monarch for his sire.

"You're certainly arrogant enough," Lily murmured. "And I seem to remember saying how handsome you look in a wig."

He scowled at her, but she knew his displeasure was feigned. His color was returning and his hands no longer worried the brim of his hat.

"Don't you see?" Fiona said. "You were his firstborn. He fled to the continent in 1651 to escape Cromwell. 'Twas the year after you were born. Your mother was dead. At the king's request, my father took you in and, for your safety, raised you as his own."

"I'm illegitimate?" he said, sounding as if it were a curse.

Like a gale wind, relief swept over Lily. She looked at her mother, who was trying not to laugh. She stared at the elegantly handsome man in the portrait. The humor of it struck her. Gazing up at the man she loved, she said, "You're angry?"

He bristled, looking very kingly. "I'm a bloody royal bastard!"

Lily hugged him. "Praise God and his angels that you are."

Into the trees, he shouted, "I'm a bloody royal bastard!" A family of nightjars took flight. Hugh's heart followed suit, and he swept up his darling Lily and squeezed her until she protested.

She was not his niece. Looking down into her lovely face, he said, "You will bear my children."

"Aye." Shyly, she added, "God willing."

Hugh intended to praise God every day for the rest of his life. "You'll go home with me to Virginia."

"Aye."

"We'll build a life together."

"Aye. But—"

As Hugh watched, she saddened. "What is it, my love?"

"What of Fiona?"

Offhandedly, he said, "She'll come with us, of course."

"You needn't speak about me as if I'm elsewhere or incapable of governing myself."

"My father thinks you're dead, Fiona," Lily admitted.

The damned Hamiltons, Hugh thought. "Your father is a bloody—"

"Be silent, Hugh!" Fiona commanded. "I'll not have you disparage him to me. 'Tis why I left the MacDonnels and came here to live."

"I'll curse him as I may, Fiona. He's a damned Hamilton—sorry, Lily."

But Fiona wasn't done. "Be that as it may, I loved him, and no matter what you or my father say, I will always love Edward Hamilton."

Hugh hadn't considered this turn of events; he'd been

too caught up in his own near catastrophy. "Lily, did you say your father hadn't wed?"

"Nay, he chose not to take a second wife."

Turning his attention to Fiona, Hugh saw her grow sad again. "Will you have him back as your husband, Fiona?"

She stared at her hands, which were knotted together. "I doubt he'll have me. I've passed my prime."

Hugh felt her pain and knew he had to end it. "You're as bonny as a day in May, and as your future son-in-law, 'tis my responsibility to see to your welfare."

Lily poked him in the ribs. "What mischief are you about, Hugh?"

Striving for innocence, he said, "No mischief. I'll simply send a message to your father asking him if he wants his woman back."

Fiona brightened. "But you won't tell him which woman."

Feeling happier than a lark in spring, Hugh resisted the urge to shout. "A clever ploy, if I do say so myself."

To his surprise, Lily said, "Then you'd better ask *your* father to send his army to keep the peace."

A fortnight later, Lily paced the floor of the common room of Blackburn Keep. Hugh was attending yet another meeting with the dukes of Ross and Argyll. After sending three messages to Edward Hamilton and receiving back three condemnations to hell, Hugh had written to his father. By royal summons, the two peers of the realm, Ross and Argyll, had come to negotiate between the Hamiltons and the MacDonnels.

Lachlan MacDonnel, Fiona's father, the man who had raised Hugh, had come at her bidding. Upon arrival, he confirmed her story, and in his blustery manner, confessed that he loved Hugh as his own. When introduced to Lily, the chieftain of the MacDonnels had flown into a rage. Fiona had shown her mettle by stepping between them, dirk in hand, and breaking up the ruckus.

By order of the king, a man-of-war was anchored in Wigtown Bay, ready to defend the port should the Hamiltons disobey his direct command and attack by water. A full complement of armed Stewart clansmen had also been sent to Blackburn Keep and now surrounded the estate, should Lily's father attack by land.

She pitied him, for he did not know that Fiona lived, and Hugh refused to tell him. "Let him be as surprised as I was. He deserves the shock," Hugh had said in defense of his omission.

Now, Lily waited to learn the details of her father's latest communique.

A door opened, and the sound of male voices drifted from the hall. Lily relaxed, for the men were not arguing. She turned and saw Hugh and Fiona enter the common room. He looked happy. Fiona looked like she had swallowed a frog in mixed company.

"What's happened?" Lily asked.

Hugh kissed her cheek. "Your father's ship just entered the bay. The dukes have gone to meet him."

Small wonder Fiona was nervous. To distract her, Lily said, "Perhaps you should wear the pink silk, Mother."

She threw up her hands and left the room, saying, "I knew this yellow linen was all wrong. I look sallow in the face and as old as Methuselah's dog."

"You're cruel, sweetheart."

"Quite the contrary. I gave her something to do, save worry over my father's arrival. What do you think he'll do?"

"Past demanding I return you, I cannot say." His arms surrounded her. "I do suspect we'll see a bit of Hamilton ire."

"A bit" turned out to be an understatement, for the moment Edward Hamilton saw his daughter on the arm of Hugh MacDonnel, his face turned as red as the stripes in his tartan plaid.

"What have you done, lass?"

Although her stomach did somersaults, Lily stood her ground. "I've fallen in love, Father. Hugh has done me the honor of asking me to marry him, and I have accepted."

Her father went for his dirk. It took the pair of dukes to hold him at bay. "You cannot, Lily." When she refused to budge, he blustered, "For the love of God, Lily. Hugh MacDonnel is your uncle."

His abhorrence was expected, but Lily was prepared. "No, Papa. He is not. My mother told me so."

His eyes grew dim with sorrow. "Your mother is dead, God rest her soul. These people have tricked you."

"I'm not Hugh's sire," Lachlan MacDonnel declared.

Her father looked to the dukes for confirmation.

"He speaks true," said His Grace of Ross, stepping away.

His Grace of Argyll also relinquished his hold on Edward. "Hugh's the king's get. 'Tis why that man-o'-war sits in the harbor."

Scanning the face of every man in the room, her father relaxed. He'd always been stern and distant, but Lily now understood that a broken heart had made him so.

"I'll not argue when the banns are read," he conceded. "But you had no right to tell my Lily that her mother lives."

The room had gone unnaturally quiet, for everyone except her father knew the truth. Suddenly calm, Lily reached for the door handle. "You are speaking of Fiona Margaret MacDonnel. You named me for her."

Squaring his shoulders, Edward looked Lachlan Mac-Donnel in the eye. "Aye, and a bonny lass my Fiona was."

The MacDonnel chieftain rocked back on his heels and glanced at the ceiling, at his hands, and at the mirrors on the wall—everywhere except at Edward Hamilton.

"Then we have a surprise for you, Father." Lily opened the door, and the expression on her father's face brought tears to her eyes. Edward the Angry, the notorious warlord of the Hamiltons, stood frozen, his mouth slack, his weathered complexion as white as his fancy silk neck cloth.

Fiona stepped cautiously into the room. "Hello, Edward."

Lachlan MacDonnel threw back his head and laughed. "I never thought I'd see the day when a Hamilton had nothing to say to a MacDonnel."

"Lily has changed all of that," Hugh said, drawing her to his side.

Arm in arm, they watched Edward Hamilton approach the wife he thought long dead. The embrace that followed was lengthy and punctuated with whispered words and heartfelt sighs. Edward cupped Fiona's cheeks in his hands and drank in the sight of her. In response, she blossomed like a maiden with her first beau.

Hugh interrupted the reunion. "I believe a toast is in order."

Just as the wine was poured and glasses raised, a signal horn blared.

"Hamilton, what wickedness have you brought?" demanded Lachlan MacDonnel. Although stern, his voice held no rancor.

Her father shot to his feet, but did not reach for a weapon. "Me? I wasn't allowed to bring so much as a servant to shine my boots."

"Comes the king!" someone yelled from outside.

A servant in royal Stewart livery dashed into the room and skidded to a stop. Behind him, four men struggled beneath the weight of a gilded throne. When the impressive chair was lowered to the floor, yet another servant unfurled a narrow carpet.

The tension in the room grew as thick as a fog. The tartan-clad chieftains adjusted the chains on their fancy badger sporrans. Fiona excused herself to check on the staff. Edward held her back with a murmured, "You always did fuss over a perfectly clean castle and a well-ordered staff. Leave it be, love."

Lily and Hugh shared expectant glances.

A moment later, the king of England strolled into the room. Draped in a dazzling mantle of sky blue velvet lined in white taffeta, he was a figure to behold and admire. He wore a full black wig beneath a cap adorned with white plumes.

Lily and Fiona executed deep curtsies, and the men swept off their hats and went down on a knee.

"Arise, lords and ladies." His lofty gaze settled on his elder son. "Lord Hugh, we presume."

"Aye, Your Majesty. Welcome to Blackburn Keep."

The king moved to the throne and allowed his servants to arrange his robes both before and after he sat down. His bejeweled fingers dangled over the arms of the massive chair.

Lily glowed with pride as Hugh presented her to the king. "My wife, sire, do you give us your blessings."

King Charles admired Lily with the experienced and notorious eye of a man accustomed to appreciating the female form. She did not wither beneath his scrutiny; she was too busy with her own. She found him handsome, to be sure, but toilworn for a man of fifty. The differences between him and Hugh were as striking as their resemblances. The king's chin bore a cleft, which Hugh's did not. Hugh possessed a stronger, squarer jaw, and his lips were more suited to a smile. But their noses were identical, as was the shade of their eyes.

The king coughed delicately. "If you've come to flatter us, lass, you succeeded admirably."

Lily blushed. Hugh chuckled.

Turning slightly, a royal brow lifted, the king stared at Hugh. "You find us entertaining, pup?"

"Nay, sire. Those are same words I spoke to her, when first she clamped eyes on me."

A rakish smile made the king look younger than his years and befitting his scandalous reputation. "We are told you plan to return to the Virginia Colony."

He took Lily's hand and placed it on his arm. "We will make our home there."

"We could command you to stay."

"True. Or you could wish us well and know that as loyal servants we do your bidding in the colonies."

"You will breed our grandchildren there?"

"And name the first son for you."

The pleased king pulled one of three rings from his right hand. It was a rampant lion set with an emerald the size of fat pea. "Bestow him with this, Blackburn, and enlarge him with the title of viscount. . . ." At a loss, he stared at his hand.

"Westward, perhaps?" Hugh said.

"Ah, Westward, indeed. Viscount Westward. We like it well."

Hugh took the ring and bowed. "Thank you for your generosity."

The king nodded, fanning the plumes in his hat. Then his attention strayed. "Hamilton," he said, beckoning Edward to him.

Lily and Hugh returned to their place near Lachlan

MacDonnel and watched Edward lead Fiona to the throne.

"Do you bless this wedding between Blackburn and your daughter?"

"Heartily so, Your Majesty. If it contents you."

The king wagged a finger at him. "We will have a pledge of peace from you and the MacDonnels, or your heads will rest on pikes."

Fiona gasped and looked from her husband to her father. The latter hurried to her side.

"Think you, Lady Fiona, that you can keep peace between these two men?"

"Nay." When the men on either side of her gaped in awe, she added, "Only Your Majesty can make that command."

Obviously impressed by both her honesty and her confidence, the king glared at the two chieftains. "We have made a similar command before, but rowdies that you are, you have chosen not to heed us. What say you to that treason?"

MacDonnel went down on a knee and placed his jeweled dirk at the feet of the king. "Your presence is enough to gain my oath, Your Grace. I swear never again to make war on the Hamiltons."

Hamilton did the same, making sure the two blades touched. "For me also, Your Grace. The MacDonnels may come in peace to Arran."

Hugh put his cheek against Lily's and whispered, "I say we excuse ourselves and be about getting my father that grandchild."

Scandalized and thrilled at once, she turned so her lips brushed his. "You're embarrassing me."

"'Tis nothing compared to what I intend to do later, my love."

Love. As she gazed into his eyes, Lily saw their future unfold. She said a silent prayer of thanks to God and another to Fiona, who had sent Hugh to Arran, bearing flowers from the sea.

AUTHOR'S NOTE

Although largely unsung, the French pinasse, or pinnace, as the Dutch and English called it, occupied an important place in the history of sailing. Swifter and more versatile than the apple-bellied giants of her age, the pinasse was employed in a variety of roles. Her maneuverability and shallow draft made her a perfect choice for scouting and exploration expeditions. The French square rigged their pinasses, and, with only twenty men for crew, successfully plied the trade routes to the American colonies. The Dutch version of the seventeenth-century pinnace became the prototype for the sloop of war.

Because the Scots often associated themselves with the French, I styled the *Valiant Lily* after the pinasse.

Indian
Summer
by Rosanne Bittner

❀❀❀

Warm were the days when we were together,
And warm was his heart.
Like the hot, fiery but elusive wind,
He caressed me; but I could not catch him.
He touched me,
My body, my heart, my spirit.
I will not forget my Cheyenne lover,
Or that Indian summer . . .

Chapter One

"Hold still, Evelyn." Margaret Gibbons quickly scrubbed her four-year-old daughter. It was so much easier bathing her here at the pond several yards behind their cabin rather than using precious water that had to be hauled by the barrel from Fort Reno. She scooped water into a deep wooden bowl and poured it over Evelyn to rinse her. The child's long, blond hair, a mass of curls when it was dry, hung in wet ringlets nearly to her waist. Margaret thought how pretty her daughter was, what a joy to her heart. She had lost two babies since having Evelyn, and she feared this was the only living child she would ever have.

Evelyn laughed with joy at being naked and wet, her big blue eyes dancing with merriment, baby teeth showing through puckery little lips, dimples in her cheeks. Margaret envied her child's freedom. It was such a hot day that she wished she, too, could strip off her clothes and fall into the water; but even though the pond was hidden by tall grass and a grove of young oak trees, and beyond that a patch of sunflowers, she still felt she would be taking too much of a chance. A hundred or so men roamed the fort grounds only a half mile away, but that was not the only danger. Just south of the fort was the Darlington Indian Agency, occupied mostly by Southern Cheyenne.

Her husband had given her strict orders not to come here alone, but stifling, late-summer temperatures had caused her to throw all caution to the wind. Disobeying his order made her feel she had some say in her life. Ever since she could remember, her parents and her husband were telling her how she must feel, think, behave, speak. Here, alone at the pond, she could just be herself. She could laugh and play with her daughter. She could let the combs out of her hair if she wanted. It was long and blond and wavy like Evelyn's, but she was never allowed to let it hang loose and free.

It seemed everything about her life was regimented, from when she was very small through her marriage at seventeen. Sometimes she imagined what it might be like to let her hair loose and run naked and screaming through the high grass, embracing the wind and the sun. She loved Edward, but when he made love to her, she wished he would show more passion. She was in turn forced to hold in much of her own passion because she feared he would think her a wanton, sinful woman if she behaved as though making love were anything but a duty, for the sole purpose of bearing children.

Was it sinful to just want to lie with a man? Edward had bedded her and planted his life in her. They had a daughter together. Yet there was so much about that part of marriage that was a mystery to her, even after five years of marriage. Neither had ever seen the other with nothing on, and they had never made love without total darkness. She couldn't help wonder what it would be like to lie together in the grass, in the warm sunshine.

She closed her eyes. "Father, forgive my sinful thoughts," she whispered. She was a minister's wife. She should not be thinking about pleasures of the flesh. Edward was a good man, a righteous man. He had come here because he had felt a calling to bring God's word to the Indians. By settling near Fort Reno, he could also serve the soldiers there, lonely men who risked their lives trying to keep the unruly Cheyenne on the reservation where they belonged. Edward was convinced that the presence of soldiers was not enough to quell the restlessness of the Indians, who had lately been sneaking off the reservation and making trouble as far north as Kansas and Colorado. Edward believed the Cheyenne needed to learn the white man's ways, and that started with converting them to Christianity. In his thinking, that was the only way to "tame the wild savages."

"This is 1875," Edward had said just last night at supper. "Most Indians except the Sioux in the north have learned they can no longer live the old way. They must conform to a new way of life, and Christianity will help calm their souls and properly civilize them."

Margaret was not so sure it would be all that easy. They had been here only a short while, and the Indians she had seen hanging around the fort seemed surly, some of them broken and miserable, certainly not eager to embrace the white man's religion. Surely they felt displaced and lost. The commander at the fort had said that at one time the Southern Cheyenne were some of the fiercest warriors the army had faced, brave fighters who were quite skilled and elusive. The sorry beggars she had seen around the fort did not depict such a people, and she had to wonder what it would be like for her own people if another race came along and pushed them off their land, forced them to live in a place they hated, robbed them of all dignity and possessions, and forced them to change their entire way of thinking and living, lording over them like masters, and handing out food and supplies in meager portions as though they were dogs.

Did Edward ever think of it that way? Did he ever try to understand how they must feel? He acted as though they should gladly embrace their new life and new religion. He was bringing them something wonderful and they should be grateful, but there was no joy in their eyes, and few bothered to listen to his preaching. She wanted desperately to talk to

Edward about her own theories on helping the Cheyenne, but she knew he would resent his wife giving him advice. Her place was to take care of home and meals and have babies, and to keep quiet in the area of decision making.

She sighed with frustration. She had not wanted to come to Indian Territory. This place was not as pretty or green or cool as Massachusetts. This little pond was like nothing more than a puddle compared with Massachusetts Bay and the Atlantic Ocean. There were no gulls here, no smell of salt water, no cool ocean breezes. There were trees here, but they were not huge and fat and old like those in Massachusetts. The soil here was red clay, not dark and rich. She felt Edward could be better serving his calling somewhere else, perhaps in a new community in Kansas or Nebraska or Colorado, where white Christian families needed a church and a minister.

"Mommy, get wet with me!" Evelyn splashed water at her mother, interrupting her thoughts.

Margaret laughed. "Oh, you're not being fair, Evy! Mommy is still dressed. Now you come out of there and get dressed yourself. We have to get back to—" Her words ended in a gasp. A horse had appeared from out of the thick stand of trees to her right. It was painted with stripes, a sun, and arrows. On it sat a dark-skinned man wearing only a loincloth, his black hair hanging long and loose and a leather band tied around his head. He was sweating and looked ill, but there was no doubt he was strong and fierce. He sat staring at them, and Margaret wondered how long he had been watching them before he made an appearance. What did he want?

She realized then that little Evy was naked. She quickly grabbed a towel and wrapped it around her daughter, devastated and frightened that an Indian man had seen a little white girl that way. She picked her up and held her close. "Go away!" she said to the Indian.

His eyelids drooped a little, and suddenly he slumped forward and slid off his horse. Margaret stepped back, keeping a tight hold on Evy, who watched in curious wonder. "Is he sick, Mommy?"

Margaret watched him quietly for a moment. Should she run away and leave him there? Was he dying? A good Christian would go to his aid, no matter the color of his skin. Her heart pounded with fear, and her thoughts raced in confusion. What would Edward have her do? He would probably say she should leave him and run to the fort for help and protection. Again the tiny feeling of rebellion stirred in her soul, making her want to do exactly the opposite. She set Evy on a blanket. "You stay right there, Evy, do you hear? Put on your dress. I know you can do it by yourself."

"Yes, Mommy." The child whispered the words, as though she was part of a wonderful, scary adventure. She stood rigid, not bothering with her dress yet, more intent on watching her mother and the wild Indian who had just intruded on their privacy. Her father had taught her she must stay away from the Indians, especially the Indian men, but she found them fascinating, and she wished she could play with some of the Indian children around the fort, but her father would not allow it.

Margaret stepped cautiously closer, and just as she reached the man, he rolled to his side with a groan, making her jump back. Little Evy gasped and covered her mouth with her hand.

"Water," the man muttered. "I need to reach . . . water."

When Margaret first saw him, she had been too frightened to notice any details about him. Now she saw that he had ugly red marks on his neck, almost like burns, and his entire neck and jawline were badly bruised. "The pond is just a few feet away," she answered, thinking it was good he at least spoke English. He couldn't be all that much of a savage if he had taken the time to learn the white man's language. Many of the Indians around the fort still spoke little English. "What happened to you? Can I help you?"

"White men . . . cattlemen . . ." That was all he said as he got to his knees.

Margaret reached out hesitantly. She had yet to even touch one of these Indians, and it seemed outright indecent to be touching one who was nearly naked. Again she was disturbed by a curiosity that was surely sinful, for she found herself looking upon his brawny, bare arms and chest with fascination. She had never seen Edward without his shirt on. She grasped his arm, felt his hard muscles as she daringly moved his arm around her shoulders and put her own arm around his waist. "Let me help you to the pond."

He stumbled beside her to the water's edge, then

walked a few feet into the water and let himself fall into it. Margaret watched him put his head back to wet his hair and cool himself. He said something in his own tongue as he angrily splashed more water onto the burns on his neck.

He seemed better with the relief of the water. He would apparently be all right, and Margaret realized she should take Evy and leave, but her legs would not move. She watched him move out of the water, a powerful-looking man with a physique she imagined was like the Greek gods she had learned about in school. She noticed scars on his breasts above the nipples, and wondered how they had gotten there.

"Mommy, button my dress."

Margaret looked down at Evy, who stood there grinning at the Indian. "I'm Evy," she said, totally unafraid. "And this is my mommy. Who are you?"

"Evy, don't—"

"I am Wild Horse," the man answered, his voice raspy and strained, as though his throat was sore.

Wild Horse! Margaret had heard the soldiers talk about this man. They called him a troublemaker, one of those who often fled the reservation to try to live the old way. He was supposed to be dangerous. He had run away again only a week ago, and it was rumored he was responsible for raiding farms farther north, shooting at settlers and stealing supplies. Fear gripped her, yet still she could not move. His dark eyes showed no animosity toward Evy when he answered her, but when he moved his gaze to Margaret, those eyes changed. He looked her over curiously, and she could see in that look a man's satisfaction in what he saw, but there was also a hint of contempt there. "You are . . . preacher's woman."

Margaret could not recall ever having seen him around the fort or the chapel. "How do you know that?"

"No other white women . . . here. My people tell me of white man who comes to bring his God to us. He brings with him a woman with hair like sun and eyes like sky."

Margaret felt suddenly warmer, touched by the way he had described her. Run, Margaret! she warned herself, yet something held her there. She swallowed against her fear, and she grasped Evy's shoulders tightly. The child's simple gingham dress was still unbuttoned in the back, but Margaret was too afraid to take her eyes off Wild Horse to stop and button it. "What happened to you? What are those marks on your neck?"

There it was! A bitter hatred moved into those frightening dark eyes. Without answering, he turned away and walked unsteadily to his horse, which stood drinking at the water's edge. He took a red bandana from his supplies and knelt beside the animal, dipping the bandana into the water to wet it. He held it to the burns on his neck.

Margaret wondered at her own bravery—or was it stupidity? She walked closer. "Please, let me help you. Tell me what happened."

Wild Horse stared across the pond at some jays that flitted about, wishing he could be free again, like them. "White men take cattle through our lands . . . in places they do not belong." He winced with pain. "They try to hang me. They track stray cattle . . . to where I was camped. They surrounded me, pointed weapons at me, and made me give up my own. They say I stole cattle. I did not. They strayed there." He shivered and dipped the bandana into the water and again applied it to the burns. "It was just excuse for those men to hang an Indian and get away with it. They put a rope over limb of a tree and they forced me onto horse, put rope around my neck, take horse away." He shivered with rage. "They laughed . . . while I hung there . . . slowly choking."

"Dear God," Margaret whispered, her heart filled with pity. Was he telling the truth? Or had he really stolen the cattle? Even if he had, was that any reason to string a man up then and there? How could any man do such a thing and watch and laugh? "How did you get away?" Why was she standing here talking to this man who was known to make trouble? Why was her fear fast leaving her?

"It was becoming dark. They stayed only a moment . . . then rode away. I felt my breath leaving me . . . felt myself dying, and my rage at those men gave me strength to wrestle my wrists free of ropes with which they tied me. I could not let myself die that way. Hanging means the spirit is cut off and cannot escape to follow Ekutsihimmiyo to land of freedom in afterlife. I reached up. I prayed to Maheo to give me strength to grasp rope above me and pull myself up to tree limb. I got one arm over it and with my other hand I loosened knot around my neck and got out of it. I fell to ground . . . do not know how long I was there. It was morning when I awoke." He sat down in the grass and put his hands to his head as though it ached. "I was confused . . . could not think where to go. I let my horse go where he pleased, and he carried me back here where my people are."

Evy ran off to chase a butterfly, her dress still flopping open in the back. Margaret felt lost in a torrent of confusion. "You need to tell the soldiers what happened," she told him.

His dark eyes flashed when he looked up at her. "And you think they would *believe* me?" he asked with a sneer. "You have not been here long. You do not know how it is for my people. Those men have surely already told their side . . . that I stole cattle. In eyes of soldiers I am called bad . . . troublemaker." He straightened with pride. "I leave this place because I hate it! This is not way for my people to live. We should be free to hunt where we like. This food they give us"—he spit—"it is bad. I go hunt for fresh meat, but I do not steal white man's cattle!"

Margaret backed away again, realizing his anger was building. She called to Evy, and the girl came running. She knelt down to button her dress, but before she could finish, the child darted away and pointed her chubby little hand toward Wild Horse, touching his cheek with one finger. "I never touched an Indian before," she said with a sweet grin.

To Margaret's surprise, Wild Horse smiled, a handsome grin that erased all the hatred that had been in his eyes moments before. "I once had little girl like you. Her hair was not golden. It was dark like mine." He took a piece of his long hair and held it out for her to see. "Still, she had pretty smile . . . like yours."

Evy frowned. "Where is she? Can I play with her?"

A terrible sadness came into his eyes. "She and her mother are gone to place where there is always peace, where grass is always green and water is always cool and clear and there are many buffalo."

"Will they come back?"

Margaret felt a deep ache in her heart at how he looked away, unable to answer right away. She came closer again, no longer afraid for Evy. "I think Wild Horse is telling you that his daughter and wife have gone to heaven, Evy." Wild Horse looked up at her gratefully, and she saw tears in his eyes. Such tragedy in that look! She had not even considered these people might have deep feelings for their loved ones the same as whites.

"Oh!" Evy answered, her eyes growing brighter again. "They're with Jesus then!"

Wild Horse smiled sadly. "We call Him Maheo." He put a hand to his throat again and bent over, choking and gasping for breath.

Margaret moved to his side, alarmed. "You must be badly injured. You must tell someone about this, Wild Horse."

He shook his head. "When white men who hanged me . . . discover I did not die they will tell even bigger lies. They will be afraid I will tell truth of what they did to me. They will . . . make sure soldiers believe I stole cattle. I must hide until they have . . . gone on north and I know they will cause no more trouble. My people will help me. They will hide me. I will stay here until tonight. Then I will . . . find my way into agency. That is last place soldiers will look for me. I have friends there . . . who will hide me in their homes until I am stronger and can get away again."

"What about your horse? Won't it be recognized?"

He took a moment to get his breath. "They will wash off paint . . . mix into herd of other horses." He met her eyes. "You are only one who knows. I must trust you . . . but how can I? You are . . . white. You will feel it is your duty to tell your husband and soldiers I am here."

Margaret thought of Edward again. Yes, he would most certainly consider it her duty to report what had happened. It seemed she might be able to help Wild Horse by telling his story for him, but instinct told her what soldiers would think of her talking to the man alone. They would probably laugh at her for believing him, and Edward would be furious that she had come alone to the pond and had subjected herself to what he would consider a terrible danger.

"I believe you're telling the truth," she told Wild Horse. "I won't say anything."

He drew in his breath, feeling his throat constricting. Was it swelling on the inside? Would he still die from this awful horror? Never would he forget the feeling of that rope tightening around his neck. It would haunt him forever. "How can I . . . trust you?"

Margaret stood up and folded her arms. "If you think you can't, then you'll just have to kill me, won't you?"

He watched her blue eyes for several long, quiet seconds. He liked this white woman whose name he didn't know. What was it about her that had compelled him to tell her his story in the first place? Why did he feel he could trust her?

She pressed Evy's shoulders. "Evy, you must not tell your father or anyone about seeing Wild Horse here at the pond today. If the soldiers find out, they will hunt for him because they think he did something bad, but he did not, so we are going to keep his secret. Can you do that? Do you understand?"

The child nodded. "I won't tell, Mommy. I can keep a secret."

Margaret knelt beside her. "That's a good girl. It's the right thing to do, Evy. You aren't doing anything bad, I promise. You're just helping Wild Horse by not telling anyone he was here." She looked at Wild Horse. "If I can find a way to help you, to prove those men had no right to try to hang you, I'll do it."

Wild Horse was astounded at her willingness to help. "It would not matter. I was not supposed to leave agency. I fear they will soon put me on iron horse that takes bad Indians to that faraway place where they say it is very hot with many insects . . . that place where many of my people die of homesickness and diseases from white men and from insects."

Margaret frowned. She had read that some of the more notorious Apache leaders and now some of the Plains tribal leaders were being shipped off to prisons in Florida, where they could not be anywhere near their people and keep them stirred up. Was that what he meant? "Wild Horse, I'm not sure just *what* I can do, but I can at least find out what the soldiers are saying and let you know."

His eyes showed his surprise. "I do not understand why you would do this."

Because it is exactly the opposite of what my husband would say I should do, she thought. "I don't know, except that I believe you and I am sorry for what you have suffered. No man should be put through such humiliation. I can't help wonder what your life would be like right now if settlers and soldiers had never come here."

He dabbed the bandana to the burns on his neck. "It would be very different . . . and my wife and child would be alive today."

She wanted to know more about him, his beliefs, about the being he called Maheo, whom had compared to her own Christ. She realized that in order to bring their own religion to these people, they first needed to understand them, what they felt on the inside, what they believed. Edward did not feel that was necessary. What difference did it make what they believed? The important thing was that they learn the white man's way.

She wished there were more time to talk to him. In only these few minutes she had come to feel comfortable around him, and she was full of questions. But if she stayed here any longer, someone might come looking for her, and Wild Horse would be discovered. "I have to get back or I'll be missed. I'm not even supposed to come here, but whenever my husband leaves to go preach at the agency, I am free to do what I please. He won't take us there." She blushed in embarrassment at the meaning of the remark.

Wild Horse sighed deeply. "He does not wish for his woman and child to be near Cheyenne." He shook his head. "Go now. Your people will say bad things about you if they find you helping me."

She turned and picked up the blanket, soap, and towel she had brought with her. "I'm sorry, Wild Horse. I wish I could do more. I will pray for you."

You are not like the others, he thought. He had met very few white women, none who showed no fear. And this one was so beautiful. He wanted to touch her, to smell her hair, but she was forbidden . . . and she already had a man. "Do not concern yourself with me. Soon I will be gone again."

"But how can I get word to you of what the soldiers are saying?"

"My people will hear. They will tell me."

Their eyes held in a strange attraction neither of them understood. She turned then to leave.

"Wait," he called in a raspy voice.

Margaret looked back at him. "What is it?"

He studied her form beneath the plain cotton dress she wore. Her waist was slender; her breasts looked full and firm. He wondered how she might look with that golden hair undone, falling over her pale skin. "I do not know what you are called."

What was the powerful force in his look? Margaret felt like a curious child who had found something new and wonderful, but it was unlikely she would ever see him again. What difference should it make to him what her name was? "Margaret," she answered. "Most just call me Maggie."

She hurried away then, and Wild Horse watched after her. "Maggie," he repeated in a raspy voice. He closed his eyes and lay down in the grass, astounded at his thoughts. He hated whites, more now than ever; yet he was imagining what it might be like to have that pretty, forbidden white woman lying naked beside him.

Chapter Two

*R*everend Edward Gibbons finished a very long prayer, after which he and his family sat down with Major Albert Doleman and his wife, Gloria, the daughter of an army general from Wisconsin. Margaret felt uncomfortable around the woman, who had an uppity air about her and who made it very obvious she hated it here at Fort Reno. She had come to visit her husband for a month or two and would go back to her mother in Wisconsin before winter. She hoped that her husband would be transferred to a "more bearable" location than Indian Territory, at which time she would gladly join him.

That is the difference between an army man and a preacher, she had once rudely remarked to Margaret. An army man does not expect his wife to always follow him, but a preacher's wife . . . well, she must follow him wherever God calls him, mustn't she? Kind of like Ruth in the Bible—'whither thou goest,' something like that. How sad for you, Maggie.

The woman had no regard for the Cheyenne at all. She refused to go near an Indian, seldom even came out of the fine, brick officers' quarters where her husband lived. They had no children, and she had joked that if the major didn't get himself stationed someplace respectable soon so that she could stay with him, there would never *be* any children.

"Your lovely little daughter looks sunburned," the woman told Margaret aloud. She sat across the table from Margaret and Evy. She picked up a bowl of mashed potatoes and handed them to her husband as her lovely, green eyes fell on Margaret with a discerning gaze. "She is much too fair for this damnable climate, you know."

"I quite agree," Major Doleman added. The man put some of the potatoes on his plate and handed them on to Margaret, who wondered if Gloria Doleman had ever cooked a meal on her own. Every time the major invited them to join them for a meal, it was cooked by army cooks at the mess hall and carried to them in warming pans, then served by one of the privates as though the major and his wife were a king and queen.

Margaret felt a flush come to her cheeks, realizing the real reason Evy was sunburned. Edward would be furious if he knew she had been swimming naked at the pond. "I'm afraid Evy played outside too long today," she answered the major and his wife.

Evy giggled, and Margaret prayed the child would remember to keep their secret. That was not an easy thing for a four-year-old, who did not fully understand why it mattered.

Margaret scooped some potatoes onto the child's plate. "Eat up, Evy. You know your daddy doesn't like any food left on your plate." She gave her only a little so the child would not have to force down the food just to please Edward. She passed the potatoes to her husband, who was watching them both closely, a stern look in his dark eyes. She thought how handsome he was when he smiled, but that was an unusual sight. Edward was eleven years older than she, a man who took life much too seriously, as far as Margaret was concerned. When she was seventeen, she had been attracted not only to his looks but also to his determined quest to bring Christ to those who still did not know Him, his zeal to "save the world."

Margaret had wanted to be the woman who supported him in that glorious vision, had felt a fire tear through her the first time he touched her. But soon after their marriage he had quickly doused the flames by chastising her for making noises of pleasure when he made love to her, which had embarrassed her to such devastation that it was several weeks before she could even bring herself to make love again.

However, a child had already been conceived from that first humiliating experience, and Evelyn was born nine months later, a very difficult birth that had apparently done some kind of damage, as she had lost two babies since then.

"What is the mission of the troops we saw riding out of here earlier?" Edward asked the major, who sat at the other end of the table. He set down the potatoes and took a bowl of gravy from Margaret.

"They're out scouting for that troublemaker, Wild Horse, again. He broke loose from Darlington, and settlers farther north have had some problems with raiding. We think Wild Horse might have something to do with it. There have even been reports of a couple of young girls being—" He hesitated, realizing there were women present. "Of course, there are a lot of other renegades out there," he continued. "It's so hard to pin down just which ones do what, so we end up having to punish all of them for what a few of them do. All I know is, things are usually more peaceful when Wild Horse is on the reservation where he belongs."

Margaret could hardly eat. Rape? Somehow she knew Wild Horse had not done such a thing. Besides, he couldn't have been that far away if he had already made it back to the agency today. "No one can actually say who did the terrible deeds then?" she asked cautiously.

"Only that it was Indians," the major answered. "The girls who were violated are too distraught to identify them, so I'm told through telegrams."

"There was more than one?"

Edward cast his wife a scowl. "Margaret, why are you asking so many questions about something that is not of your concern?"

She held his gaze, embarrassed he had chastised her in front of the major and his wife. "I am concerned with justice," she answered. "It doesn't seem fair to blame a man for something just on hearsay." She looked at the major. "I thought I heard something about Wild Horse usually escaping on his own, not with a war party. If there are several men involved in these raids, then maybe he had nothing to do with them. Maybe he just needs to get off the reservation once in a while and feel free."

"Margaret!" Edward's face reddened, and he looked at the major. "I am sorry for my wife's forwardness," he told the man. "It is not like her at all."

Margaret held her own anger in check. She knew Edward was furious by the fact that he called her Margaret instead of Maggie.

"Oh, what is the harm in asking questions?" Gloria put in. "After all, women were violated. It's natural to worry and wonder who might have been responsible, seeing as how she has to live so close to the reservation. That is why I stay inside most of the time. I don't trust those savages one bit, but I do agree that there should be some way to be more fair about who gets accused of these things. I am sure that punishing a whole group of innocent Indians for what a few of them do can only keep the hard feelings stirred and cause the Indians to continue looking for revenge. It seems to be a never-ending circle."

"If they were all dead or in real prisons instead of on reservations where they can get loose, maybe we could get on with settling the West," the major put in.

Margaret was appalled at the man's attitude, but she knew she had already said too much.

"Well, I hope I can get through to some of them," Edward told the man. "I still believe they simply need to be Christianized. If I work with them long enough, they'll come around. Each time I go to the reservation to preach, one or two more come to listen."

Margaret quietly finished her meal while the men spoke, and she smiled inwardly when the major prattled about how his men would find "that renegade Wild Horse," if they had to travel a hundred miles to track him down. He's right here under your nose, you fool! she felt like shouting.

"I like Wild Horse," Evy spoke up.

Margaret struggled to keep her composure, as the other three stared at the child.

"Evelyn, what are you saying?" Edward asked.

"He had a little girl like me," she said with a sweet smile. "I saw him today."

Margaret forced a light laugh. "Evy, such an imagination!" She scooped what was left of the child's potatoes together. "Now you finish those potatoes and quit making up stories."

The rest of them laughed, and the major shook his head. "How ironic the child should tell a story so close to the truth. Wild Horse *did* have a daughter. Actually, he had a son *and* a daughter. They and his wife were killed at Sand Creek eleven years ago, back in sixty-four, when Colorado volunteers attacked a peaceful village of Cheyenne under Black Kettle. It was quite a scandal for Colorado—a Major Chivington directed the raid—killed mostly women and children. The Cheyenne went on quite a rampage after that, and Wild Horse was one of the ringleaders. I guess you can hardly blame the man, seeing as how he lost his young wife and two children. I don't think that rage ever quite left him. He never did take another wife. Still, he's got to realize that everything is changed now. The Indian simply cannot live the way he once lived, and going out and raiding and killing will not work. It only makes life more difficult for the rest of the Cheyenne."

Edward frowned. "How old is this Wild Horse?"

"Oh, I guess about thirty-two."

"Hmm. Only a year younger than I am. Life sure is an irony, isn't it? A man the same age as I, still living like an ignorant savage."

The major swallowed a piece of chicken. "Not so ignorant as you might think. He seems quite intelligent. He actually kept and took good care of a white captive once, just so he could learn the white man's language from him. In gratitude, he kept his word and set the young man free after several months. His purpose was simply to learn the language so that he could better defend himself and his people. He doesn't trust the things that are said at treaty councils. He thinks the Indians get cheated partly because interpreters don't always properly explain what is being promised them.

He figured his best defense was to know the language. You have to admit, that's smart thinking."

Margaret felt a sweet satisfaction. For some reason it pleased her to know that Wild Horse was so intelligent. Now she knew how he managed to speak such good English. She was glad Edward had asked the questions she had wanted to ask herself. Her heart ached at the thought of what had happened to Wild Horse's wife and little children. What a terrible thing! What kind of battle is it when men murder women and children? How could a man not carry revenge in his heart when something like that happens?

She stayed out of the rest of the conversation, glad that little Evy did not bring up Wild Horse's name again. Apparently everyone believed the child just had a vivid imagination, but Margaret felt somewhat uncomfortable whenever she caught Gloria looking at her. She suspected that being female, the woman had an instinct for another woman's troubles. Was it her own guilt that made her feel Gloria Doleman suspected something was not quite right? The woman already had detected that Margaret was not happy with her marriage. Surely that was why she had made the remark about it being too bad a preacher's wife was forced to follow her husband to the ends of the earth.

Margaret was glad when the meal and dessert and a shared glass of wine were finished. Wine was the only type of alcohol her husband would touch, and then only one glass. They thanked the major for his hospitality and the good meal and finally left to walk back to their cabin, built just outside the walls of the fort.

"I am very upset with you, Maggie, for making those remarks to the major about something you know nothing about."

Margaret carried a sleepy Evy in her arms. "Edward, just because I am a female, doesn't mean I don't have opinions and beliefs of my own. I have a right to express them." She stopped walking. "Please take Evy. She's getting too heavy."

He stopped with her and took the child into his arms, arms Margaret had loved to feel around her when they first fell in love. They were strong arms, and she longed to see his naked torso the way she had seen Wild Horse's earlier in the day. Edward had a fine physique, but he showed it to no one, not even his wife. It had been drilled into him since he was small that practically every pleasure there was in the world, as well as that of looking upon one's wife or one's own body, was sinful. Margaret wondered if he, too, sometimes wanted to express his passion more; if he had feelings he kept in check only because someone else had told him it was wrong to feel that way.

"I have never known you to behave this way," he told her, scowling.

Margaret drew in her breath. "Edward, you are never going to reach the Cheyenne until you learn to truly *care* about them as human beings. You have to understand how they think and feel, what they believe, their spiritual connections. You can't just blindly walk in on them and order them to change their lives. Maybe they don't think they need salvation at all! Maybe *we* could learn something from *them*, and through what we learn, we can better understand how to help them through this terrible time of transition for them. They have lost everything, Edward! *Everything!* Now the government comes in and tries to take away what dignity they have left, and people like us come and try to steal their very religion out from under them!"

Edward stared at her in shock, speechless. "Margaret!" he said in a whisper. It was the only word he could utter.

She waited for a tirade, holding his gaze boldly and feeling better than she had in a long time. It felt good to speak her mind. If she could only get up the courage to tell him how she felt about their own personal relationship. "I will not say I am sorry for all the things I just said," she said aloud. "I am not. I married you because I loved you and wanted to help you in your quest to bring Christ to those who needed to hear the truth. I meant to join you in your teachings, not just sit home nursing children. And since it looks as though there might not *be* any more children, I might as well get more involved in your work. Let me help you, Edward. Take me to the reservation with you. Let me and Evy get to know these people, befriend them, gain their trust. That is the only way they are going to start listening to you."

He shook his head in disbelief. "You've lost your mind! Is it the desolation out here? Are you that lonely for your family and for Massachusetts?"

She closed her eyes, realizing he had not grasped a thing she had said. "No," she answered. "I am that lonely for you, Edward." She turned and walked rapidly then, fighting back tears. Surely there was a way to reach him, to make him understand she must be allowed to express her passions. She felt as though a volcano were boiling inside her, needing to erupt but unable to get out. Meeting Wild Horse today, that forbidden, intimate encounter had awakened something in her, needs she thought she could ignore, a longing for freedom, perhaps not so different from Wild Horse's yearning to be free.

The night did not bring much relief from the heat. Margaret lay awake listening to crickets. In the distance she could hear voices, soldiers on night duty. She thought how ironic it was that she lay here next to her husband, yet her thoughts were of another man. Was he safe? Had he managed to hide himself at the agency?

She smiled in the darkness at her wonderful secret, and at Wild Horse's fine trickery. Men were out there combing the hills for him, and he was right here——at least she hoped he was still here. But why did she care? She felt almost as though she were cheating on Edward thinking such thoughts, but she could not quell them. She closed her eyes and prayed for forgiveness, then turned to Edward, touching his arm. "Edward, are you still angry with me?"

He sighed deeply and did not move. "I don't know. You just . . . you acted different tonight, Maggie. I've never seen you like that."

She rubbed at his arm. "I can't sit by and say nothing, Edward. I want to help you. I want to go to the reservation with you——befriend the Cheyenne, win their confidence."

"I don't want you there."

"But Edward—"

"I don't want you there!" He spoke the words louder, and she moved away from him.

"You'll wake Evy."

"Then don't go against my word when she's asleep and force me to raise my voice."

She lay there quietly, fighting tears. "Why did you marry me, Edward?"

She heard him gasp in exasperation. "What kind of question is that?"

"A very valid one. Why did you marry me?"

He paused, shifted in bed. "Because I love you. Why else?"

"I'm not sure. Maybe you just wanted someone to give you children, a wife on your arm, to show your followers what a fine family man you are. Did you ever truly desire me, Edward?" She felt him rise to a sitting position.

"For heaven's sake, Maggie, where are you getting these questions? Of course I desired you. A man can't . . . well . . . he can't be a man if he doesn't desire the woman. How do you think you had Evy, and the two children we lost? I'm the one who fathered them."

She turned her face to look up at him in the moonlight. "Is that the only reason you want me?"

In the moonlight she saw a strange look come into his eyes. For one brief moment she thought she detected a passion she rarely saw there, but it quickly vanished. He drew in his breath and moved to get up. "You are talking about lust, Maggie, and lust is a sin. I love you. I don't lust after you."

Maybe I want you to lust after me, she thought. Was it terribly sinful of her to be thinking such things? "I just . . . I want you to love me as a person, Edward, not as just your wife and the mother of your child. And I wish you would respect my opinions."

He shook his head and moved toward the bedroom door, stubbing his toe on a stool. "Damn!" he cried out. He danced around for a moment, then came to the foot of the bed and grabbed hold of the brass rail. "Now look what you've made me do! I swore!"

"You didn't use the Lord's name in vain."

"I swore, nonetheless."

"A lot of men swear, Edward."

"What is wrong with you tonight! I don't understand a thing you're trying to tell me!"

She sat up. "I'm trying to tell you that I want you to listen to me sometimes. I want you to be your own man, Edward, not the man your parents beat you into becoming. They hit you, didn't they? You've mentioned that they took the whip to you every time you did or said anything they considered sinful, and I'm sure that's why you're afraid to allow your real feelings to show. God wants us to be joyful, to celebrate our love and our passion. And you need to do more than just preach to the Indians. God would want—"

"How *dare* you tell me what God wants! What does a woman know about such things! And how dare you tell me my parents were wrong to discipline me! I want no more such talk, do you understand? No more of it!"

"Mommy!" Evy called out from her room. "What'sa matter, Mommy?"

Margaret sighed. "You've wakened Evy."

"It's your fault, not mine! Tell her to go back to sleep and be good, or *she* will be punished! You're spoiling her, Maggie. You never discipline her!"

Margaret got out of bed and walked up to him, facing him squarely. "And if you ever take a whip to her, I will *leave* you, Edward Gibbons! You will not raise our daughter the way *you* were raised, so that she becomes an adult with no feelings!" Her voice broke on those last works. She turned and marched into Evy's room. The cabin was small—just the two bedrooms and one main room, a simple structure put up by soldiers. Their arguing could not help but be heard by Evy. She picked up the child and soothed her, telling her everything was all right and she must go to sleep. The child finally dozed off again, and Margaret went into the main room, where Edward sat at the table reading the Bible by an oil lamp. He looked up at her.

"Is that what you think, Maggie? That I have no feelings?"

She was almost glad for the hurt in his eyes. At least that meant she had stirred something inside him, and had given him something to think about. "No. But I think that whatever feelings you do have, you keep them buried because you are afraid to show them. And if *I* sense your lack of compassion, what do you think the Cheyenne think? I think they can be very perceptive, and they know when someone is sincere and when he is not. Until they feel *you* are sincere, they are not going to respond to your preaching." She moved to the bedroom door. "Good night, Edward."

He did not reply. She went to bed alone, and again her thoughts strayed to another man, one with dark eyes—eyes that had roamed her body as though she stood before him naked. Edward had never looked at her that way. She wished he would come to bed and pull her into his arms, tell her he wanted her, just because she was his woman and he loved her, and for no other reason. But when she awoke in the morning, she realized she never even noticed when her husband came to bed. He had not touched her.

Chapter Three

"Is this our secret place, Mommy?"

Margaret was not sure how to answer Evy. If she said that the pond was their secret, it might make coming here that much more exciting for her, which would mean it would be even more tempting for her to tell her daddy about it. "Let's just say it's our special place, and we can't tell anyone about it, or we might not get to come here anymore."

"Teach me to swim, Mommy. Can you swim?"

Margaret kissed her cheek. "I haven't tried for a very long time, Evy. And Mommy can't take off her clothes and go in the water with you, so you just stay close to the edge."

"Why not? Take off your dress, Mommy, and go in the water with me."

Oh, how she longed to do just that. "Big ladies don't do those things," she told the child. "Only little children can take off their clothes and go into the water. Now hurry and get cool. We don't have a lot of time."

"But how will *you* get cool?"

"I'll be fine." She pulled off Evy's dress and shoes and drawers, and the child squealed and ran into the water. Margaret smiled, unbuttoning the top buttons of her dress and then lifting her skirt to remove her slips and her own shoes and stockings. She decided she could at least get her feet wet and perhaps splash some water on her neck and chest. She lifted her skirt and walked to the edge of the pond.

Again Edward had refused to allow her to go to the reservation with him. He had spoken little to her since their argument two days ago, except to say the necessary things to everyday living, and to pray. She wasn't sure if he was angry, or if perhaps he was giving some thought to the things she had told him. His blue eyes had become unreadable, and she had decided to let him ponder the things she'd said and let him take the next step. The strangest part about the entire incident was that until meeting Wild Horse for just those few minutes, she had never had the courage to speak to Edward the way she had. Something had changed, but she wasn't sure why or what had caused it. She only knew that coming to the pond made her feel good inside, and meeting

Wild Horse had made her think completely differently about the Cheyenne.

Was he evil? Was the devil in him? Was that why she had spoken so harshly to Edward, why she longed more than ever to lie naked next to her husband, to see passion in his eyes, to long for him to lust after her? Had Wild Horse been sent by Satan, or perhaps by God? Ever since meeting him, she wanted more than ever to go to the reservation and get to know some of the Cheyenne. Surely that was not the work of the devil. Surely it was God's way of showing her how the job could be done, which meant that it was God who had led Wild Horse to the pond that day.

She held her skirt bunched in her arms so that it was well above her knees, then walked into the cool water. It felt wonderful. She tied the dress then so it would stay high and her hands would be free. She dipped them into the water and splashed its coolness onto her face and neck, rubbing it over the whites of her breasts, again feeling a sweet freedom at knowing Edward would be gone all day and she could do as she pleased. She laughed with Evy, splashed her, watched the child's blond curls dance in the sunlight.

"You can't stay in too long this time, Evy. You're still burned from the last time we were here. You've got to come out and sit in the shade. Mommy brought something for us to eat, and I'll read to you."

"Wild Horse! Wild Horse!" The child looked past her and ran out of the water before Margaret could catch her. Margaret turned, her eyes widening when she saw Wild Horse standing there. A naked little Evy ran right up to him and grabbed his hand, asking him to please come into the water with them.

Margaret wondered why her legs would not move. Wild Horse should not see her little girl this way . . . or see *her* this way! He let Evy pull him toward the bank, and Margaret's blood tingled at the way his dark eyes moved over her, drinking in her bared chest, her bare legs. For a moment she actually enjoyed the way he looked at her, *wanted* him to look. But suddenly it hit her how wanton she must seem, how sinful it was to let this Indian man see bare skin that even Edward had not seen! Where was her mind! And what made her think she was safe? This man was a known raider, probably a thief, maybe a killer and a rapist!

Her face reddened deeply, and she quickly untied her dress and let it fall, its hem drooping into the water and getting wet. She turned away from the man and frantically began buttoning the front of her dress, while Evy splashed at Wild Horse and laughed. Margaret turned back around and grabbed the girl up, shrouding her naked little body with her arms. "What are you doing here!" she demanded of Wild Horse.

"I remembered you said that when your husband comes to reservation, you come to pond. I wanted to see you again."

She hurried out of the water and grabbed up Evy's dress.

"No, Mommy! I want to play in the water with Wild Horse!"

"I told you we have to be careful you don't get burned more," Margaret explained, yanking the girl's dress down over her head. "Now be a good girl and try buttoning your dress by yourself. The buttons are in front. Show Mommy you can do it." She looked at Wild Horse, who had turned around to watch her. He wore a deerskin apron over his loincloth this time, but his legs were still bare, the sides of his buttocks revealed. Over his brawny chest he wore only a deerskin vest. His arms were bare and most of his chest revealed. His hair was pulled back and tied into a tail at the back of his neck, a neck that still showed bruises. The burn marks were a darker red and showed some scabbing, but the injuries did not distract from his chiseled, handsome face.

"You had no right sneaking up on us like that!" she told him. "No right looking at my little girl . . . and at me."

You liked it when I looked at you, he wanted to tell her. "What is wrong with looking at something precious and beautiful?" he asked aloud. "Do you think that because I am Cheyenne, I would do something terrible? I am not a man who looks upon little girls with bad thoughts. She is just a child, and she makes me think of Singing Bird, my own daughter."

"I can be your little girl," Evy said innocently.

Wild Horse smiled softly and looked at Margaret. "You see? She is not afraid of me. Why are you? Because you are a grown woman? Do you think I came here to violate you?"

Margaret's cheeks grew ever hotter. She turned to pick up the blanket and picnic basket she had brought. "We have to go, Evy."

"But, Mommy——"

Margaret gasped when a strong hand grasped her arm. She looked up into Wild Horse's dark eyes. So close! He was so close, and there was a scent of wildness about him that stirred her deeply. She felt wicked and sinful, part of her enjoying his touch, another part of her telling her she should run. "Let go of me!" she demanded.

"I want you to stay. I want to talk," he told her.

She had to force herself not to drop her eyes and gaze at his bare chest. What was this terrible temptation? "About what?"

"Just to thank you for helping me two suns ago . . . and for not telling the soldiers I am here."

"Fine. I accept your thanks. Now let go of me."

He frowned, letting loose of her arm. "What do you fear, Maggie?"

The way he spoke her name stunned her. The words were said softly, and for him to call her Maggie in an almost affectionate way brought another tingle that spread throughout her body. "I . . . I'm *not* afraid."

"I see it in your eyes. I am not here to hurt you. I told you why I am here, and it brings me joy to see and listen to your little girl."

Margaret looked around nervously. "It's dangerous for you to be here. Someone could see you. You're taking a great risk."

He smiled softly. "I am not afraid."

I am, Margaret thought, afraid of myself, not of you. Somehow she suspected he knew that, and she resented him for it. "Major Doleman has men out looking for you," she reminded him.

"I know this. My people tell me."

She watched his eyes. "You've been hiding at the reservation?"

He nodded. "I do not have family left, either my own or my wife's. I stay with friends."

Margaret moved away from him to where a tree shaded the grass. She set the blanket and basket on the ground again. "I'm sorry about what happened to your family. Major Doleman told us about it. We had dinner with him, the same day I saw you here at the pond." She spread the blanket out in the shade, wondering if God could ever forgive this sin of wanting to stay here alone and talk with an Indian man. "He also told us how you kept a prisoner with you in order to learn English. He thinks you did it to help keep your people from being cheated in treaty making." She looked back at him and saw some anger return to his eyes.

"It did little good. Even when treaties say wonderful things and promise us much, white men in place called Washington find a way to break it or to twist meaning of words. Your leaders are determined to have us all dead or pushed together on one little piece of land, and I know that they have power to do this. They are many, and we are few now. It is only a matter of time. My own fight will not help much, but I do it for pride. A man cannot just lie back and let others walk over him, even when he knows he cannot win."

Margaret frowned. "I'm worry, Wild Horse. I truly am. I disagree myself with a lot that has happened. I have even argued with my own husband over his ideas for helping the Cheyenne." She turned and called to Evy to come and sit down on the blanket and eat, then met Wild Horse's eyes again. "I brought some ham and bread and a jug of water. Would you like to eat with us?"

He looked around himself this time, and he reminded her of a wild animal. He seemed to be literally sniffing the air, his eyes studying the shadows in the trees around them. "I will sit," he told her then. "There is no one near."

She studied him in utter fascination. "Would you really know it if someone was near, even if you couldn't see them?"

He nodded. "I would know it. You whites do not keep all your senses trained. You are soft. You are used to living inside walls that destroy your sense of smell and hearing and seeing."

Margaret smiled and sat down on the blanket. "You're probably right."

Evy ran over and sat down beside her. "Are you going to eat with us, Wild Horse?" she asked.

The man smiled, and again Margaret was struck by how his whole face changed when he grinned. His teeth were even and white, his lips full. She imagined him playing inside a tipi with his own children. Were they so different after all? What was it like for an Indian woman when her man made love to her? She imagined they were much freer about it, perhaps lying naked in the light of day, taking a special joy in the act.

She nearly gasped aloud then at realizing what she had

been thinking. She kept her eyes averted from Wild Horse, afraid he would read her thoughts. "I'll make you a sandwich," she told him. She quickly cut some bread while he sat down, bending his legs and crossing them. Evy plopped down on her knees in front of him.

"Can you finish buttoning my dress?" she asked him.

He touched her cheek. "I will try, but my hands are big and clumsy for such little buttons."

Evy giggled at the remark, holding still while he buttoned the last few at the top of the bodice of the dress. Margaret thought how utterly furious Edward would be if he knew she was letting an Indian man touch Evy, or that he had seen their daughter naked . . . had seen his wife with her chest bared and her legs showing. She took secret pleasure in realizing how drastically she was disobeying her husband's wishes. She made a sandwich and poured some water into a tin cup. "It isn't much," she said, as she handed him the food.

He smiled softly, his fingers touching her own when he took it from her. "It looks like good meat. White men who make deals with government to sell them beef for reservations take money, then they sell good meat someplace else and give us bad meat. It is same for other supplies they bring us—all bad, no good. They make money from government, then make more from others who buy the good things from them and give them clothes and blankets that are worn and full of holes, fruit that is old. I could tell you many stories about how bad it is."

Margaret frowned. "But the government should know what is going on!"

He smiled bitterly. "They *do* know! They simply do not care." He shook his head, his eyes moving over her again. "You are so innocent of the truth, you and your husband both. Does he not know that as long as bellies are hungry and feet are cold, my people will not listen to what he has to say? He will not win them over until he helps to do something about how we are being cheated. Tell him to write to those who sent him here, people from his church. They can gather good things, good blankets and clothes and shoes and even food. If they would send these things, and if he would write letters to your Father in Washington, tell my people he understands how they are being cheated and that he is trying to stop it, then they would listen to his teachings about your Jesus."

Margaret's face brightened. "That is exactly what I told him a couple of nights ago! I told him he first has to truly care, that the Cheyenne know when someone is sincere. We argued about it." She handed a sandwich to Evy, who faced Wild Horse and sat cross-legged just like he did. "Evy, that is not a ladylike way to sit," Margaret chided. "Put your legs together and pull your dress down."

Wild Horse swallowed a bite of his sandwich. "Why do you care how she sits? This is most comfortable way to sit when you have nothing to lean against. You should try it yourself."

Margaret could not meet his gaze, totally embarrassed at the thought of sitting with her knees apart that way, even though her dress covered her. "It is a sinful way for a lady to sit," she said quietly, making herself a sandwich. When Wild Horse did not reply, she felt her cheeks growing hotter. Wild Horse probably had not even given thought to the implications of a woman sitting that way. She was the one who had made it seem sinful and suggestive, and was angry with herself for making it into something embarrassing.

"Can I please sit this way, Mommy? I want to sit like Wild Horse sits," the child begged. "Why is it bad?"

Margaret looked at her, then she heard a soft chuckle from Wild Horse. She was surprised to hear him laugh at all, but for the moment it irritated her. He was laughing at *her*. He knew she was embarrassed, and she was even more furious with herself for planting such thoughts in his head. She moved to the farthest corner of the blanket, wondering what he must think of her sitting in the grass like this with her. "Sit however you like then," she told Evy. "Just don't ever sit that way in front of your father."

Several moments of awkward silence followed while Wild Horse finished his sandwich. Margaret ate only a small piece of meat and drank some water, her appetite gone. It was Wild Horse who finally broke the silence.

"Why is it you *vehoe* think it is so bad to show your skin or to sit a certain way? Why must you wear so many heavy clothes when it is hot? Our little children always run naked in summer. Our women wear only light deerskin dresses with nothing under them. There is nothing bad in this. I think it is white man who *makes* it seem bad, because we have learned white men think with their manparts instead of with their heads. Because of this, little children cannot be naked and free, and their women must hide themselves under many layers of clothes."

Margaret could not bring herself to look at him. "Please don't talk that way in front of Evy." She breathed deeply to compose herself, shocked by his words, yet finding no argument for them. Did he realize how she longed to swim naked with Evy? The man was uncomfortably perceptive. She wished she could argue his point, but she knew he was right. If Indian children could play naked and Indian women could dress freely and comfortably without fear of Indian men getting the wrong ideas and attacking them, then which race was the more virtuous?

"What is a manpart, Mommy?" Evy asked innocently.

Wild Horse laughed aloud, and Margaret was mortified. She quickly rose. "Please leave, Wild Horse." She looked down at him, and he lost his smile.

"How easily offended you are. Do you not see I am trying to make you understand how my people think?" He set aside his sandwich and stood up to face her. "You think we need saving, that we cannot possibly be happy unless we live as you do. Do you not understand we were happy before you came? My people were once joyful and innocent. Our children sleep right beside the mother and father. They often see the mating, and they think nothing of it, because it a natural thing. They learn early in life that it is beautiful, a part of loving one another. Why should a child be taught it is wrong? It only makes them learn to be afraid of it so that later in life they never know how to enjoy it. I am thinking that you have never enjoyed your man."

What was this intense grip at her insides? Why did his bold and sinful words stir her to the bones? "You have no right speaking to me like that, certainly not in front of Evy."

A sneer moved across his face, and he shook his head in disgust. "Think about what I have told you. If you want to win my people, learn to share their joys and laugh with them. Learn not to be so serious all the time."

He put the back of his fingers to her cheek, and she could not bring herself to move away from him or even to take offense.

"I will come back here again when your husband is preaching at agency. If you want to understand more, you will come, too." He took his hand away. "I will tell you about what we believe, about Maheo. I think perhaps he is no different from your Jesus. Perhaps he *is* Jesus, come to us in another form with a different name. I will teach you that your God and mine are not so different."

He turned and quickly vanished into the underbrush, and Margaret stood there transfixed, her mind whirling with confusion, her body feeling on fire from his touch.

Edward watched his wife cut him a piece of bread. He wished she had not been so right about some of the things she had said the other night, wished even more that he could tell her so, but the fear of punishment for forbidden thoughts and emotions was still great in him. He could still see his father's angry, condescending looks whenever he "erred," could still feel his mother's coldness. Most of all he could still feel the paddle that often bruised his hips and legs and back, or the whip that left red welts on him. If they could be so unforgiving and dole out such punishment to their own son, what would God do to him if He took disfavor with him?

He loved his God, but his parents had also taught him to be afraid of Him. Part of his reason for coming here was to prove to his parents that he was a faithful servant, willing to go even to such a remote, dangerous, and lonely place as Indian Territory, to bring God's word to a people who had never heard it. Was Margaret right in saying that the Cheyenne sensed his heart was not in this? That he was here just to prove something to himself and his family and not because he particularly cared about the Cheyenne?

No. He must not admit to such a thing. Nor could he admit to himself or anyone else that he *did* sometimes want Margaret just for the woman she was, that he *did* sometimes feel a great passion, an absolute lusting after her, or that he *did* sometimes want to discuss her opinion about things. He wasn't sure now just how to tell her or that he should even be thinking such thoughts, for all his life he had been told all these things were wrong.

"The major says that Indian, Wild Horse, is supposedly dead," he said aloud. He noticed she hesitated in buttering his bread. What was that look on her face?

"Oh? How do they know that? Did they find him?" She handed him the buttered bread, meeting his eyes, but

Edward thought she looked startled, even afraid he might be right.

He took the bread, watching her closely. "No, but the soldiers who went after him say they ran into some cattlemen who claim they caught him with stolen cattle, and they hanged him. The soldiers went to find the body, but it wasn't there. Now they're not sure what to believe. I can't imagine a man could get himself out of a noose. The captain feels his own people found him and took down his body, but he believes, and so do I, that the Cheyenne would surely be more upset, maybe even do something drastic, if they found a leader like Wild Horse hanged. Those at the Darlington Agency haven't even seen Wild Horse, or heard anything about his dying. The Cheyenne there have a way of keeping in touch with the wilder ones who continue to roam and raid, so they would probably know."

"So the captain *doesn't* think he is dead?"

"He doesn't quite know *what* to think."

"What would he do if he found him alive?" she asked cautiously. Edward cut a piece of meat with more vigor than required, and Margaret knew he was becoming irritated again that she should dare to ask questions about army matters.

"What difference does it make, Margaret? They would send him off to prison, I suppose. He stirs up too much trouble."

Prison. Such a beautifully spiritual man in such an awful place. It didn't seem fair. And the way Edward had said her name, so cold and with anger. He had never spoken it the way Wild Horse had the other day, with a kind of touching reverence.

"Wild Horse helped me button my dress once," Evy spoke up.

She swallowed some peas, and Edward frowned. "Evy, you are going to have to stop making up these stories. God does not approve of little girls telling tall tales. I have never had to punish you for anything in your life, but I *will* if you keep letting your imagination run away with you like that."

Evy pouted, and Margaret ached to defend her innocent daughter. She was on the verge of blurting out the truth, for Evy's sake, when Evy looked at her and grinned, seemingly unaffected by her father's threats. She covered her mouth and giggled, and Margaret decided not to say anything yet. If it came to Evy being terribly upset or unnecessarily punished, she would have to betray her word to Wild Horse that she would not tell where he was, although she knew she would have to tell eventually. Maybe Wild Horse would just leave again and never be found. Then she could keep her secret forever. Yet the thought of his leaving brought an ache to her heart, stirring a loneliness she could not explain. She realized that when the day came that she could never see the man again, she would miss him.

It had been five days since their last meeting. Because of the sinful way the man made her feel, she had stayed away from the pond the last time Edward went to the reservation. Had Wild Horse gone there and waited for her? Was he angry? Disappointed? Maybe he had already fled again. It seemed incredible he would stay so close and risk being arrested by the soldiers, maybe sent to a prison in Florida, just so he could come to the pond and see her again. The thought of it gave her a feeling of worth and being wanted that Edward had never given her.

Had Edward thought about the things she told him? He behaved as though their conversation of a few nights ago had never happened. They finished supper with little more conversation, and then it was time for Bible reading and prayers. Evy fell asleep before Edward was finished, and he insisted Margaret wake her up, that she must not sleep during the reading of the Word. Finally he finished, and Margaret put Evy to bed. By the time she finished her own chores for the evening, Edward was already in bed. She changed in the darkness, crawled in beside him on the feather mattress and curled up to go to sleep, but he turned to her, pushing up her nightgown.

"We need to try again for a child," he told her.

That was how he always approached her—never "Maggie, I love you. Maggie, I want you, I need you." Margaret knew that sometimes he really did want her out of pure physical need, but he always used the excuse that it was time to try to get her pregnant again. Didn't he understand how deeply she ached to hear the right words? To have him pull off her gown and rub his naked skin against her own? To kiss her deeply, to touch her in secret places?

No. There was just this. She must obey by opening her legs so that he could quickly invade her. She must not arch up to him or make any noises that might suggest she enjoyed this. Edward, too, remained silent. While he took her,

Margaret was astonished to realize she was imagining someone else doing this to her. His skin was dark, his brawny chest hovering over her. His hair hung over his shoulders and brushed against her own naked breasts. The thought brought such a surge of passion that she almost cried out his name, but she could only imagine Wild Horse invading her this way.

Edward finished with her quickly and rolled off of her, getting up to go into the curtained-off washroom near the bedroom. Margaret felt him get back into bed then. "I will pray that this time the seed will take and that you will keep this one," he told her. "You can go and wash now."

Margaret silently got up to go to the washroom, stifling a need to burst into tears.

Chapter Four

Margaret lifted her skirt and walked through the underbrush to the pond. It had stormed last night, and today was cooler but humid. She had promised Evy she could look for frogs and tadpoles, but that was only an excuse to come here, and she came against her better judgment. Why didn't she just continue to stay away? Why was it so important to know if Wild Horse had gone away again? If he had, she had missed her chance to learn what she could from him about the Cheyenne way, and maybe that was a big mistake. Maybe God had sent him to her after all.

And maybe that was all just her own manner of reasoning, so that she did not feel guilty about coming here. It was much too dangerous for her heart and her sense of moral values to be here, hoping to find an Indian man for whom she had lusted while her own husband made love to her; yet here she was, looking around, hoping. Evy ran to the edge of the pond with a little strainer and a bucket.

Margaret stood silent, watching the reeds, the underbrush, the bushes and trees. It would be just like Wild Horse to be here without her even knowing it—watching her. What did he think about her? Did he want her as a woman? She was sure she had seen it in those dark eyes.

"So, you finally chose to return."

The voice came from behind her and she gasped and turned. Because of the cool day, he was fully dressed today, and he looked magnificent in fringed, deerskin pants and shirt. The shirt was unlaced at the neck, and his chest sported a beautiful turquoise stone that hung around his neck on a piece of rawhide. Another necklace was tied around his throat, and she noticed his neck had healed nicely. His hair hung long and loose, except that some of it was tied at the side of his head with a beautiful, round, beaded hairpiece held in place by what looked like a piece of bone.

"I wasn't sure you would come," she told him.

Yes, you were, he wanted to answer. But that would embarrass her, and she might run off. "Why did you not come the last time?"

She swallowed. Because of what you do to my heart,

Wild Horse, and my common sense. "I was afraid if I came too often, I would be found out, and then you might be caught."

He smiled and nodded, and Margaret suspected he did not believe her. Damn him! His eyes seemed to drill right through to her heart. She looked away. "You look better, and your voice sounds stronger."

"I am healing."

She felt him walk up close behind her. "Major Doleman thinks you're dead, or at least he probably hopes you are," she told him. "The cattlemen reported hanging you, but they couldn't find your body, so he isn't quite sure what to think."

"The captain is a fool. But I suppose he is sure to discover I am alive. I cannot stay here for much longer."

But I don't want you to go, Wild Horse. "You're right."

"So . . . why did you come?"

She shrugged, watching Evy chase after tadpoles. "Be careful, Evy. Don't fall in!" How could she answer him? With the truth? No, she must never shame herself that way. "I just wondered if you were all right, if you were even still around."

"Wild Horse!" Evy noticed him then and came running, carrying her bucket, which looked much too big in her small hand. "Look what I have!"

Wild Horse walked past her to greet the child. He knelt down and looked into the bucket, dipping his hand inside to scoop up a few tadpoles. "Ah, you have found beginning of new life," he told her.

Evy frowned. "Huh?"

He held out his palm, in which two tadpoles wiggled and squirmed. "Some day they will be frogs and toads." He put them back into the bucket of water. "You were once a tadpole. Did you know that? The Great Spirit gave you life, and now here you are, much prettier than any frog!"

Margaret thought to object. Edward would be outraged if he knew an Indian man was telling Evy such a story.

Evy giggled. "I'm going to find some more babies!" she exclaimed, running back to the pond.

Wild Horse rose and watched after her, then turned to meet Margaret's eyes. "When Indian children reach seven or eight summers, they know all about life, how it is made, how it grows. They have seen their parents mate, watched their mothers give birth. They know beauty of life. Children mean everything to my people. They mean continuation of our blood, our race."

She folded her arms and walked closer to him. "Tell me more, Wild Horse, about this being you call Maheo, about your beliefs."

He spread his powerful arms. "Great Spirit is in all of us, Maggie, not just in heavens looking down on us and judging us, as your husband preaches. He is *in* us, and in earth, trees, sky, water, animals—everything. We call our God Maheo. You call yours Jehova."

Her eyebrows arched in surprise.

He looked proudly down his handsome nose at her.

"You think I know nothing about your God, but I know much, and I believe your Jesus is same as our prophet, who is called Sweet Medicine. Sweet Medicine appeared to my people many, many winters ago, and taught them right way to live. He also told them to beware of men with pale skin and hairy faces who would one day come to destroy us."

He held her gaze with his own dark eyes, and she felt lost in him as he spoke. "Unlike you, we do not believe our God sits in judgment and punishes us. He is inside of us. He speaks to us through spirits that are in everything. There is Heammawihio, Wise One Above, and Ahktunowihio, God Who Lives Under Ground. Every living thing contains a spirit, and that is why, when we kill an animal for food, we thank its spirit for offering its body to give us strength and nourishment. It is through these many spirits that we find our visions. Like your Jesus, Cheyenne men fast and make blood offerings in order to have a vision and find our special spirit path. My guiding spirit is a great, white, wild horse. Spirit of that horse dwells within me, and that is why I must be free."

"Mommy, I caught a frog!" Evy exclaimed. She held the green, squirming creature up, then screamed and dropped it when it began wildly flailing its legs. She laughed and went running after it, and Wild Horse joined in the laughter. Margaret watched him, thinking again how handsome he was when he smiled. Why had she never pictured Indians laughing before she met Wild Horse?

"I want to meet again, Wild Horse, so that I can write these things down. I wish I had brought a tablet and pen today. I could never properly spell the names of some of these spirits of yours, but I will do my best."

They walked together to the edge of the pond, and Margaret opened the blanket she had brought along. They both sat down to watch Evy. Margaret wished Edward would sit like this with someone like Wild Horse and just listen. It would help him so much in reaching these people to understand their own perception of God.

"What do you believe about life after death, Wild Horse?"

He closed his eyes and breathed deeply. "When our bodies are dead on this earth, our spirits continue. Our spirit follows the hanging road made of stars up to a new land, where grass is always green, and there are still many buffalo . . . and no white men. Those who go before us are happy there, always warm, bellies always full, free to ride and hunt at will. They play games and live in fine lodges, and children are happy. I will be glad to go there. We always bury a man or woman's most precious belongings with them when their bodies are dead, things their spirit can use in hereafter—clothing and weapons for hunting."

He turned to meet her eyes. "All nature is sacred, Maggie. That is why we cannot understand why white man wants to put his sharp plow into Grandmother Earth, tearing at her. Earth is sacred. White man cuts down trees that he does not even need for fire, just so he can clear land. Spirit in tree cries out every time man puts his ax to its soul. At one time, earth, sky creatures, animals, buffalo—they all gave my people everything they needed for survival, and nothing was wasted. White man wastes everything. He skins sacred buffalo just for hide, leaving all good meat and other parts to rot in sun. My people use every part of buffalo. They burn only old, rotten wood from trees already fallen, trees that have given up themselves to us. Even the smallest rock is not moved by my people without great care."

He raised up on one elbow, realizing that she seemed intently interested. This was a rare white woman. She cared. She wanted to learn. "We do not try to say how our God thinks and feels. We do not fear our God. We live in Him and through Him. We do not concern ourselves with how this world began. It is not necessary for us to understand these things. We accept our world as it is, thank the spirits for gifts they give us. We do not try to rule our world or animals or try to change things as white man does. Life is simply a circle, Maggie. It is formed by union of man and woman; it is born, it lives, it dies and goes back to spirit form. Before it dies, it creates more life, and on and on. This earth is here for us to use while we are upon it, and we do not try to understand how it got here, how we got here. We are here, we live, we love, we laugh . . . and we cry. Life is life. White man tries to make it so confusing, when it does not have to be. Life is simply to be enjoyed. Man should embrace all spirits around him and in him. He should be happy in today, like a little child, like your Evy, taking pleasure simply in catching little frogs."

Margaret felt mesmerized. She saw this man in a new light, and to her amazement, she understood exactly what he was trying to tell her. Life did not have to be the somber burden men like Edward seemed to think it should be. Life was joy, and it was not wrong or sinful to be full of that joy, to embrace life and love, to want to let one's spirit soar. How she wished she could share all of this with Edward, but he would never understand.

"Wild Horse, look!" Evy came back to them with even more tadpoles in her bucket.

Wild Horse grinned. "You should thank their spirits for allowing you to catch them. It has been a good game, but before you go, you should put them back in water so they can be free again."

"But I want to keep them!"

Wild Horse touched her arm. "It is not right, little one. You would not want to be put in cage, would you, where you can never run free and see your mother and father, eat what you want, go where you please? Things that cannot be free soon die. You do not want them to die before they have a chance to become frogs, do you?"

Evy puckered her lips. "No. I'll put them back, but first I want to sit and watch them a little while."

Wild Horse nodded. "That is fine." He turned to Margaret. "Can you understand that is how it is for my people? Being on reservation makes them feel like they are in a prison. Many die just from a broken heart, because they cannot go home to land farther north from which they come. They cannot go to the cool mountains. They cannot ride and hunt freely. This is why many turn to firewater. It helps them forget, soothes their sad spirits."

Margaret's eyes misted. "I think I do understand, Wild

Horse. I wish I could change it all for you, but it's never going to be the same again. Surely you know that."

She was astonished to see his own eyes tear, and he turned away. "I do know it." He sighed and rose. "I must go now. I will come again, but not for much longer. Soon I must go away."

Margaret got to her feet, her throat feeling tight. How she hated the thought of him going, but it would be such a waste if he got caught and sent to a horrible prison in Florida. "I understand that, too," she told him. "Don't let them catch you, Wild Horse. A man like you would be better off dead than——"

She could not finish. He met her eyes, and she knew he had been thinking that very thing. For several long seconds she could not bring herself to look away from him. There was so much in that look, so many unspoken words. "I don't want anything to happen to you, Wild Horse."

His eyes moved over her almost lovingly. "The spirit of the horse will decide what happens to me. Either I will leave and be able to live free, or I will die. There are no other choices. I can see that you understand."

And if I did not belong to someone else, I think I would go with you, she thought. "I understand. How soon will you go?" She felt drawn to him, unlike anything she had ever experienced.

"I should already have gone. I stayed because of you. If telling you about my people and how we believe can somehow help them, then I will stay until you understand all of it." Finally he turned away from her. "Come here again when your husband is gone. Bring your paper and pen so you can put what I tell you onto paper. I cannot read white man's writing, but I trust you to say it right." He looked around, again the wild animal being cautious. "I go now."

He walked off into the stand of trees, and Margaret watched after him until she could no longer see him. "God, protect him," she whispered.

For another two weeks Margaret lay beside her stiff and silent husband at night, dreaming about another man, and every chance she got she met Wild Horse at the pond. It was he who taught her about freedom and spiritualism and how to feel close to nature and to God. Sometimes he brought a flute and played for her. Evy had made a new friend at the fort, Rose Hart, a girl two years older who was the daughter of a new lieutenant who had been assigned to the fort and had brought his family. Margaret welcomed the chance to send Evy someplace else to play so that she could be alone with Wild Horse, all the while realizing what a dangerous thing she was doing—more dangerous for her own heart than for any other reason. She told herself that meeting him and learning the Cheyenne customs and beliefs was impor-tant to understanding his people, and that was partly true. But she knew the real reason she kept going back to the pond.

She loved Wild Horse. It was a different kind of love than what she felt for Edward. She could and would never tell Wild Horse how she felt, although she suspected he knew. In fact, she was sure she saw love in his own dark eyes, but neither of them spoke of such things. They talked only about their different cultures, and sometimes she just lay back on the blanket and let the summer breeze flow over her while he played the flute for her—haunting, touching music that floated across the pond and into the trees and made her feel so serene, so close to God, so free. Sinful as it was, she could not bring herself to stop meeting him, nor was she quite sure it was truly wrong. Sometimes she still brought Evy, who seemed to adore Wild Horse. She was more open and happy around him than she was around her own father.

She knew through Wild Horse that his people did have a wonderful sense of humor, a special joy about them in spite of their suffering. She wrote down everything he told her in a notebook she kept hidden from Edward. Wild Horse talked about life on the open plains, about how a Cheyenne man sought his vision, about the Sundance ritual. Now she knew how he had gotten the scars at his breasts. He had also told her about Sand Creek, his words bitter, finally trailing off into a quiet sob. Yes, the Cheyenne loved and grieved like anyone else. How sad that most of her own people thought of them more like animals, just because they lived differently.

She was taking terrible chances, yet could not bring herself to put an end to the meetings. She wondered at her own boldness of taking her heart into dangerous territory, where it could be shattered at any time. Nothing could ever come of her feelings for Wild Horse, and she knew that soon it would have to end, for he must go away, or die fighting the soldiers that might come for him. She also realized she had to think about Evy, the shame on the family if anyone ever knew about what she was doing. Yet every chance she got, she came back, and Wild Horse was always there waiting for her.

Part of her fought madly against forbidden emotions, and another part of her yearned to break free and be wild and wanton, to be held by those strong arms, to know the ecstasy of making love for the sheer pleasure of it. When she said her prayers at night and asked for forgiveness of her sins, the magnitude of what she was doing would nearly overwhelm her, and she wondered if she would burn in hell for it. Yet she could not help feeling sometimes as though there was not one thing wrong in any of it . . . as though God had led her into this strange new world for a purpose.

They grew closer, happy in each other's company. Again she met him. How many times was this? Ten? Eleven? She had left Evy behind this time to play with Rose. It was a lovely day—warm, but not too hot. She lay back on the blanket and let Wild Horse play the flute for her again. The music made her feel so serene. Apparently no one at the fort could hear, or else they thought the music was coming from the agency.

She closed her eyes and listened, full of ideas about how she could help the Cheyenne, wishing Edward would listen to her. Suddenly the flute playing stopped, and a shadow blocked the sun from her eyes. When she opened them, Wild Horse was leaning over her, resting on his elbows . . . so close! She started to sit up, but he pressed her shoulder back against the blanket.

"You know that we are falling too deep, Maggie."

She swallowed back a sudden lump in her throat. "We're just friends."

"Are we?" He touched her hair, and she shivered. "This cannot last, but there is one more thing I will teach you before I go away."

A tear slipped down one side of her face. "I don't want you to go away."

He put a finger to her lips. "I want you to come to the agency, even though your husband forbids it. When he goes again, follow him. My people will welcome you. I have told them how good you are. Your husband will be surprised at how open they are to you. He will see that you have been right, that you must make friends first. Will you come?"

She sniffled. "If that's what you want."

He leaned down and licked the tear from her cheek, and she gasped at the literal pain of want that ripped through her. "Wild Horse," she whispered, thinking how good he smelled, like fresh air and the earth. His face was close, and she could not quell the surging desires he stirred in her. She raised up and met his lips in a hungry kiss, wishing Edward would let her kiss him this way.

Wild Horse drew in his breath when she bit lightly at his lower lip. Margaret was not even sure why she had done it, surprised at the lustful feelings he stirred in her. He pulled away, a grin on his face. "What is this you do with your mouth?"

She smiled. "I kissed you! Don't your people kiss?"

He frowned, touching his lips. "No." He smiled again.

"But it is a nice thing, this kissing." Suddenly his smile faded, and look of wild desire came into his eyes. He quickly sat up. "It is not time yet," he said softly.

Time for what? she wanted to ask, but she already knew the answer. There would never be a right time, for it was forbidden. I love you, Wild Horse! She could not say it, for saying it would only make it hurt all the more when she finally had to admit nothing could be done about that love. He had added that word "yet." Did he mean something *should* be done about this? How could it, when she belonged to another man, and he belonged to another world?

He got up and picked up his flute. "Come to reservation," he repeated.

"I will."

He looked down at her like a conquering warrior, and she knew that if he were to kiss her again, she would be lost in him completely. He turned and quietly left, and every bone, every part of her flesh ached for her forbidden Cheyenne lover. That was how she thought of him, although he had not touched her that way . . . yet.

She closed her eyes and crumpled into the blanket weeping, begging God's forgiveness and guidance, for she was fast losing control of all her emotions. Her world had been turned upside down by a man who was supposed to be less intelligent, less educated, less civilized . . . but she didn't think any of those things about him. To her he had become superior. It was as though he held some special power over her so that when she was with him, she could not think straight.

"I can't come here anymore," she told herself. "I simply can't. It will destroy my marriage, my self-respect." She got up and wiped at her eyes, picked up the blanket, and hurried away. She decided she would go to the reservation the next time Edward went, and not to the pond. She would *never* go back to the pond!

Chapter Five

*E*dward preached about Jesus to three old men and two middle-aged women, who all spoke and understood just enough English to have some conception of what he was telling them, but who also looked at him with rather blank faces. He knew he was fast losing their attention, and he lost it completely when a commotion stirred to his right and a little behind him. He turned to see several Cheyenne gathered around something or someone. They were mostly women and children, but there were also a few men there. They were all carrying on in their own tongue, the women apparently very excited about something. There was some laughter as they passed something around among them, and the few people who had been listening to him got up and abruptly walked away to join in the excitement.

Disgusted, Edward closed his Bible and donned his hat. He marched over to the babbling group of Indians, hoping to get all their attention away from whatever was so interesting. He was beginning to wonder why he bothered to come here. Maybe Maggie was right. Maybe they should go to some white settlement where there were good, Christian people hungry to hear God's word. Besides, his wife had been so changed since coming here that he hardly knew her. He thought that perhaps if he got her away from here, where she would be around women more like herself, he might get the old Maggie back. The only other women here were the major's wife, who was cold and not much of a visitor, and the new lieutenant's wife. He was glad the lieutenant had a little girl Evy could play with, but the lieutenant's wife also did not intend to stay long. Evy would again need other children with whom to play, and Maggie certainly needed the company of other Christian white women.

He quietly moved into the crowd of Indians to see what had gotten their attention, and there spread out on the grass he recognized one of Maggie's prettiest quilts, a colorful star pattern that the Indian women were ogling as though it were gold. Displaying it was his own wife! While several of the women eyed the quilt, Maggie was handing out pieces of ribbon in many colors, as well as buttons and some cloth. "Who among you speaks English?" she asked with a smile.

"Maggie! What in God's name are you doing here!"

Margaret lost her smile as her husband pushed his way through to stand in front of her. Before she could answer, he noticed Evy playing in the distance with some Indian children. Because the weather had grown hotter again, the Indian children ran naked, including the little boys! Evy herself wore a dress, but her feet were bare.

"I am trying to win these people's friendship," Margaret answered.

He met her eyes, his own showing rage. "How did you get here!"

"I walked. It's a nice day."

"The agency is a whole mile from the fort! You walked here *alone*, with our daughter, exposing yourself and her to the dangers of savages?"

Margaret faced him, unflinching. "I simply took a walk on a beautiful day to come here and make some friends, which will ultimately help you in your work, Edward. I felt no risk and no fear. Perhaps if you would stop thinking of these people as savages, you would see them for who they really are—lost souls, a lonely, displaced people. They have a wonderful sense of humor and dignity. I have brought them gifts. I want to show them I care and that I trust them enough to let my child play with their children! Now stand aside. I want to give my quilt to someone. Do you know if any of these people here speaks English?"

Edward stared in disbelief.

"I speak some white man tongue," an old woman told her. She was skinny and almost toothless, and her thinning, gray hair was tied in two tails at either shoulder. In spite of her age and size, she was obviously strong, as she marched up to Margaret and literally pushed Edward aside. "Who gets pretty blanket?"

Margaret smiled. "Who among you is most recently married? She will need a warm blanket this winter for her and her husband."

Edward reddened, but the Indians laughed when the old woman interpreted Margaret's statement. A shy young woman who looked to Margaret as though she could not be more than fifteen, stepped forward. She was chubby, and her face showed marks from either measles or smallpox, but she was still pretty.

"This is Summer Storm," the old woman told Margaret. "She took a husband only five suns ago."

Margaret picked up the quilt and handed it out to the girl. "Then please accept this from me and my husband as a wedding present."

The old lady told the girl what Margaret said, and Summer Storm's eyes widened with delight. She took the quilt with a wide smile. *Ha-ho*, she told Margaret in a quiet voice.

"She says thank you," the old woman told Margaret.

Several women who had been given ribbons and buttons also thanked Margaret. One stood holding a rolling pin. She touched it as though it were a most wonderful thing, then said something to Margaret. The old woman interpreted for her. "She says she will use the wooden instrument you gave her to crush corn for flour and berries for juice and to use in making pemmican."

"What is pemmican?" Margaret asked.

"It is a special food we make from meat and berries and fat. They are dried and crushed together and cut into strips. It lasts long time. Our warriors carry pemmican when out on hunt or in battle." The words were spoken as though the woman still expected life to be that way for her people again.

"I see," Margaret told her.

"Margaret!" Edward interrupted. "How dare you tell that girl we've given her a wedding gift! Don't you realize none of these people gets married the Christian way? That girl is living in sin, and you have *encouraged* it!"

Margaret held her chin high. "Most of these people marry for the same reasons we do—for love, and to have children. The women remain chaste until they take a husband, and they do not cheat on their husbands. Where is the difference, Edward? They have their ways of marrying, with a special ceremony and all, just like we do. Who is to say our own people are any more married than theirs, just because we marry in a church and have a piece of paper that supposedly makes it legitimate? In fact, I don't doubt there is more love in some of the marriages among the Cheyenne than there is in some of our own marriages!"

Edward paled. Was she referring to *their* marriage? Had his wife lost her mind? "How do you know anything about the feelings of the Cheyenne or their marriage ceremonies?"

She turned away, thinking, Because I am in love with one. Because I have been meeting with the notorious Wild

Horse, and he has taught me many things. Poor Edward would probably have a heart attack if she told him the truth. "I studied about them before we came here. I wanted to know."

Edward put his hands on his hips. "I am very disappointed in you, Margaret."

She finally met his eyes again. "Did you ever stop to wonder if sometimes maybe *I* am disappointed in *you*?" She turned to the old woman. "Tell the women that they may keep their presents only if they listen to my husband talk to them for a few minutes. Tell them he and I truly care about them and wish to share our God with them. We understand they have a God, and he is called Maheo. Tell them we believe Maheo is the same as our God."

The old woman smiled and called out to some of those who had started to leave. She told them what Margaret said, and most of them wandered back. In spite of the heat, Summer Storm had the lovely quilt wrapped around her shoulders. A few of them had some words for Margaret, and the old woman turned to her. "They say they will listen, only if *you* stay. They do not much like your husband, but because he has such a good and kind woman, they say he must be a good man, too. They will listen about his God. I will tell them what he says."

"Promise to tell them true," Margaret said to the old woman. "We have to trust you to say exactly what my husband says."

The woman nodded. "I will do this." She looked at Edward and smiled, and Edward turned to Margaret with confusion in his eyes. She realized he didn't know whether to be angry or grateful.

"Please get Evy away from those naked boys," he told her quietly.

Margaret stood her ground. "Evy is just fine. She is a child, Edward. She does not see their nakedness. What better way to learn about such things than through innocent eyes, through joyfulness and playing? There isn't one sinful or evil thought among those children. All you have to concern yourself with is preaching God's word to these people who have promised to listen. Tell them you are grateful for their attention. Tell them you know about their prophet, Sweet Medicine. Tell them you believe he is the same as our Christ."

"What?"

"Just do it, Edward. I will explain later. If you tell them that, they will listen to you, because you will be relating to something they know about and believe in. There is no sin in that, Edward. God will understand why you compared Jesus to Sweet Medicine."

Edward blinked, looking down at his Bible. Margaret put her hand over his. "Do it, Edward. You came here to preach to them. I have found a way to make them listen, at least for today."

Edward turned to them and opened his Bible. He began hesitantly, his astonishment at his wife's behavior making it difficult for him to concentrate.

Margaret glanced over to where Evy was playing. She had taken off her dress and underclothes and was running naked with the rest of the children, her long, blond hair dancing in the wind. She grabbed a little Indian girl's hand and they began picking wildflowers together.

"So, tell us, Maggie, some of the men here told my husband you walked off to the Indian agency alone, you and Evy. Why in the world did you do a thing like that? And why didn't you just go with Edward?"

The pointed questions came from Gloria Doleman. The woman served Margaret a glass of lemonade. She had invited Margaret and Lieutenant Hart's wife, Josie, to the major's quarters to visit, and Evy played with Rose in the courtyard in front of the building.

Margaret thanked Gloria for the lemonade. She relaxed into the wicker chair on the front porch of the building, the overhanging roof protecting all three women from the hot sun. "Edward has never allowed me to go with him to the reservation," she answered Gloria. She sipped some of the lemonade, hating talking with someone like Gloria about what she had done. The woman could never understand it in a hundred years.

"Then why did you go?" Gloria persisted. "Surely you know you did a very dangerous thing, Maggie."

"Yes. I would never dream of going there alone," Josie Hart put in. "Let alone subject Rose to those savages. God only knows what you and Evy could pick up there; lice, for one thing."

"The Cheyenne are very clean," Margaret answered. "I was not afraid. People only fear what they don't understand,

and I have studied the Cheyenne enough not to be afraid of them. Actually, it was quite a nice experience." She met Gloria's discerning green eyes. "I went without Edward's permission because I wanted to prove to him that I could help him in his work. I think I proved my point."

Gloria's eyes narrowed. "And how is that, dear?"

Margaret tried to appear unaffected by that gaze, but she felt as though Gloria Doleman could see right through her. Maybe it was her own guilty conscience over meeting Wild Horse at the pond so many times that made her imagine everyone else knew what was going on. "I took gifts," she replied. "They were very receptive to that. I found an old woman who speaks English, and I had her tell the others I understood about their God and their prophet, Sweet Medicine. I compared Sweet Medicine to our Christ, and they seemed to understand then what my husband had been trying to tell them."

Edward had been very quiet in the two days since she went to the reservation. His feelings were hurt to realize his wife had been able to reach the Indians when he had not; yet Margaret knew that deep inside he was grateful for giving him a way to approach the Cheyenne. He didn't quite know what to make of her, and she didn't know what to make of herself. She felt removed from her body. The person others saw was the same Margaret Gibbons she had always been, but the Margaret on the inside was confused, feeling a new power, new desires.

"And how is it you know so much about the Cheyenne religion?" Gloria pressed. "You learned all of that in books?"

Margaret felt the unwanted flush come into her cheeks. "Yes." No. I learned it from a man, a spiritual and very handsome man who makes me feel like a beautiful, wanted woman just by the way he looks at me.

"Quite a wonder," Gloria answered. "One would think you have been talking with one of those Cheyenne. I doubt there are many books that go very deeply into the religion of the Plains Indians. What is this book that you read, Maggie?"

"What?" Margaret had been hardly aware the woman was speaking. Her thoughts had drifted to a dark vision hovering over her . . . to a quiet pond. . . .

"I said, what is this book you read in which you learned so much about the Cheyenne?"

"And why would you care?" Josie added.

Margaret watched Evy and Rose play, unable at the moment to meet either woman's eyes. "I have forgotten the name of it. I borrowed it from a library in Massachusetts before we left to come here. I took a lot of notes," she answered, hoping God would not strike her down for the partial lie. She had taken notes, but they were straight from Wild Horse's mouth. She finally looked at Josie Hart. "I care because Edward cares. I care because he came here to bring God's word to the Cheyenne, and I wanted to find a way to help him do that."

Evy and Rose came up on the porch then. "Wild Horse says we used to be tadpoles," Rose told her mother.

"Wild Horse?" Josie frowned. "Rose, wherever did you get such an idea, and why would you make up such a story? You have never seen that bad Indian called Wild Horse."

"Evy has. She said he helped her get tadpoles one day at a pond, and he told her they were baby frogs, and we used to be babies like that."

Josie looked in dismay at Margaret. "Margaret, where does your daughter come up with such stories?"

Margaret felt the heat in her face, but she managed a look of deep concern. "I can't imagine. I'll have a talk with her. She has had this idea lately that she knows Wild Horse. I suppose it's because there has been so much talk about him."

"I suppose," Gloria put in, her eyes drilling into Margaret. "Such an imagination."

Margaret finished her lemonade. "I really must get home. Edward will be coming back soon, and I have to start supper."

"Why didn't you go with him today to the agency?" Josie asked.

"I don't want to interfere too much. I just went the other day to see if I could find a way to help make them listen to him. I don't need to go with him every time." She could have gone to the pond. Wild Horse had probably gone there looking for her, but she had vowed to stay away. She must not go back, not ever! She had nearly lost her heart the last time, and something more. If Wild Horse touched her again, she would do something she would regret for the rest of her life. She was Edward Gibbons's wife, and Wild Horse was a man doomed to flee or die. Nothing could change either of those situations, and she was a fool to carelessly submit herself to terrible sin and worse heartache.

Margaret rose and bid her good-bye, taking Evy's hand and walking off with her. Gloria watched them. She did not believe for one second that Evy was making up her stories. She was a sweet child, very open . . . and children had a habit of usually speaking the truth. "Out of the mouths of babes," she muttered.

"What did you say, Gloria?" Josie spoke up.

"Oh, nothing. I was just thinking." Should she tell her husband her thoughts? Would he laugh at her for suggesting she believed Wild Horse might be right here under his nose? It certainly couldn't hurt to make a search at the agency. If he *was* here, what on earth did Margaret Gibbons have to do with any of it? The woman had guilt written all over her pretty face. How delicious to think that the good minister's wife might be secretly meeting with a wild Cheyenne man!

Margaret could keep her vow no longer. Surely Wild Horse would leave soon, and she could not let him go without seeing him once more, if for nothing more than to thank him for sharing so much with her, for showing her a joy she had never known before. The heat today was miserable and stifling, but she would not let it keep her from walking to the pond. Evy was with Rose, and Edward was at the agency. She did not bring a blanket, for she did not plan to stay long, and she did not dare sit or lie back on a blanket again with Wild Horse sitting near her.

His kiss had burned into her like a brand. For the rest

of her life she would not forget the taste of it, the feel of his full lips opening to her. It had been thrilling for that little moment to be the one in control. She had been the teacher then, showing Wild Horse something pleasurable and exciting. Never did she think she could be so bold, but he brought out a wildness in her she had not even known was there, a dangerous passion that after today must be reserved for no one but Edward. If only her husband recognized that passion and allowed her to share it.

She knew it had hurt him when she went to the agency, but she had not meant to make her proud husband feel inadequate. She had only meant to help, and through helping, perhaps find a way to be closer to Edward. So far it had not worked. She had tried so many times to get him to talk to her, to tell her of any feelings, dreams, fears he wanted to share, but right now they seemed farther apart than they had ever been. She knew it was partly because of this secret love she shared with another, and it must end. After today . . .

"So, at last you come again."

The words interrupted her thoughts, and she turned to see Wild Horse standing behind her. She put a hand to her chest to still her heart. He looked magnificent, wearing only a loincloth, his hair clean and shining, hanging loose, down past her shoulders. "How do you do that, Wild Horse? I never hear you."

He grinned. "You are not supposed to hear me. When one lives off the land, one must know how to stalk the enemy and how to track his prey without being seen or heard or smelled."

"Is that what I am to you? Your prey?"

He smiled sadly. "Maybe." He walked closer, and she wondered if a more perfect specimen of man existed. "You have come to say good-bye. Tonight I leave, but that is not why you would say good-bye. You belong to another, but your heart is beginning to betray you, so you came to tell me you will no longer meet me here."

She looked away, always surprised at how he knew everything she was thinking. "It's wrong for me to feel this way." She felt a strong hand on her shoulder then, and she shivered at the touch.

"It is never wrong to love, Maggie, and if you did not belong to another, if our worlds were not so far apart . . ." He ran a thumb into the bun at the nape of her neck. "Why do you always wear your hair so plain and tight? I want to see it hanging long, just once, before I go. Take these combs from your hair, Maggie."

She still could not look at him, yet already she was under his commanding spell. Why could she never say no to this man? She reached up and pulled out the combs that held the bun in a twist, then undid the barrette that held it pulled together. She shook out her long, blond tresses and trembled when she felt his hand run through them.

"You have the most beautiful hair I have ever seen. Does your husband like it this way?"

She swallowed. "Please, Wild Horse, I came here to thank you for everything you have shared with me . . . and for showing me a way of life I never realized was so beautiful. I will never forget—"

"Maggie."

The name was spoken with such tenderness that she could not finish. The tears came then, and she turned. In the next moment she was in his arms, a wonderful, strong, warm embrace that made her move her own arms around him. She had never rested her face against a man's bare chest before. It was comforting. There was nothing to be said, for they understood that it could not be put into words. He rubbed one hand over her back, used the other to grasp her thick hair and force her to tilt back her head.

"I want to kiss again," he said softly.

"We can't—"

His mouth met hers in a warm, delicious kiss that set her aflame. She moved her arms up around his neck and returned the kiss with groaning passion. Never had Edward shown such desperate need, such near worship of her. He moved his lips to her hair then. "Maggie, my beautiful Maggie," he whispered. Suddenly he moved a foot behind her ankle that made her fall back, but he kept hold of her, lowering her gently onto the grass. For the moment she was lost in him, unable to think rationally, pent-up needs burgeoning forth as she returned more kisses with eagerness. His hand moved along her side, to a breast. She cried out at the touch. Edward never touched her this way. He pulled at the shoulder of her dress, tearing off buttons when he suddenly ripped it downward and moved his lips to her bare shoulder, to the white softness of her breast.

"Wild Horse, we can't—"

"Take off your clothes, Maggie. Come into the water

with me." He licked at her breast, pulled her dress and camisole farther away to expose a nipple.

"Wild Horse," she whimpered, grasping his hair, gasping in utter ecstasy when his lips found the pink fruit of her breast. He sucked gently, groaning with the want of her. "Please, stop, Wild Horse."

He moved his lips back to her throat. "Your husband has never done this. You have never been so free, have you?" He raised up on his elbows. "I told you I had one more thing to show you. This is what I wanted you to know, how to give yourself freely to a man, that it is not wrong to feel this way. Come and swim naked with me, Maggie. See how it feels to have the cool water caress your body. Then we will make love. It will not be like anything you have ever felt before. Let me show you, Maggie. No one else ever needs to know. It is right. You know that it is right."

Oh, how she wanted him inside of her! She wanted to be Wild Horse's woman, but she knew it was wrong. In his eyes he saw no wrong with it. He came from a people who acted freely on their feelings. When a Cheyenne man and woman felt this way about each other, they simply went off and acted on their passion, and they were then man and wife. If a Cheyenne woman was disgusted with her husband and wanted out of the marriage, she simply cut their blanket in two and set his half outside the tipi with his moccasins and other belongings, and that was the end of it. If only life could be that simple for her own people, but at this moment she realized just how different they were.

"You must let me go, Wild Horse," she whispered.

"Don't make me do something that will leave me feeling unhappy for the rest of my life."

He raised up a little, his dark eyes studying her face. "It would make you unhappy to be one with Wild Horse?"

A tear slipped down her cheek. "No." She reached up and touched his face. "It's the regrets I would have later, the regrets and the guilt that would make me unhappy. I have never wanted to give myself to a man the way I want to give myself to you right now, but I can't let it happen. That is the difference between us." She breathed a deep sob. "I wish I could be as free as you. You're stuck on a reservation . . . soldiers looking for you, and yet you are more free than I. Maybe if I had more time, but I can't change overnight what I have been brought up to believe is right, no more than you and your people can change in just a few days. Can you understand that?"

His own eyes teared. "I understand that I love you. If you did not belong to another and you were my captive, I think perhaps you would not want to go back to your people. You would want to stay with Wild Horse and be his woman."

She sniffed and sobbed. "I love you," she told him through tears. "But I can't do this."

His eyes moved over her, and one tear dripped onto her chest. He leaned down and kissed her breast once more, then rolled away from her. "Go," he said flatly. "Go quickly."

There was so much more she wanted to say. Her whole body screamed for satisfaction. She knew now that there was a beauty and a wonderful joy in giving herself to a man with passion, with wanton desire. She longed to know the full extent of that pleasure, but it simply could not be this way. She choked in a sob and got up, pulling her dress back over her shoulder. "Good-bye, Wild Horse," she sobbed. "I shall never forget you."

She hurried off into the trees, hardly able to see where she was going. She cried harder with the aching need to go back and let him have his way with her, to experience just once such wonderful freedom of her womanhood, but she had to think of Evy. If such a thing were discovered, it would be bad for her little girl, who would have to grow up among whispers about her "soiled, bad mother." She didn't care for herself, or even for Edward. It was Evy who mattered. Why destroy her child's future for one brief moment of passion with a man she could never have. Still, she knew this hurt would not leave her for a long time, and the worst part was, she would have to suffer it alone. She could never tell a soul.

Chapter Six

"Did you hear? My husband is going to search the agency for that savage, Wild Horse." Gloria Doleman twirled her parasol as she stood talking to Josie Hart. "It was my idea," she said proudly. "I told him that Indian was just tricky enough that he might be hiding right here with his own people."

"Do you really think that's possible?" Josie asked, enjoying the gossip.

Gloria glanced at Evy, who looked up from where she was digging in the sand with Rose. "I think it's very possible." She paused, noticing a rather alarmed look in Evy's eyes. "*You've* seen Wild Horse, haven't you, Evy?"

Evy watched the woman, her child's inner senses telling her there was something bad about what Gloria was saying—something dangerous for Wild Horse. She remembered her mother telling her so many times that she must not tell she had seen the man, but sometimes it was very hard to keep the secret. Now she sensed it was very important. "No," she answered.

Gloria frowned. "Oh, now, Evy, it isn't nice to tell lies. Surely your father has taught you that."

Evy stared in confusion. Was she being a bad girl? Her mother would never tell her to do something bad, so it must be all right to not tell about Wild Horse. "I'm not lying," she answered. Her little heart pounded, and she could not keep the tears from coming to her eyes. She was afraid for her mother and for Wild Horse.

Gloria sniffed. "Then why are you crying, Evy?"

"Gloria, leave her alone," Josie urged. "She's just a child with a big imagination."

Gloria smiled in a kind of sneer, looking back at Josie. "I don't think she's making it up. I think she and her mother both have seen Wild Horse, and for some reason they're hiding the truth. I can't imagine how they might have met him, or why they would not tell anyone, but I think I'm right, and Albert will *prove* me right when he finds Wild Horse at the agency. When they do, he'll be arrested and sent to Florida, and his troublemaking days will be over." She looked back down her nose at Evy. "Your friend, Wild Horse, is in a lot of trouble, Evy."

She turned and walked off with Josie then, talking in a near-whisper. Evy noticed Josie looked surprised, and she was sure the two women were talking about her mother and Wild Horse. She got up from the sand and looked into the distance. Beyond the fort sat her parents' cabin, and beyond that was the pond. Wild Horse was always at the pond. Maybe her mother was there right now herself. She decided she must go and warn them. Wild Horse should know soldiers were going to look for him and arrest him.

"I can't play anymore," she told Rose. "I'm going home."

"You're supposed to wait for your mommy to come and get you," Rose warned her.

"I know the way." She brushed herself off. "Tell your mommy my mommy came for me. She waved at me from over there by where you come into the fort. Bye!" She ran off, but decided she would not even stop at her house first. The important thing was to warn Wild Horse, and as far as she knew, he lived at the pond. Wild Horse had been good to her. He was so different, full of stories. He made her laugh. She liked her Indian friend, and she didn't want the soldiers to catch him.

Margaret felt numb, realizing how close she had come to committing a terrible sin, yet not really regretting it. She would suffer her broken heart in silence, try to mend it by finding a way to get closer to Edward. Maybe someday she could tell him the truth. For today, she could barely face the truth herself. She managed to compose herself, changed her clothes, and after a fit of crying, retucked her hair and had come to get Evy. It was nearly dusk, and she brought a pie she had made yesterday. She needed an excuse for waiting so long to come for Evy, so she would tell Josie she spent the day catching up on some baking.

She should have come a long time ago, but it had taken time to overcome the trauma of what had happened at the pond, more time to soothe her eyes so that the swelling went down and no one could tell she had been crying. This had been the most unusual day of her life, and she wondered how long it would take for this sick feeling to leave her.

She noticed no children playing outside Lieutenant Hart's quarters, and she supposed Josie had taken the girls inside because it was getting dark. She took a deep breath and knocked on the door, and Josie Hart opened it. Margaret thought she looked at her strangely, with a note of disapproval. "Margaret! What brings you here so late?"

Margaret felt instant alarm. "I came to get Evy. I'm awfully sorry I'm late. I brought you a pie. I've been baking all day, and the time just got away from me."

Josie frowned. "Evy isn't with you?"

Margaret looked past her to see Rose sitting at the table. "No. You mean, she isn't here?"

"Well . . . no. Rose told me you came for her. I was off talking with Gloria, and Rose said you came around the fort entrance and waved for Evy to come home."

Margaret looked at Rose, fear gripping her. She

handed Josie the pie. "Rose, why did you tell your mother that I came for Evy? I never came at all."

Rose puckered her lips as though to cry, worried she might be in trouble. "Evy told me to say it. She said she wanted to go home and to tell Mommy you came for her."

Margaret put a hand to her chest. "But she never *came* home!" She looked at Josie. "Where is my daughter?"

Josie set the pie aside. "I swear, Maggie, I thought she was with you! I'm terribly sorry—"

"Why did she suddenly leave like that and ask Rose to tell a lie?"

Josie turned away, trying to think. "I . . . I don't know. Gloria was here, and she was talking about—" She faced Margaret. Were Gloria's suspicions true? Perhaps she should not be too quick to judge. "About Wild Horse. How the soldiers were going to look for him at the agency and he would be arrested."

Margaret turned away. "Dear God," she muttered. Had Evy gone to try to warn Wild Horse? Where would she go? Her heart pounded harder at the answer to that question. The pond! What if she fell in while no one was there? "Where is your husband?" she asked Josie.

"Why, he's at the agency with some of the other men, searching for Wild Horse. Gloria felt perhaps he was hiding there."

Gloria! What a meddling, pompous woman! Her stupid remarks must have upset Evy, who probably thought she had to help Wild Horse! She turned to face Josie. "Please, Josie, go ask some of the men to form a search party! And have someone go to the agency and get my husband! He was going to stay the night there. Tell him Evy is missing! We have to find her! It's getting dark! Tell some of the men to come to the pond a half mile or so behind our cabin. She might have gone there!"

"But why would she go there?"

"I don't know! I . . . I left the house for a while, and sometimes I take Evy to that pond so she can swim and bathe there. She might have gone there looking for me." Or for Wild Horse! If soldiers were looking for Wild Horse, Evy could get hurt! "Please, Josie, will you ask some of the men to start searching, and get Edward?"

"Of course! I'm so sorry, Maggie. I really thought you had come for her."

Margaret did not reply. She ran out and headed out of the fort toward the pond, calling for Evy, her precious baby, perhaps the only child she would ever have. How could she live without her daughter? She never should have stayed away so long! Guilt overwhelmed and consumed her—guilt for having fond thoughts of another man besides Edward, guilt for leaving her daughter to meet that man secretly. Her beautiful, sweet child! Anything could happen in this wild land, especially in the dark. The woods between the cabin and the pond were thick. She could turn in the wrong direction. She could fall and get hurt. She could drown. And this was Indian Territory—outlaws often hid here. She had no fear that a Cheyenne would bring the child harm, but there were all other elements of men out here, scurvy whites who exploited the Indians with rotten whiskey whenever they could, traders from all parts of the country. She was such a pretty little girl, so innocent and trusting.

It seemed to take forever to get to the pond, and when she arrived there, she was breathless and sweating. The night had remained warm and muggy. "Evy!" she screamed. She shouted the name over and over, but there was no reply.

"You must go, Wild Horse," old Wise Owl Woman told him in the Cheyenne tongue. "It is only a matter of time before the soldiers find you."

Wild Horse came out from behind the inner wall of the old woman's tipi. The Cheyenne had erected a second wall of skins within the outer layer, so that there was a space in between where Wild Horse could hide, yet to the soldiers it looked as though there was only one layer of skins. Wild Horse had hidden by staying with the old woman, who the soldiers thought lived alone. Whenever soldiers or other white men came around, he hid between the skins; but Wild Horse knew that this time was different. This time the soldiers were being extra cautious, checking every dwelling twice.

"It will be night soon," Wise Owl Woman told him. "You can escape then. The soldiers will soon give up their search until morning, and for now they have something more important to look for."

"More important? What is that?"

"They came for the white preacher. They told him his little daughter is missing. She cannot be found anywhere."

Wild Horse's eyes widened, and he grasped the old

woman's arms. "Evy? The little white girl with the golden hair?"

"*Aye*. That is the one. The search for her has gotten their attention. It is a good time for you to get away now."

Wild Horse went to the tipi entrance and peeked out. Things had quietened, but there were still a few soldiers about. Far in the distance he could hear men shouting Evy's name. What had happened to that precious child? It would kill Maggie if her daughter should come to harm. Where had she gone? If she had run away, then why? He realized the first place she might go was the pond, perhaps to find him. His heart pounded with dread at what could have happened to her. Maggie must surely be beside herself with fear and dread. "I cannot leave yet, not until the girl is found," he told the old woman.

"But this is the best time! They will find her, Wild Horse! Do not concern yourself. Many men look for her."

He pulled on a shirt. "But none have the skills to find her that I have."

"It is too dangerous! Do not do it, Wild Horse! Get yourself away from here!"

He turned away, his heart crying out for the child . . . and for Maggie. For one brief moment he thought he might be able to possess her, but he should have known better than to try. She was too honorable to give herself to another man, but he knew she had so wanted to belong to him, just for a little while. Now it could be his fault that Evy was missing. He could not leave this way, without knowing what had happened to the child, without knowing Maggie had her little girl back in her arms.

He shook his head, leaving his shirt open as he pulled on a pair of buckskin pants and laced them. "I will look for her," he told Wise Owl Woman. "Get my horse and supplies ready. When I have found the girl, I will come back for them and then I will go." He picked up a rifle he had stolen from a settler weeks earlier. If he found Evy, she might need some kind of protection. He also picked up a blanket and slung it over his shoulder. "Do not worry about me, old woman. Just have my things ready for when I return."

"It is a very unwise thing you do, Wild Horse."

He thought about Maggie . . . the pond. "It will not be the only unwise thing I have done today." He looked out again. For the moment there were no soldiers in sight, and he was out of the light of a distant campfire. He ducked outside and disappeared into the darkness.

Margaret felt numb and unreal. She shivered, even though the night was warm and she sat with a blanket wrapped around her head and shoulders. An oil lamp burned beside her, and all around the pond and through the trees and underbrush beyond it other lights danced, men searching and calling for Evy. Some even waded in the pond, which because of the late-summer drought, was no deeper in the center than a man's chest. They, too, held up lights, as they dragged ropes and blankets and anything else they could find through the water, hoping that if Evy's little body was under that water, they would catch it and get her out.

She couldn't be dead! Sick dread overwhelmed Margaret until she thought she might vomit. She had cried until everything ached. Her throat hurt, her eyes burned, sharp pains jabbed at her chest. She watched Edward come toward her then. He was soaked to the skin from searching the pond himself, and his eyes showed the same desperation she felt herself. He sat down wearily beside her. "At least she hasn't turned up in the pond," he said, his voice dull with sorrow. "That gives us some hope. Maybe she didn't come here at all, Maggie. If she got lost, a little child like that couldn't get far. One of these men will find her." He ran a hand through his hair. "I just don't like the idea that some Cheyenne man might find her."

"They would never hurt her," Margaret answered.

"You don't know that. You think you know them so well, but the soldiers think some of the Indian men could be fascinated by your and Evy's light hair. You're a grown woman with a husband, but Evy . . . she's the kind of child the Cheyenne would love to have as a captive, to raise as their own and save for some warrior's special wife."

Margaret closed her eyes. "Honestly, Edward, do you really think these reservation Indians would be stupid enough to try to keep a little girl on the agency without anyone knowing about it? The days of making war and taking captives are over. The child is simply lost. Maybe it will be a Cheyenne who finds her. If it is, he or she will bring her to us and that will be the end of it."

He sighed deeply. "I don't know. Right now I just hope she's still—" He could not finish the sentence, and he rubbed at his eyes. "My God, Maggie, why had you been coming here in the first place? I told you a long time ago to stay away from here. It's too close to the agency, and it's so hidden. Anything could have happened."

Something did happen—something wonderful, beautiful, special. "I came here because this was our special place," she answered aloud. "Here Evy and I could be ourselves." She faced him. "We could laugh and play. Evy could splash naked in the water and chase butterflies and catch tadpoles and know the joy of life." She looked away. "If anything has happened to Evy, I won't let you blame me for it, Edward. *You're* to blame, for forcing us to seek out a place where our spirits could be free and where it wasn't a sin to smile."

Edward rose and paced. "I don't know you anymore."

"You have *never* known me, Edward. You have never bothered *trying* to know me. You have never asked what makes me happy, what pleases me. All these years *I* have been trying to please *you*. But here, at the pond, I didn't have to please you . . . only myself and Evy."

Men shouted back and forth to each other but still no sign of Evy. "We'll search all night if we have to," a sergeant yelled to one of his men. "Men have been sent to search the agency again. God only knows what could happen to her if some damn, drunk Indian gets hold of her."

"Dear God, help us," Edward muttered.

"No Indian is going to hurt her," Margaret repeated matter-of-factly.

He ran a hand through his hair. "You're so sure of that."

"Yes, I am. The Cheyenne cherish children like they were little angels from heaven." Her voice broke on the words, for Evy truly was that.

"I still don't understand how you seem to know so much about the Cheyenne," Edward told her, needing to talk about something besides Evy. "One would think you were in personal contact with one of them."

Margaret kept quiet. Wild Horse's presence must be kept a secret. She looked at her husband. "What matters is that I managed to get them to listen to you, didn't I? I haven't heard you thank me for that, Edward, or praise me for it. I wanted to help, and I did, but it doesn't seem to make any difference to you."

He knelt in front of her then. "It made a great deal of difference, Maggie. It was a hard pill to swallow, and I haven't quite known how to tell you that I'm grateful. I am not accustomed to a woman taking charge like that, stepping in for the husband. I've always been taught that the woman and children are to be silent. They are to stay home and tend the home and learn their prayers and read the Bible diligently, and——"

"Edward." Margaret interrupted him, leaning closer and studying his eyes in the lantern light. "Haven't you ever wanted to do something fun? Haven't you ever wanted to tell a joke and laugh, or to dance, or take off your clothes and feel the sun and wind against your body?"

He blinked, dumbfounded. "What?"

"*Evy* liked to laugh. She liked to be naked and to let the sun burn her skin and dance in the wind. She liked to learn about nature, and we did those things here. If she died here, then she died happy." She choked in a sob. "My God, Edward, *listen* to what I am trying to tell you. Think what a joy Evy has been to our lives. Maybe God has put in us this fear of losing her just so you can understand what she means to you. You love her with so much passion that right now you want to weep for the want of her. We can *share* this sorrow and our love can grow stronger from it."

He watched her for a very long time, then turned away, crouching on his knees and bending over. His shoulders shook, but his weeping was silent. She touched his shoulder. "Edward, let me hold you."

He breathed in a deep sob. "I don't . . . know how to . . . do this, Maggie."

In all their years of marriage, it was the most touching thing he had ever said to her. She stood up, taking his arm. "Come here, my darling."

He rose, and in the next moment he grasped her and held her tight against him, weeping, clinging to her in a way he never had before. "I can't . . . live . . . without Evy," he admitted.

Margaret could not reply. A wave of mixed emotions flooded over her. How ironic that possibly the only way to reach her husband had been to lose her child. It was not a fair price to pay, and she could not believe that God would ask it of her. He would bring Evy back to them.

Chapter Seven

*W*ild Horse's keen ears could hear the tiny whimperings on the wind. He paused and listened again, walked quietly toward the sound. After several hundred yards the sound grew more distinct——a child crying. It was dark, but he knew this land well, and he realized he was near a steep bank, at the bottom of which was a creek. His eyes were accustomed to the darkness now, and by the moonlight he could tell he was on the edge of the bank. The crying came from below.

He wrapped the blanket he had brought around his shoulders and carefully made his way down the bank, his moccasins slipping twice on the tall grass. When he finally reached the bottom, he paused again. The creek was nearly dried up from the heat, so that the trickle of water made hardly any sound. Now he could tell that the crying came from what looked in the darkness like a large boulder. He walked toward it, then smiled with relief. Who else would be out here crying but little Evy? He walked around the boulder, and there she sat, crouched against it. "So, here you are," he said softly.

Evy, startled by the sight of such a big man looming in the moonlight, let out a little scream and started crying harder. Wild Horse set his rifle aside and knelt in front of her. "I am sorry, little one. I did mean to frighten you. It is I, Wild Horse. You do not have to be afraid."

"Wild Horse," she whimpered.

She threw her arms around his neck, and a wave of emotion swept over him. Memories of another little girl clinging to him made him want to weep. He had let go of his Singing Bird for just a moment, so that he could turn around and fight off a soldier, and in that quick moment another soldier had run his sword through her heart. He knew now that the men who had attacked Sand Creek that day were not regular army, but civilian volunteers from Colorado, men determined to rid their territory of its scourge—the Cheyenne. Their act of bravery had involved murdering and mutilating hundreds of women and children. Among them had been his precious Little Eagle and Singing Bird, and his beautiful Rain Woman.

He held Evy close. That first day he had seen her

playing at the pond with Maggie had brought back memories of his own wife and little girl doing that same thing in another time . . . another place. He realized that his love and desire for Maggie were really just a longing to have back that which he had lost. Maggie was right in stopping him. Nothing could ever come of allowing such passion to blossom.

"Everyone is looking for you. Your mother is very worried, little one," he said aloud, patting her bottom. "Did you not hear soldiers shouting for you? They are not so far away."

"I was afraid," she sobbed, still clinging to him. "I didn't know if they were good men . . . or bad men . . . and I'm afraid my mommy and daddy will be mad at me for going to the pond alone."

"But why were you going there? And how did you end up here?" Wild Horse pulled away and took the blanket from his shoulders. He wrapped it around her shivering little form and moved her onto his lap.

"I was . . . looking for you," she whimpered, using part of the blanket to wipe at her dirty, tear-stained face. "I got lost. It got dark . . . and I fell down that big hill."

Wild Horse grinned. Yes, to a child the bank would seem like a big hill. "Are you hurt?"

"I don't know." She shivered in a sob. "I hurt my knee and my arm. And I bumped my head. I think I fell asleep or something. It wasn't dark when I fell. When I woke up it *was* dark . . . and I didn't know where I was, or what to do."

Fell asleep? Perhaps she had hit her head harder than

she realized. "You lie still. When you are warm and rested, I will take you to your mother." He patted her back. "Why were you looking for me, little one?" She seemed to be calmer, now that she knew she was safe.

Evy rested her head against his broad chest. "I heard a lady say the soldiers were looking for you . . . and that they would kill you or send you away. She said they knew where you were." She straightened, looking at him in the moonlight and crying harder. "I didn't tell, Wild Horse! I didn't tell!" she sobbed.

Wild Horse put a big hand to the side of her face. "Do not cry, Evy. I believe you. You are my special little friend, and you keep a good secret. They must have found out some other way." This time it was he who used part of the blanket to wipe at her face. "You must promise me that never again will you go off alone without telling anyone."

"I . . . promise," she sniffed.

Wild Horse grinned, holding her against him again. "You rest, little one. The sun will rise soon. I will take you back, and then you and your mother and father will be happy again."

Evy felt safe in his arms. "Don't let the soldiers catch you, Wild Horse."

He realized he had to take her back to Fort Reno. "I may have no choice," he answered, "but do not fear for me, little one. I will find a way to keep from being caught," he assured her so that she would stop crying. "I will find a way." He knew he should take her back right away, but it felt good to hold her . . . to remember another little girl who had clung to him this way.

Wild Horse rose with Evy in his arms. Birds were greeting a gray sky that had lightened slowly because of clouds. Thunder rumbled in the distance, suggesting that soon a much-needed rain would come. He knelt down and picked up his rifle, keeping Evy in one arm. She stirred and rubbed at her eyes.

"Where are we, Daddy?" she asked in a tiny voice.

"It is not your daddy. It is Wild Horse, remember? Are you all right, little one?"

Evy blinked and looked around, her cheeks rosy from the warmth of sleep, her lips puckered in curiosity. Her big blue eyes rested on Wild Horse then, and there came the dimpled smile that he so loved. "You found me when it was dark!"

He smiled. "Yes. Now you have slept and are rested. I will take you back to your mother. Keep the blanket around you. I think it will rain soon." He started up the bank, and Evy touched feathers he had tied into his hair.

"Why do you wear these?" she asked.

Wild Horse reached the top of the bank and looked around cautiously. "Feathers have many meanings to my people," he answered. "Some are for war, some for prayer, some represent number of enemy a man has touched or killed."

"Are the soldiers your enemy, Wild Horse?" She rested her head against his shoulder as he started walking with her.

"To someone like me, yes, they are enemy. But you should not think of them as all bad. They are just men doing what they are told to do. One day you will understand, when you are older." He stopped for a moment, looking into her face. "You will not forget Wild Horse, will you?"

She shook her head, her curls bouncing. "Never! Mommy says someday we'll go back home to Mass— Mass—Masschooets. Nobody there knows any Indians. Mommy and I can tell everybody we had an Indian friend." She sobered. "You could go with us, Wild Horse."

He smiled sadly. "I do not think I would much like it there. People like the places where they come from. They miss them, just like your mommy misses her home in that place in the East. I miss my home, to the north. I will take you home, and then I will leave. I will go to *my* true home. Then we will all be happy."

Evy rested her head on his shoulder. "But I will miss you, Wild Horse."

"And I will miss you, little one, you *and* your mother. But we must not be sad about it, for you will know that I am happy, and I will know that you are also happy. It is a good thing we do. Do not ever cry for me, Evy. Whatever happens to me, I will be happier than if I must stay here and live. Do you understand that?"

"I think I do."

It was in that moment that Wild Horse realized he had allowed his love and concern for Evy get in the way of his usual alertness. He had not heard the horses in the distance, and because they were downwind of him, he had not smelled them. Now, suddenly, they appeared from out of the trees—soldiers, still searching. They spotted him carrying Evy. He dared not turn and run. Evy could get hurt. He stopped still, clinging to the girl in his left arm, holding his rifle in his right hand.

"Soldiers! It's soldiers, Wild Horse!" In all innocence, Evy had told the men farther ahead in the clearing who he was. "Run, Wild Horse! Run!" An excited Evy began twisting and wiggling to get away from him so that he could run away.

"Hey! What the hell are you doing with that poor little girl!" one of the soldiers shouted.

Evy, confused and afraid for Wild Horse, began crying. Wild Horse's eyes, which only a moment before had been filled with love and joy, were now dark slits of hatred. He set Evy down. "Get out of the way, Evy."

She let the blanket fall away from her, and she clung to his leg. "No! They'll hurt you, Wild Horse."

"Go!" he shouted, startling her with the anger and firmness of his voice. "Go to the soldiers!" he ordered her. She began crying harder, and she turned away, walking toward the soldiers, her little shoulders jerking with her sobs. Wild Horse held up his rifle. I am not going to that place far away, he promised himself. He knew instinctively these men were not going to listen to anything he had to say. They already thought the worst. It was either turn and run and be shot or go to prison in Florida or perhaps stand and fight. All three choices meant death, and he could not think of a better way to die than to face these men and die in battle.

"I bring the little girl back to you!" he shouted. "Now I go away!"

The soldiers, four of them, had already ridden closer, all of them aiming pistols at him. "You're not going anywhere, you heathen bastard!" one of them answered. "We were looking for you long before you abducted that poor little girl! What did you do to her, you filthy Indian? Did you figure to sneak off with your little white captive and then wait for her to grow up so you could make a woman of her?"

Wild Horse slowly lowered his rifle. "I found her lost and alone. I was bringing her back."

"Sure you were," another put in. "Just doin' your good deed for the day, were you? You know we've been lookin' for you, so why would you risk bein' caught just to help a little white girl? You had plans of sneaking off with her, didn't you? You figured that would be a good revenge. You just didn't figure on getting caught."

"If I was going to steal her, why would I still be so close to fort? And why do I not have my horse and supplies with me?"

They all kept their pistols leveled. "He's got a point there, Johnny," another spoke up.

"He's full of bullshit!" the one called Johnny answered. "Put that rifle down, Wild Horse. You're comin' with us. You've got some explainin' to do, and a little trip to make. Some of your buddies are waitin' for you down in Florida."

Wild Horse kept a tight grip on his rifle. "I am not going to that place."

One of the soldiers chuckled. "Looks like you don't have much choice, Indian."

Wild Horse eyed them all with a steely glare. He watched a couple of them swallow—knew they were afraid. He was not afraid at all. For this one moment he could be a warrior again. It was a good day to die, for he knew Evy was safe. "I *do* have a choice," he answered. He glanced toward Evy to make sure she was out of the way. "Good-bye, sweet child. Be good to your mother."

Evy nodded, staring in wonder, not sure what to expect. Suddenly Wild Horse raised his rifle and fired. One soldier screamed out and fell from his horse. A volley of shots poured forth then from the pistols of the other three soldiers. Evy gasped in fear when bloody holes appeared all over Wild Horse. His body lurched backward, but still he stayed on his feet. He raised his rifle again. More shots rang out, and finally he stumbled backward and fell to the ground.

"Wild Horse!" Evy whimpered. She started to run to him, but quickly one of the soldiers was off his horse and had hold of her.

"You stay away from there, little girl. It ain't nothin' for you to see."

"Let me go! Let me go!" Evy struggled against him. "He's my friend!"

He kept hold of her in one arm and managed to get onto his horse. "Yeah, well, maybe that's what he told you, but he was lyin', kid. Believe me, we're all better off with him dead."

Evy continued to scream and cry and fight the man. She had to go to Wild Horse and tell him she loved him before he went to heaven, but the soldier would not let her go back. She vowed in that moment to always keep her promise to never forget Wild Horse, or the stories he told her, or the way it felt to be held in his arms and know that while there, nothing could hurt her.

"Mrs. Gibbons, Private Johnny Kinzale here. We've got your girl."

Margaret and Edward were already on the porch of their cabin, having heard the sound of several horses riding up in the early morning. Kinzale had barely finished his statement before Margaret was at his side, grasping Evy out of his arms and hugging her close, weeping with relief. She had been too absorbed in the sight of her little girl to notice that another soldier dragged a travois behind his horse. On it lay a body.

"Evy, thank God!" Margaret wept. "Oh, Evy, where did you go? Why did you go off alone? What happened to you?"

Evy hugged her around the neck, and Edward embraced them both.

"I went to find Wild Horse," the child answered. "I was scared the soldiers would find him. I wanted to tell him to get away, but I got lost!"

"Wild Horse! Why on earth would you want to find him?" Edward asked. He stroked her hair.

"Because he's my friend," she answered.

"Evy, you've got to stop these fantasies about that man."

"They are not fantasies," Margaret told her husband. She kissed Evy's cheek. "Wild Horse *is* her friend."

"What!"

"You sure about that, ma'am?" Johnny Kinzale asked her. "We found Wild Horse carrying her. Looked to us like she was trying to get away from him. We figured—"

"Wild Horse found me, Mommy!" Evy interrupted. "He saved me from the dark. He put a blanket on me and kept the monsters away till it was daytime again."

Margaret felt a torrent of emotions rush through her. What had the soldier been saying? They found her with Wild Horse? Where was he now? It was then Evy started crying again.

"They killed him, Mommy! The bad soldiers killed Wild Horse!"

A horrible coldness gripped Margaret's heart. "What?"

"I wasn't trying to get away because I was scared of Wild Horse, Mommy. I was scared of the *soldiers*! I tried to get away so Wild Horse could run!"

Her eyes filled with tears, and Margaret looked up at Kinzale. "What happened?"

"We had to shoot him, ma'am. I don't know what the hell is goin' on here with you and your daughter, or if maybe Wild Horse really was just bringin' her back. All I know is he leveled his rifle at us and started shootin'. He injured one of my men. It was obvious he aimed to kill us all, so we had to shoot back. The damned Indian is full of bulletholes, but he's still alive." He looked behind him. "Back there on the travois."

"My God!" Margaret groaned. She handed Evy to Edward and ran to the last soldier's horse, kneeling beside a bleeding, shivering Wild Horse. "No! Wild Horse!" She hardly knew where to touch him. In spite of his dark skin, he was obviously terribly pale, and his eyes were glazed. blood covered the blanket that had been put over him. Margaret carefully took hold of his hand and bent his arm up so that she could rest the back of his hand against her cheek. "Oh, Wild Horse, what have you done?"

He swallowed, giving her hand a weak squeeze. "It is . . . best . . . this way." His whole body trembled, and he gasped in pain. "Maggie," he groaned.

Edward had followed his wife to Wild Horse's side. He was astonished at the gentle way in which the man spoke her name.

"I'm so sorry, Wild Horse," Margaret sobbed. "If not for me and Evy, you might be gone now. Free!"

"But I *am* . . . free now. I go to . . . be with my Little Eagle . . . Singing . . . Bird . . . and with Rain Woman. I am truly happy now. I go to hunt . . . ride free . . . in land where . . . there are many buffalo. It is . . . a good place."

"Wild Horse—"

His dark eyes gazed upon her face for one last time. "So . . . beautiful. My . . . Maggie."

Margaret felt his hand weaken as he took one last, shuddering breath. She moaned his name once more, resting her face against his shoulder then, realizing that for the rest of her life her regret would not be that she had loved this man while belonging to another. It would be that she had refused him the one thing he had wanted most, the one thing *she* had wanted most. Now he would never hold her again, never touch her lips, never whisper her name.

A confused Edward touched her shoulders. "Come away from here, Maggie. You're making a spectacle of yourself."

"I don't care!" she shouted. She shook him off, then gently closed Wild Horse's eyes. She touched his face lovingly, then rose, watching him a moment longer before looking up at Johnny Kinzale. "You made a terrible mistake! Wild Horse was a good man. My daughter and I knew him well. He never would have hurt Evy. *Never!* He risked his life to help find her. How can your dirty little minds make something bad out of what he did. *You're* the ones who should be shot."

Johnny looked at Edward. "You'd better calm your wife down, mister, and maybe leave the Fort Reno area. This ain't gonna look too good to the rest of the men."

Edward stood there red-faced. "I don't understand this any more than you do."

One of the other soldiers grinned. "I think *I* understand it. Your woman preferred a wild Indian to her husband." He chuckled, and to Margaret's complete surprise, Edward walked past her and lit into the man, trying to grab him from his horse.

"How dare you malign my wife that way!" he growled.

The soldier kicked at him, sending him sprawling. Edward got back up, and already Evy was crying harder. "Edward, don't!" Margaret pleaded. "Let them go!"

Edward backed away, panting and brushing off his clothes. "Get out of my sight!" he growled.

"Wait!" Margaret asked. "What will you do with Wild Horse?"

"We'll take him to the agency and let his people bury him," Johnny answered. "This will be a good lesson to them to show what happens when you disobey the rules and try to flee the reservation."

"You make sure you take him there!" she demanded, tears streaming down her face. "He should be buried properly—the Cheyenne way!"

Johnny snickered and shook his head. "We'll make sure he gets there."

A couple of the others chuckled, and Margaret did not trust them. "Leave him with us," she said as they turned to go. "*We'll* take him to the agency."

Johnny turned his horse, frowning. "That could be dangerous, lady."

"She ain't no lady," one of the others spoke up.

"You take that back!" Edward seethed.

Margaret touched his arm. "It's all right, Edward." She was astounded at his anger. She looked back at Private Kinzale. "We will be in no danger. I'm not afraid to take Wild Horse to them myself. It's you and your men who had better be on the lookout when the Cheyenne find out what happened to him."

She held her chin in a commanding presence, and a nervous look came into Kinzale's eyes. "Cut him loose, Jim," he ordered the soldier who dragged the travois. The man dismounted and untied the rawhide straps that held the makeshift stretcher. Johnny tipped his hat to Margaret. "I'm glad we found your daughter, ma'am. She seems to be unharmed."

"Of *course* she's unharmed, you fool!"

The last soldier remounted his horse, and all four men rode off. Edward ran a hand through his hair and turned to face his wife. "You have some explaining to do, Maggie."

She picked up Evy and hugged her close. "Not yet, Edward. The only thing I will tell you for now is that I loved him." She watched the color drain from his face. "It was different from the way that I love you. I *do* love you, Edward. I was never untrue to you, but Wild Horse taught me something about love and joy and life that I never knew before. Evy knows. She loved him, too."

Edward shivered. "Maggie . . ." He uttered her name with such emotion that it touched her. She held Evy in one arm and touched his face.

"It's all right, Edward. Hitch our horse and wagon. Come with me to take Wild Horse to the agency. Stay with me while he is sent to the afterlife the Cheyenne way. Will you do that?"

He swallowed, a tear slipping down his cheek. "If it means not losing you."

Thunder rumbled nearby, and a light rain began to wet her face, but Margaret hardly noticed. Love welled in her heart, both for her husband, for his unexpected display of emotions, and for Wild Horse for being the cause of it. She closed her eyes. Wild Horse was worth more than all the soldiers inside the fort. Her only consolation was that he had died exactly the way he would have wanted to die—fighting to the last.

The evening brought little relief from the long, emotion-packed day. Margaret lingered near the scaffold upon which Wild Horse's body had been placed, with all his personal possessions. It was now late afternoon. For hours old Wise Owl Woman and other women from the agency had carried on their eerie wailing over the death of one of their most loved, most honored warriors. Nearly every Cheyenne from the agency had come to the sacred grounds they had blessed through their own special ritual, to be used to bury their dead. Because they knew Margaret and Evy had been special to Wild Horse, they had allowed them to watch the burial, but because they were white they could not step onto the sacred ground. They watched from a hillside, and Margaret still sat there, her heart aching for Wild Horse. If only she could hold him once more, touch him once more, tell him she loved him.

Edward had also stayed. He sighed deeply. "It's be-cause of him that you understand them so well, isn't it? He's the one who taught you all those things you knew about the Cheyenne."

Margaret wiped at her eyes, and Evy wandered off to

pick wildflowers that she wanted to give to Wise Owl Woman. The child was not fully aware of the gravity of death, and she looked upon it with innocence. She was no longer sad. She only knew that Wild Horse had gone to a wonderful place where he could be a hunter and warrior again, and where he could find his wife and little children. He was happy now.

"He wanted what was best for them," Margaret answered her husband. "He knew their lives had to change, and he thought that it would be easier for them if they could see that what we came to tell them is not so different from what they already believe. He just wanted to help me find a way to reach them, and I in turn tried to show you."

Edward rubbed at his eyes. "Now we'll have to leave."

"No. We have all the more reason to stay now. Wild Horse died saving Evy. He loved her. He was caught only because he stayed here too long, and he stayed here too long because of me, because he wanted to help me understand his people. We owe it to him to stay on and do what we can for them. I'm not afraid to face the soldiers, Edward. In time the talk will die down. We could come and live on the agency, start a school here, maybe encourage more to come—doctors, teachers. God brought Wild Horse to us, Edward. I know you think I'm crazy, but I believe it." She faced him. "And it wasn't just to help us know how to reach the Cheyenne. It was to help us know how to reach each other." She touched his hand. "I have so much to tell you, Edward."

He frowned, and his eyes teared. "I was raised to believe it's sinful to feel anything." He looked away. "Deep inside I understood a little of what you've been trying to tell me the past few weeks. I just thought it was wrong to think about those things."

"Anything to do with love and joy can't be wrong, Edward. I don't believe God is a terrible being waiting somewhere up there to strike us down for the first wrong deed. I believe He loves us much more than we can ever imagine."

He put a hand to the back of his neck. "It's hard for me, Maggie."

"I know that." She took a tighter hold of his hand. "Edward, will you do something for me?"

He sighed. "What is it?"

"Let's go to the pond tonight. We'll take a lantern and eat our supper there. After Evy falls asleep, you and I—" She hesitated. "Edward, I want us to undress and go into the pond."

He looked at her in shock. "What!"

She touched his face. "I want to know that freedom, Edward. We're man and wife. Nothing we do together can be wrong, because we love each other, and God means for us to enjoy each other's body. I want to go into the water together, Edward, to feel the water's coolness against my skin . . . to feel *you* against my skin. I want to feel free to enjoy my husband. I want you to hold me, to make love to me simply because you love me and want me and it's natural for us to want to be together that way." She leaned up and kissed his cheek. "You're a handsome man, Edward. I want to look upon you. I promise that when you let go of your desires and emotions and learn the joys of life, you will begin to understand the Cheyenne. They are closer to God than you know."

His eyes moved over her in a way they never had before. "I don't know if I can do that, Maggie."

She smiled through her tears. Perhaps once she stood naked before him, it would be much easier for him. "I will help you." For now she would have to make the first moves. She would do the teaching, and she would enjoy it. "Let's go home, Edward. I'll make some sandwiches and we'll go to the pond."

They got to their feet and Margaret called for Evy. The girl came running with a handful of flowers. "Look, Mommy! Aren't they pretty?"

"Yes, Evy." She looked out at the scaffold on which Wild Horse lay. "I don't think Wise Owl Woman or the others would mind if you took them down there and laid them where Wild Horse sleeps. His spirit will keep you safe in the sacred burial grounds. Why don't you take the flowers to Wild Horse? He can give them to his own little girl."

Evy smiled and ran down the hill. Edward and Margaret watched her lay the flowers under the scaffold, and she blew a kiss to Wild Horse. Somewhere nearby an Indian man began playing his flute, a mystic, touching song that floated on the soft afternoon breeze and on upward to another place, another time when the grass was green and plentiful, and many buffalo grazed across a beautiful land. Where Cheyenne warriors rode free and wild to hunt and make war and came home to their women to celebrate victory and life.

Margaret took hold of Edward's hand, and Evy ran to join them, taking hold of her father's other hand.

"Can we go on a picnic by the pond, Daddy? I'll catch you some tadpoles."

Edward grinned, looking at Margaret. "Yes, we can go on a picnic." He stopped to kiss his wife, something he had never done in broad daylight before. "I love you, Maggie. Right now that's the only thing I'm sure of."

"And it's all I need to hear," she answered.

They continued walking, and in the distance Margaret saw several horses running. The lead horse was white, its mane and tail flying in the wind, its shiny coat glistening in the sun, its muscles rippling with every movement. The beautiful animal reminded her of Wild Horse.

"The spirit of the wild horse will decide what happens to me," he had told her once. Now the answer had come. He was as free as the spirit of the horse that had lived in his soul. The white horse seemed a symbol of that freedom, as though to tell her Wild Horse still lived.

Run, Wild Horse! Run, and never look back!

She left the burial grounds with Edward and Evy, never noticing a small girl with long, black hair and dressed in a deerskin tunic, run to pick up the flowers Evy had left under Wild Horse's scaffold. She smelled them and she smiled, little dimples showing in her cheeks. She held up the flowers, as though to hand them to someone. A handsome Indian man appeared from nowhere and took the flowers, then took the little girl into his arms. They both laughed when he whirled her around, then suddenly vanished.

Scarlett O'Hara. *The Thorn Birds'* Meghann Cleary. Emma Harte from Barbara Taylor Bradford's *A Woman of Substance.* They're the spirited, indomitable heroines from some of the biggest block-buster bestsellers of our times—women who've made us remember them all our lives.

Get ready for the next great heroine. Her name is Tully. And once you meet her, you'll never forget her.

TULLY by Paullina Simons. An excerpt follows:

Jack had fallen asleep underneath her, underneath her thighs, underneath her lips.

Sometime later Tully came to, still on top of him. Feeling her stir, Jack woke up. They made love again, had a quick shower, muttered at each other, and then got back into bed, bleary-eyed and exhausted.

"I gotta get home," said Tully. "I ought to at least make a pretense at some propriety."

"Who cares?" said Jack rudely. "He's never home, anyway."

That's true, thought Tully. But he is working, or playing rugby. It's not quite the same. "Still, though," she said vaguely.

"Still, though, nothing," said Jack. "You can't go. You said you would tell me everything."

Tully elbowed him in the ribs. "Did not. I said, what do you want to know?"

"I don't know," said Jack, smiling. "What is there?"

"This is not a restaurant," Tully declared. "Ask now, or I'm asleep in two seconds."

"Tell me about your father," he said quickly.

"Daddy, yes, uh-huh. Yes, he was with us awhile. You know, they were both uneducated and poor—"

"Kind of like me?" Jack interjected.

She smiled. "Nothing like you. Both worked in factories all day and we never had anything. But that was okay, you know, because, well, he was a real nice man. He always kissed me good night. I just think he never knew what to do with me. He didn't read very well, so he couldn't teach me to read. He was an only child, I think, and didn't know how to play with me. I think me going to school must have been the best thing that could have happened to them both. Suddenly, after five years, they breathed a sigh of relief that I was no longer just running around a fenced yard by myself all day while they weren't there. Anyway, it was when I started school that Hank was born. They didn't tell me I was going to have a brother, they just brought him home, like a done deal, and said, here, here's your little brother. There was none of that 'Come feel your brother or sister kick your mommy's tummy' nonsense beforehand.

"They named him Hank after my dad, Henry. He was kind of cute. He managed to outlive his infancy and was growing up into a little person. After school, Jen, Julie, and I used to come up to the Grove and play with him.

"My dad, as you can imagine, flipped out over Hank. He still didn't know what to do with him, like feed him or bathe him or play with him, but he just had that look on his face of a smitten man—a man in love.

"Dad and Hank used to have this routine where every Saturday and Sunday morning after breakfast they would toddle to the candy store down the block and buy the newspaper and some candy. I used to have this routine where every Saturday and Sunday morning I would ask Dad to take me, too, and he would say, 'Natalie, we'll be right back. I'll bring you something, Natalie.'

"One Saturday morning, Dad had breakfast with us, washed his cereal bowl, put shoes on Hank and on himself, and said, like he always said, 'Hank and I are going for a little walk. We'll be right back. We'll bring you something, Tully. Right, Hank?' and Hank, who must have been around two, said, 'Yup, Tuwy wants candy.'

"Dad put on his hat and Hank's little cap. It was July— very hot and dry. 'I'll be right back, Hedda,' Dad said, as he said every Saturday. My mother nodded, didn't even turn from the sink.

"Leave your GI Joes," Dad said to Hank. "We'll be right back."

"Every Saturday for about a year they had gone without me, but this particular Saturday, Dad came over to where I was sitting, bent down, and kissed me very hard on the top of my head, and kept his lips there for a moment. I saw his face in one of the glass cabinets. His eyes were shut tight. Then he scooped up Hank, and in his beige shorts, a white Topeka T-shirt, and old sneakers, walked out the kitchen door, down the steps, onto the driveway, and down the road to the corner.

Tully paused for breath while Jack stroked her leg with his fingers.

She continued. Fifteen minutes went by. Mother and I cleaned the table. Half an hour went by, we washed the dishes. An hour went by, we started vacuuming. Two and a half hours later—at noon— my mother said, 'I'll be right back.' I said, 'I'll come with you.'

"'I'll be right back, I said!' she told me, and left.

"I sat in the kitchen for a while, walked into the yard, walked outside to see if they were coming back. I rewashed the dishes and cleaned the windows. I changed my clothes. I packed my bag. I was seven. I just had no idea what was to happen next. I kind of walked around and imagined they all had left me—Henry, Hedda, and Hank, split and not looked back.

"I still remember I had this airless gut feeling for hours, this whooshing hole. I usually had it when I was by myself in the yard and no one was with me and the sun was going down. I never liked that much as a kid. I finally realized, though, that the whooshing noise wasn't actually inside me, it was just the din of the Kansas Turnpike. When I was little I used to actually like that turnpike. I used to look at it from the upstairs window and imagine all the places where it could possibly take me. There were so many places.

"But this time I wasn't thinking of the turnpike. I was inside the house and still heard the whooshing. So I sat there imagining monsters. I thought that if I had to be alone in that house when it got dark, I'd lose my mind. All I thought of was running into the street screaming, and being hit by the first passing car, the first passing car with *lights*.

"Hours went by, and then I kind of cheered up. I cheered up because I thought, Well, where would I go? And immediately thought, Jennifer."

"Why Jennifer and not Julie?" Jack asked her.

"Oh, there was never any question," said Tully. "Jennifer and I were just too much alike. When I was with Jen, I was home. I was never alone. Even at seven. For years we played together and we hardly ever talked. One might think we didn't know each other, but we knew nothing but each other. And I envied her her parents. Envied her their devotion.

"Anyway," Tully went on. "I almost started looking forward to my own parents not coming back. I started, in a kid kind of way, making up a life without them, without that yard, without those chickens and the chickenshit. I imagined another life and it didn't seem so bad, you know. I thought of all the sympathy, all the comforting, of all the people saying behind my back, 'There she goes, there's that girl whose parents ran away.' It started to seem funny to me. 'There is that girl, what do you think she could have done that they ran away from her?'

"So I sat on the couch, thinking all those things, and it began to get very dark and I got scared again. I didn't know what to do. I put my knees up to my chin and rocked myself back and forth on the couch and cried. God forbid I should have turned on any of the lights, right?"

"Did you believe in God then?" asked Jack.

"Hell, yeah," replied Tully.

"Was that what kept you from going nuts?" he wanted to know, kissing her shoulder.

"In the dark? No, God could help me. No, not at all," Tully answered, kissing him back. "It was her coming back that did it. It must have been nine in the evening. I had been alone for nine hours.

"I kept saying, okay, I'll count to sixty and then I'll call Jen. Okay, I'll count to sixty again, slower, and then I'll call Jen. Okay, I'll count first to another sixty and then I'll definitely call Jen. I must have done that a hundred times.

"And then she came. She turned on the light in the living room and said, 'Natalie, take your feet off the couch.' And then she went to bed."

Jack stared at her.

Tully nodded. "Yes. Went to bed."

"I must have sat there and counted a thousand sheep before sleep slapped me. I woke up on the couch the next morning and then I went to bed."

Jack and Tully were silent.

After a while, he said, "Did she ever say anything to you about it?"

"Yeah," said Tully. "That Sunday. I asked her. I said, 'Ma, where are Daddy and Hank?' She said, 'I don't know.'"

"I asked if they were coming back. 'I don't know,' my mother said to me. 'Would you?'"

"And that's it?" asked Jack.

"That's it," said Tully. "Needless to say, they never came back. Dad must have been planning it for some time because he disappeared off the face of the earth. The police looked for them for months. Dad must have known that unless he was meticulous, she'd hunt him down."

"Did anyone inquire at the candy store?"

"Of course," said Tully. "Apparently they came in as usual, bought the usual, and left. My dad tipped his hat, the saleslady said, and he never did that before."

"And that's it? No one saw them?"

"That's right."

"You've never heard from him at all?" asked Jack.

"That's right," replied Tully, her voice catching.

"Oh, hey, Tull, don't, babe, don't do it, please, hey, now, come on." He patted her back. She waved him off, fumbling on the floor for her bag and then feverishly rummaging through it.

"Tully, what are you looking for?"

"A cigarette," she said, and threw the bag on the floor.

"A cigarette? You don't smoke anymore."

"Yeah, right," she said. "I want to, though. I can't seem to get the cigarette out of my mouth."

He stroked her leg. "Take it easy, Tully," he said. "It's all right. It's the past. Forget it."

"Jack, you don't understand. You know what the worst

part is?" She put her hand to her throat.

"The worst part is not him leaving us, leaving me, taking himself and my little brother who called me Tuwy forever. The worst part is not even his running away and not leaving a note: 'Sorry, gal, couldn't close my eyes and imagine the futureless future with your mother.' No. The worst part is that he left without *me*! He left me with her. With HER! He didn't just run by himself, he took Hank, he took him because he loved him and didn't want him growing up with that monster, but he didn't take me! He didn't think enough about me, that I wanted to run away, too, and never come back! No, no, he abandoned me with her, and I could throw up my hands for a thousand years, but it won't change the fact that for five thousand days I did nothing but pay for his leaving. Won't change the fact that he did not think enough of me to take me with him..."

Tully lowered her head, furiously biting her lip, while all Jack could do was stroke her hair and whisper, "Tully, Tully, it will be all right, babe, it will be all right, I promise, it will all be all right."

She wiped her bleeding mouth with trembling hands. "Don't you see, Jack?" she said, shaking her head. "*Ceaselessly* into the past. It'll never be all right. Never in my life, never between us, never. It will just come to pass, but my life will never leave the Grove."

"But that's not true, dear Tully," said Jack, wiping the blood off her mouth. "It will. One way or another, it will. Beat on."

TULLY—now available from St. Martin's Paperbacks!